ONE S

Also available from Headline Liaison

Your Cheating Heart by Tom Crewe and Amber Wells
Sleepless Nights by Tom Crewe and Amber Wells
Hearts on Fire by Tom Crewe and Amber Wells
The Journal by James Allen
Love Letters by James Allen
Aphrodisia by Rebecca Ambrose
Out of Control by Rebecca Ambrose
A Private Affair by Carol Anderson
Voluptuous Voyage by Lacey Carlyle
Magnolia Moon by Lacey Carlyle
The Paradise Garden by Aurelia Clifford
The Golden Cage by Aurelia Clifford
Vermilion Gates by Lucinda Chester
Seven Days by J J Duke
Dangerous Desires by J J Duke
A Scent of Danger by Sarah Hope-Walker
Private Lessons by Cheryl Mildenhall
Intimate Strangers by Cheryl Mildenhall
Dance of Desire by Cheryl Mildenhall

One Summer Night

Tom Crewe and Amber Wells

HEADLINE
Liaison

Copyright © 1996 Tom Crewe and Amber Wells

The right of Tom Crewe and Amber Wells to be identified as the
Author of the Work has been asserted by them in accordance with
the Copyright, Designs and Patents Act 1988.

First published in 1996 by
HEADLINE BOOK PUBLISHING LTD

A HEADLINE LIAISON paperback

10 9 8 7 6 5 4 3 2 1

All rights reserved. No part of this publication may be reproduced,
stored in a retrieval system, or transmitted, in any form or by any
means without the prior written permission of the publisher, nor be
otherwise circulated in any form of binding or cover other than that
in which it is published and without a similar condition being
imposed on the subsequent purchaser.

All characters in this publication are fictitious and any resemblance
to real persons, living or dead, is purely coincidental.

ISBN 0 7472 5222 X

Typeset by Avon Dataset Ltd, Bidford-on-Avon, Warks

Printed and bound in Great Britain by
Cox & Wyman Ltd, Reading, Berks

HEADLINE BOOK PUBLISHING
A division of Hodder Headline PLC
338 Euston Road
London NW1 3BH

Saturday night and I just got paid
Goin' down town and I'm gonna get laid
Studd, *One Summer Night*

Chapter One

Richie peered out of the misted-up window at the rain blowing in from the North Sea. He pressed his nose almost up against the glass and, with his finger, he traced a single word: *bollocks*.

It was his day off and, by rights, he ought to have been out there in that big wide world enjoying himself. The sun had been absolutely boiling all frigging week and then, when it really mattered, this had to happen. Why was he so bothered that it was tipping down outside? Where he came from, it was pissing down most of the time. It wasn't quite the same at Roker if a force nine wasn't blowing in off the water, the rain drifting in your eyes so you could hardly see what was happening on the pitch – though, the way Sunderland had been playing most of last season, that might have been no bad thing.

Sometimes, he quite liked walking in the rain, feeling it against his skin. He especially liked the thundery summer downpours, where the raindrops were as big and fat and wet as a French kiss. That was the kind of rain there was out there now. It was just a shower, it would be over soon enough – or at least that's what he tried to kid himself. But he wouldn't go out in it all the same, even though it would probably have stopped by the time he got to the bus stop at the other end of the camp. He didn't dare admit, least of all to Rob, that his trainers were leaky. They were the only pair he had at the moment and he was boracic, so they'd have to do. If it rained, he stayed in. It was as simple as that.

He could hear the thunder getting nearer, the lightning arcing. The rain was coming down like stair-rods now. This was one hell of a big summer rainstorm, right enough. The whole place seemed to shake as it beat a tattoo on the roof. It was like living inside a tin snail, this sodding caravan. He was sure there was more room inside Debbie's Mini. It was certainly noisier and smellier.

He shut out the noises coming from the far end and ran his eyes over a three-day old copy of the *Daily Mirror*. A Nuneaton man had been awarded record damages after choking on a deep-fried moth in his takeaway. A Chesterfield pensioner had been barred from his local Asda for dangerous driving – in his electric wheelchair. Samantha Fox explained why she had turned to Jesus, page six.

What a bunch of shite, Richie breathed, and knocked his coffee over. The stain spread slowly over the worn beige carpet. He let it go. They were the same colour, coffee and caravan carpets. No one would know the difference. What pissed him off was that that was the last of the coffee. In fact, there were so few grains left in the jar that he'd actually poured the boiling water in and swilled it around to try and bring it up to strength.

He put his Walkman on, nicked a couple of batteries from Rob's shaver and listened to *Dance Massive 94*. The tape was two years old and they were all records he'd heard a hundred times before but not in that order, so he let it ride. One of those girls from Leicester had brought the tape to the party the week before last and left it behind. A party in a caravan? It seemed incredible now, but there must have been thirty people jammed inside, boozing and groping and puking. But the girl – he'd forgotten her name – was a hundred miles away now. She wouldn't let him, either. No one had, not for frigging days, weeks even. Things were getting pretty desperate.

After a while he relaxed and sprawled out on the couch-sleeper, his feet swaying in time to the music. He might have fancied a ciggie but there weren't any and he wasn't going to leg it over to the camp shop in the sodding rain.

He sensed rather than heard a movement and opened his eyes. Debbie, Rob's girlfriend, was just coming out from behind the curtain that was draped discreetly across the caravan. She was wearing Rob's second-best white shirt, loosely buttoned at the front, and very little else. Her hair was all over the place. She had that just-fucked look about her.

'Do you want some tea?' she mouthed at him.

Yes, he mimed vigorously. There wasn't any tea either. Maybe when she'd got dressed she might go over to the shop and get some. He'd ask if she would pick up some ciggies at the same time, he'd pay her for them later. She was nice like that, Debbie.

He studied her as she filled the kettle at the sink. Long, burnt-blonde hair, biggish boobs, her legs slightly dimpled at the back but a nice shape, barefoot. She lived on the other side of town, had a flat with a couple of her mates but he'd never been there. She was a student at the local poly, doing social sciences, whatever that was. Half the population of Dunwich were students, in one form or another. When Rob was finished with her . . .

He heard a fart and then Rob poked his head round the curtain.

'Oh, you're wearing it,' he said to no one in particular. He caught sight of Richie. 'I thought you'd gone out,' he said.

'It's pissing down.'

'That doesn't normally stop you.'

'It did today. It's pissing down cats and dogs.'

'What fucking time is it?'

'Ten past fucking eleven.'

'Fuck me.'

'Someone already has.' This last under his breath.

'Jesus, I'm supposed to be at work at twelve.' Rob worked as a bingo caller at the end of the pier. He'd never done it before the two of them came down to Dunwich on the off-chance of a bit of easy money but the Excelsis was desperate and he'd talked them out of ten quid a session, two or sometimes three times a day. He didn't know all the bingo words yet so he made them up. 'Two fat tadpoles, ninety-six. Eastern Avenue via Bus Station, number seventeen.' The guy was a regular fucking scream. The pensioners didn't know what had hit them. There had been a number of complaints.

'I thought it was about half-past ten,' he said as he tugged on the lime-green rayon trousers he had to wear. With the jacket as well, he should have been done for GBH. It was an offence against the eyes, especially at that time of day. 'I'll never get there,' he cursed.

'There's no teabags, Rob,' called Debbie.

'I haven't got time for teabags now. Where's me shoes?'

'Look under the bed. Do you want some coffee, Richie?'

'No thanks, I just put one out.'

'I'll make you some coffee then I'll drive you there,' she said. Debbie's Mini didn't go very well, but it ran a sight better than the vile beige Fiesta that Rob owned. Loaded with Tesco bags full of clothes and tins of farty peas – in case you couldn't get them down south – it had just about got them down from the North East without too many bits coming off, but the experience had left it tired and drained. It gave up on the way back from Norwich when they went to score some grass and it had been *hors de combat* for a fortnight now. Richie was sure the car was the main reason Rob was still going out with Debbie. Normally he chucked them in after a week or so but, with her, it had been over a month now. Having a girlfriend with a car was better than waiting for the bus at the entrance to the site. It was always late and there wasn't a shelter. There used to be one, but the kids from the estate kept knocking big lumps of concrete off it and lobbing them over the cliff, so the council did the decent thing and knocked the whole frigging lot down to save them the trouble.

Rob got into his blue-arsed fly mode, scorching round the caravan in his lime-green horror suit, trying to find his comb and his wallet (not that there was anything in it) and the batteries for his shaver. Debbie got the car started and then they were off.

By the time they'd gone it had brightened up outside. The rain stopped, more or less just like that, and a big fat sun came out from behind the clouds and said 'Boo'. All around the caravan site you could see the steam rising off the grass, the raindrops glinting like little jewels. The air, which had been getting very humid until the cloudburst, had a welcome freshness to it now. Standing in the open doorway of the caravan, keeping a leery eye out for any holiday-making talent, Richie had a bowl of cornflakes for lunch. It was that time of day on a holiday-resort Saturday when one lot had finally packed up all their kids and buckets and spades and all the plastic ghastlies they'd bought and clattered off back to Rotherham, and before the next lot of hopefuls arrived with their new flip-flops and tubes of factor five. He hoped it would be better than the past week. There were a couple of good ones about eight caravans down on the other side, but they had blokes with them. There were two student teachers from Peterborough next door who'd been giving him and Rob

5

gladsome smiles, but they weren't in the least bit fanciable. It was all so bloody depressing.

In his mind he went back to that last night at home before he and Rob set off. He'd gone out with Linda to a club near the town centre and then they'd gone back with some friends of hers – they were students too, like her – and he'd ended up, inevitably, spending the night with her. They were uncomfortable in an unfamiliar bed but what did that matter?

He was really keen on Linda, he'd realised that over the last few weeks. He'd sent her postcards, rung her up a few times. She'd written him a couple of letters. Once he'd even fixed up to go back home for a weekend and see her – Tosser Green was having a party and you'd have to be mental to miss one of Tosser Green's parties. People would crawl on hands and knees across broken glass to get there. But something had come up and he couldn't do it and he could tell, when he'd called her, that she was really pissed with him.

She fancied him, that was why. In bed at her friend's house down near South Dock, she'd launched herself at him like a ship going down the slipway. She had fabulous tits, did Linda, and she was really good at sucking his cock. She hadn't ever sucked anyone else's cock before she met him, she told him eventually, although she hadn't told him at first because she didn't want him to think she was innocent or something.

So they'd lain there on the bed in that untidy room, with someone else's clothes and records all around them, and he'd licked her out while she tongued him. Then she'd knelt up on the bed and he'd gone into her doggie-fashion, the way she liked it because she said she got more of it in her that way.

He loved the moment he went into her, the way his foreskin slipped back. Linda was nice and tight and licky and she could squeeze his cock with her vaginal muscles like it was a hand or something. She was on the pill so he didn't have to wear one – he hated wearing one – and it was nice to do it like that, skin to skin. Even now, peering out of the window with unseeing eyes, he knew what it felt like to slide inside her.

They did it a couple of times, just the usual way with him on top of her, and then they must have dozed off because the next thing he knew it was Sunday morning. Linda was next to him, all sleepy, still in her make-up from the night before, and he pulled her over and she climbed on top of him and somehow he got it inside her. Then she came fully awake and she was bucking up and down on him and making him lick her tits and he realised that he felt more for her than for any girl he'd ever been out with. He'd been with a few girls since he'd come down to Dunwich but it wasn't the same. It was as if you'd been watching Inter or Juventus all your life and then you had to watch Crewe or Torquay.

A few early families began to roll up, eyeing the rusting metalwork of their holiday homes with ill-concealed dismay – what did they think this was, Billy fucking Butlin's? – and the kids running loose after their long hours spent cooped up in the back of the family Sierra while Dad negotiated the tailbacks around King's Lynn and Mum warned him to keep his temper. Richie manned the observation post for half an hour and then went for a walk along the cliff. They weren't really cliffs, not like they had at Whitby or Robin Hood's Bay, but they weren't bad for this part of the world. They would do for a suicide bid.

He left the caravan park far behind and stood on the headland, not looking back at the town. Out at sea he could see a container ship slowly making its way along the horizon, inbound for Felixstowe from Rotterdam or somewhere. The waves were grey and heavy, exactly the same North Sea he could glimpse from the spare bedroom of his nan's house at Tynemouth. The Costa del or the Riviera it definitely wasn't.

A narrow strip of beach ran along the foot of the cliffs below him. It was mostly just shingle out here so not many people came out, preferring the yellow sand closer in towards the town. There were just a couple of kids looking for crabs and a bloke with a sketchbook. There was a little gallery in the town that sold local scenes and Richie had looked in there a couple of times. All the pictures seemed the same, full of mud and flapping canvas. Nobody painted the pier and the amusement arcade and the dance club where he worked – the only interesting places in Dunwich. There was never anywhere that he knew and could recognise, just these places further along the coast, these little places built around estuaries. Before the Fiesta had packed up he and Rob had been along there, exploring. They were so gloomy that they gave him the creeps. Still, they seemed to match his mood. He tried to talk to Rob about it once but Rob didn't understand what the fuck he was on about. Rob didn't have much time for estuaries and salt marshes. If something didn't have tits and a nice mouth – for the blowjobs – he wasn't interested.

Richie walked along the clifftop, the wind blowing in his hair. The sun was round behind him now, warming his back. He liked the way the long grass seemed to ripple in the breeze, like it was liquid or something. Sunderland were playing at Norwich next Saturday, the first match of the season. Rob was going to try and work on Debbie so she would lend them the Mini to go in. So far, from what he was saying, he was winning. He was going to take her out for a pizza tonight and try and clinch the deal. Was this how things were between Pamela Anderson and that rock star guy she'd married (what was his name). Did he buy her a five-quid pizza to try and persuade her to lend him her Ferrari F50, so he could go watch the Knicks and the Jets.

Thinking of the pneumatic pleasures of *Baywatch* brought him back to his present predicament. There were usually plenty of boobs on display on the beach at Dunwich. Not naked ones – this wasn't the South of France – but enough of them to give you an appetite. Rob was definitely a tit man but Richie, well, he thought he liked a bit of everything. Linda had nice boobs but then he'd gone out for a long time with Jancis Starbeck when he was seventeen or eighteen and she was very, what was the word, petite. Still, she had lovely big nipples on her and she'd taught him how to wrap his foreskin round them, which was difficult in the extreme because by the time they got to that stage, he would usually have a thumper on him like the handle on his brother Dave's socket wrench.

She was funny, was Jancis. Sometimes she would and some-times she wouldn't, he could never tell with her. They might go out for a chinky or something and she'd be all lovey-dovey. He'd take her home and her mam and dad would be in bed, both of them seemingly dead to the world, and he'd think he'd get her on the couch or on the rug by the electric fire but then, all of a sudden, she'd go cold on him and push him off and he'd miss the late bus back, frustrated beyond belief.

And yet there were times when she was desperate for it. Once they'd been in her front room and he'd got his fingers right up her snatch. She was still in her school uniform – tight white knickers – and she was tonguing him and breathing heavily and he could see how big her nipples were through her crisp school blouse, and yet next door was her mother, running up a set of curtains on the dining-room table. He could still recall the sound of the sewing machine. How each time it paused he would think, Oh Christ, the old cow's going to come in.

But Jancis just carried on, rubbing her hot wet pussy against his hand as he cupped it, palm upwards, and then she got his dick out and pumped it up and down, still with her tongue in his mouth, in his ear, all over his face, and he knew he couldn't hold out any longer. He came, all over her pleated school skirt, right at the exact moment that she came off too, the sewing machine whirring merrily away on the other side of the wall.

He could have done with something like that right now, he said to himself. Sooner or later, logic told him, he would get laid. It might be tonight, it might be next week, but surely to goodness it would happen. Only believe, he told himself. He had watched some Open University programme on their tiny black-and-white portable only yesterday. It was all about motivation and planning for success. Tell yourself you are successful, some American professor of jerking-off had told the camera, and you will be successful. What a load of old toss, Richie had muttered to himself. Tell 'em that in Sunderland.

Nevertheless, Rob had stood in front of the mirror for half an hour or more. You are successful. You are successful. You are successful. You are successful. You are successful. All he succeeded in doing was spotting this giant zit beginning to emerge, just below his hairline, not big enough as yet to give him the satisfaction of bursting, nor yet so small that it would be inconspicuous when he launched himself on the lovely holidaymaking ladies of Dunwich.

Something about the sun and the breeze and the sky made him feel better, all the same. Tonight would be the night. He knew it, he knew it, he knew it. Maybe he shouldn't chuck himself off the cliff. Not yet, anyway. They would get the car off Debbie and go to Carrow Road Saturday week. The lads would run rings round their back four. He'd seen them at Roker last season and their defence was crap.

He walked back along the beach. It was a nice beach, clean and well cared for. Some of the ones at home were like that, too, miles and miles of open sand with only the screaming gulls for company, but some of them weren't. There were places like Easington where they'd tipped the colliary spoil straight into the sea, all the oily crud where the little 'uns played, all the leakages and stuff they tried to pretend didn't happen but which certainly did. What did they do out there at sea? Were they dumping stuff because they thought people didn't care? It was all very different down here, though. The tide was going out and the sands were beginning to fill up again as people came back from their dinners. It seemed like a nice place to be.

It was a funny-looking place was Dunwich, he always thought, as the town came back into view. It didn't seem to have a beginning and an end, it just straggled. It was like the town had been spilled on to the East Anglian coast, then washed around by the sea. There didn't seem to be any sense to it. Up in the North East places were compact, self-contained, you knew where you were. Dunwich looked like it had just sort of happened by accident.

Right in the middle was what was left of the old part of the town. This, referred to wittily as the Old Town, was all smart restaurants and antique shops now, the clothes places that sold designer labels and three-hundred-pound shoes. There were little narrow lanes that led down little winding steps where the cliffs had once been, to the pier head below. Once upon a time, there were shops that sold live crabs and nets and buckets and spades, but they'd been pushed out by the chi-chi jewellery and stuff. He didn't go there much, except when he had nothing to do. He couldn't afford any of it, not on the hundred and fifty he got each week from working in the bar at the Zero Six and the Giro money that he and everyone else like him was tricking out of the government. It was like a forbidden city to him, the Old Town.

Spreading out around it on either side were the solid Victorian streets that had developed when the town first began to grow as a holiday resort and cheap excursions brought in the masses. They ringed the Old Town like they were trying to spring an ambush on it. They started at the railway station, spreading outwards like big red-brick ripples until they reached the sea. Right along the front there were some big bloody places, these hotels that looked like fairy-tale palaces, all bristling battlements and clever little patterns in the brickwork. They had big front windows too, so you could look in and see all the well-heeled people tucking into their locally caught fish, the wine glasses on the table. There were still plenty of BMWs and Volvos parked outside but it had gone a bit downhill in the last twenty or thirty years, or so the local guys said. Richie had never known any different. All he knew was that the rich got richer and the poor got poorer. The Adelphi Hotel, where once Prince Albert, no less, had stayed in bygone times, was now a hostel for recovering addicts. And where respectable families had once come with their Ford Anglias and deckchairs to sample the Bayview Tea Room and the Giant Scenic Model Railway, now it was all noise and lights and frying. He heard all this from forty-year-old guys like Billy Brilleaux who was in charge of security at the Zero Six. He had been born in Dunwich and had never got away. His local accent was so thick Richie used to ask him for subtitles. Anyone else would have got a belt round the lug for cheeking him like that, but he and Billy rubbed along.

He peered into the distance, at the pier and the sunlight dancing on the waves. Beyond that, almost invisible now in the haze, were the newer bits, the factories along the arterial road, the housing estates that, with their bland uniformity, could have been anywhere. There were definitely two ends to the town – the part he was walking towards now, out beyond the pier, with its amusement arcades and cheap B&Bs, and the posh bit in the opposite direction, past the wide green sward that ran behind the cliffs and turned eventually into the golf club beyond which, improbably, was the caravan site where he and Rob were staying. All around here – the guide book called it Northdene, but everyone just knew it as Nob Hill – were the three and four-star hotels, the retirement homes, the big houses overlooking the sea. This was the part that had remained virtually unscathed. The place was as crisp and respectable as a ten-pound note and Richie hated it. A *Vote Labour* poster at election time would have been as welcome hereabouts as a vindaloo in a nuclear submarine.

As he walked along the beach he kept his eyes open for talent. There were a couple of language schools up among the big hotels and they could usually be relied on to come up trumps. French, Italian, Spanish, Portuguese – it didn't matter to Richie, who spoke English and English only with a Geordie twang, but whose hands and tongue and naughty bits could, he reckoned, make themselves understood in any language. Most of these girls could speak a bit of English, anyway, that was why they were here.

It wasn't quite *Baywatch* but it was pretty good, all the same. There were some nice-looking girls there sunning themselves on the beach, some nice skimpy costumes, some nice everything. A fortnight of going without made him feel pretty edgy still, but there was the sense that it wouldn't last. He stopped, chucked a few pebbles into the sea, got one to bounce and skip six times – eight was his record. He turned round, his back to the sea. Which one of you lovely ladies will it be tonight? he asked his admiring audience. You, perhaps, with the short black hair and the even shorter black swimsuit? Or you, the blonde with the green one-piece? I wish it were you, he beamed at a Kylie-clone – he daren't admit he lusted nightly after Kylie – but she had a bloke with her, a big good-looking bastard with a suspicious bulge down his beach shorts, like he'd stuffed a Black and Decker drill down there or something.

It had gone past being warm now, it was hot. There'd not really been any rain for weeks now, just these sudden showers like they'd had that morning, and then before you could say *oops mister, your flies are undone* it would be back in the seventies and eighties again. Secure behind his sunglasses, he took off his T-shirt and let the sun play around his upper body. He'd kept himself fit all through the summer and his muscles were in good shape. The league he and Rob played in with the Waggon and Horses didn't start its fixtures until nearly the end of August, but there was no harm in being prepared. They might get a few matches with the tech side, although Rob had said he wasn't sure about whether he was going back there for next term. There was a gym there where they could work out with weights, develop their upper-body strength. Besides, women seemed to like that kind of thing, a guy with a few muscles on him, not some baboon like Arnold Schwarzenegger, mind – that fucking guy looked like half a pound of walnuts stuffed inside a condom – but with a bit more meat on him than Ryan Giggs. People reckoned Rob looked a bit like Giggsy which was a bit ironic – was that the word? – because Rob played centre back and wouldn't know a feint if he fell over one in the dark. He was more the midfield hitman, was Rob. Richie fancied himself as an old-fashioned winger, like George Best or one of those guys he'd seen on his dad's videos. Sunderland had had a look at him once but nothing ever came of it. He was resigned to a future of muddy Sunday-morning battles with Internationale Consett or Babcock Valves.

So he scanned the beaches and saw one or two nice bods, but they were all either too young or too old or with husband-stroke-boyfriend in tow, and some who gave him a drop-dead look as he passed. He tried hard not to think that his two-week drought might be likely to stretch into a third before he got the chance to do the juicy with some nubile bimbette. Not like Rob who had been knobbing that Debbie something rotten at all hours of the day and night.

They had been down here three months – since late May, in fact, two weeks after the Cup Final and right at the start of the holiday season. At first, they'd both scored pretty often but of late it was Rob who was pulling everything. All Richie was pulling was his pud. He smiled as he remembered the song he and Rob used to sing on the bus back from school.

Robin Hood pulls his pud
Riding through the glen
Friar Tuck likes a fuck
Every now and then
Poor little John
Couldn't get it on
Robin Hood
Like to fuck
Friar Tuck

They would sing it over and over and over again, the whole of the fourth year on the top deck of the bus. Fatty Hammond always claimed it was him who made the words up but some of the lads he was mates with at the sixth form college knew the words as

well and a whole lot of other verses besides, about how Alan
A'Dale would settle for a male and all that, which was proof that
Fatty couldn't have written it, so they gave him a good scragging
and pinched his bag of M&Ms and threw them one by one out of
the window of the physics lab at the third years who were lined
up below them, waiting for old Ratchett to find the key for the
woodwork room.

There was something about Maid and laid but he'd forgotten
it now. One time they'd sung the Robin Hood song so loud and
so often that a woman on the bottom deck had complained
and the driver had stopped the bus right there outside the
old Doxford Shipyard where his dad used to work and given
them what for, and there was this stony silence until Lefty Wright
let rip with this absolute fucking monster of a fart, that sounded
like someone ripping calico sacking in two, and everyone had
cracked up and Richie pretty near pissed himself, and the driver
gave up and started the engine again and they heard no more
about it.

Richie was laughing to himself even as he walked along, bare-
chested, a big stupid smirking grin on his face, his ruined trainers
kicking up the sand. And then this girl, no, this fucking vision
walked right in front of him and he couldn't believe what he'd just
seen or whether she was a mirage, very tall, not at all English-
looking, with long blonde hair and legs that didn't know when to
stop. And moreover she'd smiled at him, looked at him from
behind huge dark glasses and actually smiled, and then turned
back to her friend and made her way up towards the Esplanade
while Richie stood there, frozen in time and space, arms by his
side, wondering whether the universe had come to an end or
whether she was just taking the piss because she'd seen him
walking along laughing to himself.

The first worthwhile totty he'd seen in weeks and he had to blow it, shuffling along by the water's edge grinning and sniggering to himself like he was some sort of chucklehead. *Shite, shite, shite,* he said to himself and in his confusion trampled all over this kid's sandcastle and had to help the little bugger remake it. Still, he had nothing else to do till the bar opened at six and he quite enjoyed sticking the flags in. He kept his eye out for The Vision in case she made a reappearance, but the beach was filling up fast and after fifteen minutes there was still no sign of her or her friend.

'I tell you man, she was absolutely fucking gorgeous,' he was still telling Rob an hour later. They were sitting in the staff rest room at the end of the pier, Richie with a plastic chair sticking to his bare skin in the heat and Rob still in his vile lime-green suit, like the kind of thing in which you might dress some deranged axe murderer in case he escaped and you wanted everyone to see him coming. He'd seen fire engines that were less obtrusive.

Rob seemed surprisingly uninterested in Richie's account of the blonde girl on the beach. He'd gone to see him specially, mainly because three to three-thirty was Rob's afternoon break but also because there was no one else he could talk to.

He was disappointed, though. He'd expected to be asked for full details but all he got was a sequence of non-committal grunts. Rob had a preoccupied air about him, as though Richie's lusts were somehow beneath him, not worthy of his serious interest. Finally Richie bit the bullet and asked him what the fuck was up with him.

'Nothing.'

'Come on, man.'

'I told you. There's nothing up.'

'You and my arse, man. I can see it a mile off. It's writ all over your face.'

'And I'm telling you man, there's nothing wrong with me, all right?'

'You're sitting there with a face like a wet week and you're telling me there's nothing wrong?'

He could see Rob hovering, like a fish about to bite. He bit. 'Well, this lad come to see me.'

'When?'

'Just now. Just before you came in.'

'Here?'

'No, at Buckingham fucking Palace. Jesus, where else do you think?'

He sure was irritable, Richie could see. 'Who was he?'

'He's called Mick Rowlandson or something. Fancies himself a bit.'

'And what happened? What was it about, like?'

'Aw, it was just about Debbie, that's all.'

'Debbie? What's she got to do with it?'

'This guy reckoned she was his property.'

'I thought she was going with you.'

'So did I.'

'So where's this Rowlandson bloke come in?'

'She was going with him before she met me. She told me about him. He thinks he's Jack the lad, you know. Nobody's going to muscle in on his patch.'

'That's her decision, isn't it?'

'Course it is. That's what I said to him.'

'What did he say to that?'

'Told me to fuck off out of it.'

'And what did you say back?'

'I said don't you fucking tell me to fuck off.'

'Too right.'

'That's not all.'

'I thought it might not be.'

'I told him if he goes round bothering Debbie, me and you'll be round to sort him out.'

'Where did I come into it?'

'You didn't. I told him you were my minder. That you'd done three for assault and you were mental.'

'Thanks a bunch, pal. I could use that. How did you leave it?'

Rob turned round away from the window. In the light Richie could see a small cut above his right eye.

'Where'd you get that?'

'From our friend.'

'That's a nice present. Did you give him one back?'

'Smack in the goolies, man.'

'What did he say to that?'

'Not a lot. Not a lot he could say. So I said I'd break his fucking nose if he came near me or Debbie again.'

'Do you think he will?'

'Dunno. He looked mean enough.'

Jesus. That was all they needed, some local hard man having it in for Rob. He probably had mates and mates spelled trouble. It must have been the weather, the heat made them all go mental, especially after five or six cans of Special Brew. He reckoned that was why he was feeling like a time bomb himself. Or was it just because he'd not got laid for so long? These past few days he'd been suffering from stiffies that were more like rolling pins. His ma had a rolling pin in the kitchen cupboard that he and his brother Ken used to play baseball with till he hit one straight through his da's greenhouse. He still remembered how sore his arse felt afterwards.

Rob was looking glum, which was always a bad sign. Why should he worry? He had a girl, he had money coming in, he had shoes that didn't leak.

'Are you still coming down tonight?' Richie asked eventually.

'Might as well. Nothing else to do, have I?'

'Billy's on the door tonight. You know Billy, don't you?'

'That big gorilla with the moustache and the sideburns?'

'He's all right. He's on my side, is Billy. Say you're with me and he'll let you in for free.'

Rob was at the washbasin, dabbing at his eye. It wasn't much of a cut and there didn't seem to be any bruising. He reckoned he'd live, even if a nice big shiner might have been more of a talisman.'

'Happen I might, then,' he said. 'But I'll see you later anyway.'

Music was coming through from the auditorium, that anonymous, anodyne music that always fills such places when nothing much is happening, as if the management were afraid that, without something to distract them, the audience might rip up the seats or tear off their clothes. They were already filing into the hall for the second house of the afternoon, comfortably fat old women from Warrington and Wigston with puffy sleeves, red with unaccustomed sunburn, unable to forsake their afternoon fix at the bingo for the sake of an hour or so of sun. There were younger women too, locals a lot of them, the kind who would run four or five cards at a time. There were big cash prizes to be won at the Excelsis Bingo Palace and every little helped these days, especially with a husband on the dole and new school clothes to buy for the autumn term. It wasn't the lottery but at least it got them out of the house.

Rob straightened his jacket and ran a comb through his hair. A man in an electric-blue tuxedo stuck his head round the door and looked straight through Richie.

20

'Ready when you are, Rob,' he said. Rob grunted, psyching himself up for another two-hour stint before returning to Debbie's welcoming body. He was a jammy bugger, thought Richie. Why didn't Debbie have a friend or, better still, a twin sister, an exact double of herself on whom he could expend his tortured energy? For weeks now he'd been listening to the two of them behind that curtain and it wasn't doing him a power of good.

The pier was burning white in the sun, the glare from its wedding-cake architecture almost hurting the eyes. There were a couple of girls sunbathing on the pier decking, one piece swimsuits, nice tits. Richie took it all in at a glance, like a racing tipster assessing horseflesh. He liked the dark-haired one. He gave them a big smile and, encouragingly, they smiled back. We might be on to something here, he thought, wishing Rob were with him instead of calling out his mathematical inanities to his uncomprehending audience, but then a couple of guys came up with cans of Coke, big guys with tattoos and army haircuts, probably squaddies from Colchester or somewhere, and sat down with the girls without speaking, and Richie got the message.

He played a couple of games in the arcade, won a few quid and just as soon lost it again. That left him with just spare change in his pocket until he got paid that night at the Zero Six. He fancied a cool tube himself but decided he couldn't afford it, so he used the drinking fountain on the pier instead. At least that was free. At his feet, a little Jack Russell lapped thirstily at the bowl a thoughtful management had left out for just such a purpose. Jesus, he thought, splashing water on his body, it was hotter than ever now. The Jack Russell caught his eye and barked, and then went back to the bowl of water.

His bare skin was beginning to burn a little on his shoulders so he put his shirt back on. He saw a bunch of guys he knew who were off to drink at the Pier Head Hotel, but he said he had something else to do, even though he didn't. He just didn't want them to know he was skint, that was all.

Richie wandered off along the sea front, his mind and body going in separate directions. Without really thinking too hard about it – in fact, he didn't think about it at all – he climbed the winding stairs that led up from the sea front and found himself among the streets of the Old Town.

There was an arcade there he liked to walk down, nice and cool, lots of airy space. It was called the Imperial Arcade, a throwback to the Edwardian heyday of Dunwich, all cast-iron columns and glass roof lights. The shops here were small and expensive, but they were interesting. There was one shop that sold telescopes and maps and globes, another that had old toys at bizarre prices. He looked in the window. There were a couple of Dinkies there that he was sure his older brother Dave still had, up in his parents' attic. He remembered playing with them as a kid, the coal lorry with the sacks and the weighing scales, the Lady Penelope car from *Thunderbirds*. They were asking a hundred and twenty pounds for each of them, in the shop window.

There was a tiny little sweetie shop too, not the kind of place where you might buy a Mars or a packet of Rizla, but one where the chocs came individually and were put into a box for you by a girl wearing too much make-up. He stood by the open doorway, breathing in deeply. It was almost overpowering, a smell of chocolate and luxury and wild indulgence. He studied the glass bowls in the windows, the six different kinds of truffles, the Belgian dessert chocolate. He tried to work out the prices – maths had never been his strong suit at school – but realised that one individual Montelimar, about fifteen seconds munching, tops, would set you back more than a Twix. Still, he could have demolished a bagful and he liked the look of the girl behind the counter.

He walked on. Near the end of the arcade was a lingerie shop which was definitely not for the kind of girl who bought her knicks in a three-pack from Marks and Sparks. He gazed in the window. An almost totally transparent black bra for eighty-five pounds, a long creamy length of froth that resolved itself into a nightdress priced at three hundred and twenty pounds. There were curious half-torsos in the window dressed in different kinds of things that didn't look as though they'd be all that practical on a keen November afternoon in Whitley Bay, with the wind whipping in from Norway and the whitecaps scudding in the breeze. He thought about the pampered backsides that would slip inside them and it made him feel horny all over again.

Through the plate-glass frontage he could see there was a couple in the shop, a man of about thirty-five, the woman a few years younger, late twenties maybe. She was tall, medium-length blonde hair, not at all the kind you saw working on the pick 'n' mix in Woollies. No, she looked as though she'd be at home behind the wheel of some white convertible GTi. Cars like that always attracted that kind of woman.

They were looking at bras on a spinner inside the shop. Most guys in that situation would be shuffling about, looking out of the window, trying not to look too embarrassed, wishing they had a paper to read or something, wishing they could just get the hell out of there and down to Halfords or B&Q or somewhere they could relate to. This guy seemed entirely at his ease, however, chatting to his girl, smiling at the assistant who hovered behind them, looking knowledgeable. Everyone seemed to be enjoying themselves. Richie stopped and looked, trying to imagine what was going on.

The girl doing the buying turned round and Richie could see she had one hell of a figure on her. She was holding out some bra to show the guy, a wispy sort of a thing in purple lace. Richie closed his eyes and tried to imagine what she would look like with her top off. The one she was already wearing didn't leave too much to the imagination.

When he opened them again the girl was disappearing into a little curtained cubicle at the back of the shop. The big plate-glass window let him see everything. He was aware of a sense of desire and longing. He wished he had x-ray eyes. The counter girl tidied some things up in the shop while the man just stood there, still smiling.

Richie wondered what he was doing there, rooted to the spot like some voyeur. It wasn't the usual way he got his kicks – well, not since he and Rob and Vinnie Caldwell and a few of the guys from the youth club used to sneak round the back of the nurses' home with the telescope they borrowed off Tommy Flanagan – but there was something that kept him there, just the same. Lounging against a pillar on the frontage of the shop opposite, he tried to look like he was just watching the world go by, but without much success.

He saw the girl's face at the curtain and then the guy went over to her, looking through. Jesus, thought Richie, she's showing him what she looks like. He tried to imagine what the guy must be seeing and thinking, his girlfriend flaunting her tits at him in the middle of Imperial Arcade on a sunny Saturday afternoon, and realised he had got an erection just through watching. He shifted his feet uncomfortably, hoping no one would notice.

Big, warm breasts. Richie recalled the first time he had squeezed a pair – they were Tina Harthope's knockers, in fact, and he'd done the dirty deed in the hallway at Kecks Richardson's sixteenth birthday party. He recalled how astonished he'd been at their softness – he'd thought, for some reason, they'd be quite hard. He'd wondered why, through her Miss Selfridge halter top, she didn't seem to have any nipples, whereas the girls in the mags seemed to have titties like chapel hat-pegs. And then, even as he groped her in his fumbling, amateur-seducer way, they had perked up wondrously, hard against the palm of his hand, and he'd have practically come there and then in his 501s if he hadn't had the good sense to drag Tina off into the darkened living room where a good half-dozen couples were already snogging, and there discover more of the secrets of the female anatomy.

He looked back at the shop, afraid for a moment he might have missed something. The girl had come out of the changing room now and was smiling broadly. She must have found the right size. She said something to the assistant who went to another of the spinners and held up a pair of extremely skimpy panties, the exact match for the bra. The girl nodded and pointed to something else, down below. The man was smiling.

I'm not surprised, thought Richie. He could just picture him now, slipping his hand down the front of her jeans, unzipping her, fingers probing inside, running over the purple lace. He could imagine her parting her legs for him, his fingers slipping over the waistband or perhaps in at the side, running through her pubic hair – and he was sure she wouldn't have much, blondes never did – and gently but inexorably moving down towards that warm dampness between her thighs. He could almost hear the way her breathing would change. You could always tell when women were getting aroused, Richie knew, because their breathing changed. At the moment he felt like he was panting like a horse himself. He was surprised at how much his heart was thumping. Perhaps people thought he was some kind of pervert. Maybe they'd send for a copper, have him arrested.

The assistant was crouched down now, out of sight. Richie wondered what was going on, what she was looking for. The couple didn't seem too bothered, they were standing close together like there was some big secret they were sharing. The girl whispered something in the man's ear and he laughed. It was making Richie feel pretty isolated, no girl, no job, no money and nowhere he could really call home.

The assistant stood up, looking triumphant. She was holding up a suspender belt in purple lace, just like the other stuff. The man and the girl both nodded, still smiling. Jesus, thought Richie, a girl like that with lovely big tits and she wears suspenders as well. He swallowed hard. This was getting too much to take.

He always liked the look of women in stockings like they wore in the magazines, but he'd never been with a girl who wore them. Karen Brady's sister Jill did, they said, but that was because she got bad thrush or something which came on worse with tights. Richie didn't fancy getting an itchy willy off her and, besides, he didn't fancy Jill much anyway. Her tits were nice but she had a big bum and she looked too much like that girl on *Brookside* that he loathed. So Richie's fantasies were all on paper, for the moment at any rate.

He wondered what kind of stockings the girl would wear, nice and long and sheer. She'd look good with a short skirt, he thought. At Christmas time women seemed to go mad over all these fancy tights and stockings with patterns all over them – never at any other time of year, for some reason. He liked fishnets too, leather mini-skirts and fishnets, very punky, that was more like it. He liked the way girls had dressed back then but he was too young, really. He was born ten years too late. There was nothing like that now, not in North Shields or Sunderland or anywhere that he knew.

He could imagine the bloke in the shop – God, he really was starting to resent him now – running his hands over those smooth, silky thighs, her dress riding up high over her stocking tops. He wondered what it would be like to touch her there, where the smooth skin met the rougher fabric of her stockings, the suspenders taut against her legs, an air of expectancy as his hands moved higher, a half-smile playing around her lips. He'd seen too many videos – Tommy Charlton had a rare old collection of them that he used to show at parties and things, especially if there weren't any women around – to bother much with subtleties of sexual fantasy but this girl in the shop, so confident and assured-looking, so natural, well, she was different somehow. It made him think differently about her, lusting after her there on that hot afternoon as the Saturday shoppers bustled past him, the scent of money in the air.

They were paying for it all now, or at least the bloke was, getting his wallet out and choosing a card. They'd turned Richie down flat when he applied for a card. Rob had had one but he'd defaulted on the repayments once too often and they'd taken it off him. Now it was cash for everything, if poss. He would have liked to have been there in the shop, paying for all that underwear for his girl and then going straight home and shagging her rigid. The best he could hope for was to pull someone tonight at the bar and, if that failed, a quick one off the wrist while Rob and Debbie writhed and struggled and sighed behind the curtain. The trouble was, he wanted somebody now, right there and then. He was rock-hard with desire and feeling as light-headed as if he'd just done a couple of poppers.

The couple came out of the shop, their arms around each other.

Richie studied them closely, the atmosphere of confidence and assurance that hung around them. He caught a whiff of the girl's perfume as they passed barely a couple of feet from him. He tried to hold his breath for as long as he could just to savour it and keep it within himself, watching her tight little backside as she walked down the arcade away from him and out of his life forever. One day, darling, he said to himself, as he set off in the opposite direction. One day I'll find someone like you.

He walked along, dodging through the mingling crowds of shoppers and holidaymakers. He felt very confused, a lot of resentment beginning to surface in his mind. He was standing on the pavement at the entrance to the arcade, not knowing which way to go and, in truth, not really caring. There was a lot of traffic moving up and down the narrow street and he was finding it difficult to spot a gap so he could cross.

Then a movement caught his eye. Oh shite, he thought. It was the girl again, The Vision, the one from the beach, the one with the legs. She was on the opposite side of the road, walking away from him. He lost sight of her for a moment but suddenly there she was again, going past Boots. She was with a bunch of other girls, three or four of them. They were laughing their heads off about something. He hoped they weren't talking about him, this idiot boy who wanders the beach by himself, giggling and sniggering.

He ducked across Portland Road, narrowly missing being hit by a delivery van. There were a lot of people streaming along the pavement towards him but he was able to weave in and out of them, trying to keep her blonde hair in sight. He seemed to be gaining on them when, his eyes fixed thirty yards ahead, he walked smack into Billy Brilleaux, the bouncer from the Zero Six. He was with his girlfriend, Sue.

28

'Richie,' the Neolithic security man exclaimed, all sideboards and tache. 'You trying to find an opticians or something? You need a white stick.'

'Aw, not now, Billy. I'm in a hurry.'

'So I can see. Look, mate, I got that fifty you lent me—'

'Give it us tonight, Billy.' At any other time he'd have been glad of it, he hadn't more than about three quid in loose change on him.

'No, it'll be spent by then. I just been to the cashpoint, see.'

'Billy gets through cash like there's no tomorrow,' said Sue helpfully. 'I should talk. I'm just as bad.'

Richie smiled, trying to humour her. The trouble was, he quite fancied Sue Browne himself but had more sense that to start messing about with a guy like Billy. For Rob, though, it would be different. Rob's brains were in the end of his dick.

'No, I really got to go,' Richie protested, but Billy was already pulling tenners out of his wallet and pushing them into his unwilling hand. Richie peered over Billy's shoulder. He could see The Vision up ahead, that gorgeous ass, crossing Portland Road at the lights, at the junction with Connaught Avenue, right by the Kardomah. For two or three seconds he could see those long elegant legs outlined in their white jeans against the halted traffic and then she was lost to view.

Shite, he muttered to himself. Nobody had ever pissed him off by giving him fifty quid before, but there was a first time for everything.

'Thanks, Billy,' he said absently, as the lights changed and the traffic began to roll down Portland Road once more.

'There's a branch of Specsavers next to W H Smith,' said Billy, a big daft grin on his big daft face. 'I'll lead you there if you like.'

Richie gave him a wan smile and pocketed the notes. At least he could buy a few cans of lager now and spend the afternoon watching the racing on the portable back at the caravan. It was a bit too dangerous walking around town. There was something explosive in the air. All these fucking women and he couldn't lay his hands on a single one of them.

In the end, he spent most of the afternoon dozing on a rock at the posh end of town, not far from where he'd first seen the girl. He was instinctively sure she'd not be coming back but, he reasoned with himself, you never knew, especially with women. People had favourite spots at the seaside that they liked to come back to day after day and why should she be any different, just because she was young and beautiful and tall and blonde, with nice tits and an ass you could sink your teeth into on a winter's night?

Billy's girl, Sue Browne, now she had an ass on her all right. He was convinced she liked him. She reminded him in a way of his girlfriend back home, Linda. Sprawled out on his rock, his eyes red against the glare of the sun, his mind went back to that party at Kevin Coiley's place not long before they'd come down to Dunwich for the summer, when they'd first met.

It had seemed obvious right from the start that she was mad keen on him. He'd been in the kitchen, drinking beer – well, where else was there better to stand around at a party and keep an eye on what was knocking around? They always said that Gazza, when he played for United, used to sit near the ladies' lav when he went out clubbing, so that they'd all pass before his basilisk gaze sooner or later.

Anyway, she'd come in with her mates looking for a bottle of Lambrusco or something. She was half-pissed already, which was just as well in the circs, and they got talking and one thing led to another and before too long they were out on the back porch together necking.

'Do you fancy going upstairs?' Linda breathed in his ear.

He'd known, right from the start, that he was on to a winner. All the same, he was sure his heart must have missed a beat.

He didn't answer, just held her close and gave her a squeeze and she got the message. Trying not to look like they were doing what they were doing, they brushed their way through the throngs of drink-sodden students towards the stairs. Kevin Coiley's dad was an industrial chemist with ICI in Wilton and they had a big place with loads of rooms, just right for a party and a bit of shagging upstairs.

They climbed the thickly-carpeted stairs arm in arm, and Jimmy Bilsland gave Richie a big wink as he came out of the upstairs bog. Richie was quite glad in a way to have been noticed, even if it would be all around the tech the following Monday. He got lucky with the first room he tried, a guest bedroom by the look of it, not very lived-in but it would serve his purpose fine. There was even a lock on the door.

He kissed Linda hungrily in the light of the twin bedside lamps. He liked the way she ground her hips against his loins – it made him feel wanted, desirable. She must have registered how big and stiff he was, because she asked him if he'd got anything. Of course he frigging did, he wasn't that stupid to come to a party like Kevin's without a catering-sized packet of freds.

'It's just that I forgot my pill this morning,' she said. 'We won't need it another time.'

Another time? Jesus, he'd hardly got her knickers off and already she was talking about screwing him again. The rest of her words were muffled as he thrust his tongue into her mouth.

She was wearing a clinging black dress that did little to conceal her nineteen-year-old body. He pulled it up over her hips, his hands running over her tights. Still with her mouth glued to

31

his, she began to unbutton his shirt and pushed it back over his shoulders. She let go of him for a moment, looked him deep in the eyes and then bent forward and began to lick each of his nipples in turn. That always worked wonders with him, having his nipples licked, as he pulled her hips closer to him and rubbed his cock hard against her.

She moved from one nipple to the other, her tongue flickering, sometimes nipping him with her teeth so that it made him wince. Loaded with desire, he waited until she paused for breath and then pulled her dress up and over her shoulders, shedding his own shirt as he did so. She wasn't wearing a bra under her tight-fitting dress and her breasts were bigger than he'd imagined they would be, the nipples already formed into hard little points that could and did invite his probing tongue.

Still sucking hard at her tits, he kicked off his shoes and struggled out of his chinos as best he could. Then they were lying down on the bed together, he in just his shorts and she in her tights. He left it to her to take them off – he never could get the hang of getting the tights off a girl without ripping them.

They were lying together, necking, and he slipped his hand in under the waistband of her knickers, feeling the hard crinkly hair under there, the warm moisture lower down. The crotch of her pants was soaking wet – she was dying for it and so was he.

He ran the tips of his fingers over her vaginal lips, slick and moist with her secretions, and he could feel them parting for him. She felt nice and tight as he slipped first one and then two fingers into her. She moaned and bit his earlobe, pushed her tongue into his ear, something else that was guaranteed to enhance his already turbo-charged erection. God, she had an incredibly agile tongue, he acknowledged. He hoped she was going to suck him, if not now then later maybe, or another time. For the moment, all he wanted to do was cram as much as possible of himself inside her.

As if she could read his mind, she took hold of his cock, squeezing it through his cotton pants. He hoped she liked it. Like most lads, he was convinced his willy was at best only average size, but a couple of girls in the past had said how nice and big it was. Maybe it went with the job, that kind of male insecurity. It didn't really bother him all that much.

Their mouths together, they both pulled off their own underwear and then, pausing only to slip it on, he was on top of her, her hand guiding him in. He felt immediately how wet and tight she was – not like Laura Tunnicliffe who had one like the Tyne Tunnel – and for the moment he just paused there, as if taking in the view.

'What are you waiting for?' she breathed and then he was pushing into her, the balls of his feet against the foot of the bed, pivoting his body backwards and forwards. She had her legs wide apart as if to welcome him and her eyes were open too, looking up at him, large grey-blue eyes heavily rimmed with eye shadow, her red lipstick seemingly unscathed despite their passionate assaults on each others' mouths. Her hair had fallen back on to the pillow and he was surprised by how her small features looked almost childlike in the glow of the bedside lamp.

But there was nothing childlike about the way she powered her hips back against him, slewing and swerving her body to meet his every thrust. Screwing someone for the first time could be difficult but – whether it was the beer or something that made the difference – there were no problems here with Linda. She seemed to anticipate his every move, to go with him every step of the way, using the wet, muscular walls of her vagina to massage his hard and thrusting maleness.

When she came she bit his shoulder hard enough to bring out

a nasty bruise the following morning, and he could feel the small, butterfly flutterings in her abdomen begin to spread out until it seemed like a tremor, a small earthquake even, was passing through her small and immensely desirable body. He gazed down at her contorted face, her eyes tight closed now as the spasms passed through her, her nipples pink and engorged. He could feel his own orgasm coming on as he pushed and pulled on top of her, the low bass note that spanned the universe from deep inside him, and then he was pumping his own hot, boiling seed into her, eight or nine big shuddering spasms from the root of his manhood. He hadn't come off in nearly a week and he let her have the whole lot at once.

Afterwards, they lay quietly in each others' arms. He wished he had a ciggie but he realised he'd left them downstairs, in the kitchen where he'd been drinking. Linda, he knew, didn't smoke but a lot of girls her age did. Now that his passion was at least partly spent he was surprised at how loud the music was from downstairs, the thump of techno coming up through the walls of the big, stone-built house. He wondered how it was going at the party down there, what Rob was up to. He twisted round to look at his watch and it was only just after half-eleven, plenty of time left. He hadn't a care in the world. It was the best he'd felt for ages.

They talked for quite a while, not about much in particular, clubs and music and people they knew. Richie was surprised how well he got on with Linda, a lot better than some girls whom he'd screwed at parties and things. There were times when he couldn't wait to flush his johnny down the bog and get the hell out of there, but this wasn't one of them. He felt very easy with her, felt it could go further. He asked her if she knew Cave Nine, a new club that had opened near the Metro Centre. No, she didn't. Well, would she like to go on Friday, with him? 'Sure,' she said, without a moment's hesitation.

The second time they did it, it was really easy with her. He didn't scale quite the heights of desire he'd felt for her before – the beer was beginning to take its effect on him – but it was good all the same. He took his time about it, spent a lot of effort on stroking her and making her feel good, and then he got busy with his fingers down there, just brushing against the tops of her thighs where the skin was most sensitive. He liked the perfume she was wearing, something deep and musky like Ysatis or Opium or whatever, very grown up for a nineteen-year-old, and that helped to enhance his mood of confidence and expansiveness. He had one finger inside her and with the other he was just brushing her along the outer lips, incredibly gentle, like Annabel Lewin had told him to be after accusing him of all but raking her because he was so rough. No, they liked it very gentle down there, it wasn't like you were trying to rub off a scratchcard, and he got the jackpot this time, because suddenly she just murmured at him to stop and then let him put it into her. She pulled her legs right up around his waist and it was like he was falling forward into her, he was in so deep, and they did it like that for quite a while, she thrusting up at him while he moved to and fro inside her, her breasts crushed against his chest, their perspiration mingling as they made love together on the warm white quilt cover of the Coiley's second guest bedroom.

They'd gone out a few times after that, had done it a lot, but then it just seemed to calm down of its own accord. It wasn't that they'd had an argument or anything, just that neither of them seemed to be that desperate to see one another. Once in a while he'd ring her up and they'd go out somewhere, and once she called him up and invited him to spend the night with her at her house, her parents being away staying with rellies. It was like she was a friend rather than a girlfriend, someone you felt you had to go out with every Friday and Saturday because it was expected of you, and you'd do this for a few weeks until either you realised you were getting nowhere or because something better came along. It was a good arrangement, one that would last. He'd sent Linda a couple of postcards from Dunwich, had promised to come and see her when he got home in September. He even rang her once or twice, just to hear the sound of her voice. He was very fond of her, he realised, in a quiet way.

He opened his eyes, hardly aware of where he was for the moment till he heard the sound of the waves. He sat up on the rock, blinking, took his sunglasses out of his pocket and put them on. The tide was coming in, so it must have been about three o'clock. He felt a lot calmer now, not quite so overheated and overexcited. He was glad he'd run into Billy – the fifty, nestling in his back pocket would come in useful. He didn't really fancy going back to the caravan, especially if Rob and Debbie were going to be there and, besides, there were some things he needed to get, not least a shirt he'd seen in the window of one of the shops on Eastern Avenue. It was thirty-five quid, but he'd get more that evening once he'd worked at the Zero Six and he reckoned he could afford it. It would mean going back into town but, what the hell, it might give him the chance to see the girl again. The Vision. Feeling excited by the prospect, he slipped off the rock and made his way back along the beach at the foot of the cliffs.

Chapter Two

Giselle Lescarboura lay back on the bed in the warm, summer-afternoon sunshine and smiled. A breeze gently stirred the net curtains as it came in through the open window, bringing with it the salt tang of the sea and the distant, muted hum of traffic along Eastern Avenue. The room was small and intimate, its walls bathed in a creamy glow, the furniture discreet and functional. There were thirty others almost exactly like it in the building. Most of them were considerably more untidy than hers. This was, after all, a student residence. Garfield Hall School of Languages taught young men and women from the ages of sixteen to twenty and they made their mark on its fabric in characteristic style.

She turned her head on the pillow, looking out of the window at the old bay tree outside, its leaves parched and dry in the summer heat. Every morning, Giselle loved to see the sun rise from her bedroom window. There was a big garden at the back of the school which had, once upon a time, been the home of a wealthy Victorian industrialist who had retired to Dunwich some time in the 1870s, just as it was becoming a favourite resort for the rich and fashionable. Some of the surrounding houses in Northdene were still in private hands but most had been turned into hotels and residential homes. These stately, white-painted classical buildings gazed out over the North Sea as they had done for a century and a quarter, watching the town grow and contract, silently overseeing the transition from barouche landau to Jaguar and, these days, to Mercedes and BMW and Toyota.

'Do me again, just there,' she murmured, without breaking her gaze.

Her loins were as warm as the day. Camille Minette's tongue flickered out again and sought Giselle's labia, opened up before her like an oyster revealing its treasure. It felt good, the way she played with her. Camille certainly knew what to do. She had a finesse and delicacy about her that was unusual in one so young. Boys, in Giselle's experience – and for an eighteen-year-old she had accrued a considerable amount of it – could never be quite so gentle. Hard fucking, yes, but gentle coaxing and touching – almost never.

Giselle parted her long, colt-like legs to make it easier for her, and to bring more of her body into contact with Camille's probing tongue. Again she lay back and relaxed, letting her feelings flow through her, her thoughts and urges merging into one delicious stream of desire. It was the second time Camille had licked her out that afternoon, and she was feeling warm and drowsy.

Her hips moved on the tangled quilt in a slow, easy rhythm, mimicking the movements of her friend's tongue. She looked down at her, crouched at the foot of the bed, the way her firm young breasts hung down like little pears ripe for the plucking. Giselle enjoyed nuzzling and sucking them, sometimes several times a day.

She and Giselle would sleep together maybe a couple of times a week. It got so they organised it to tie in with their timetables at the language school. Wednesday was always a good night to make love well into the small hours because both of them had a free until eleven the following morning and, anyway, the women only came round to clean on Tuesdays and Fridays. Sometimes, between lessons, unable to wait until the evening, she and Camille would hurry back to her room and have sex quickly and passionately, the way it often was with men but not so often with women. Giselle liked long, comfortable sex and she also liked it quick and urgent. They shared a vibrator which they used for such moments, when they were both too excited to be gentle.

She liked women and she also liked men, sometimes both together. Anything that gave her pleasure was fine by her. Camille, it seemed, felt pretty much the same way. She was glad they had found each other. They had had some good times since they had met at the language school earlier that summer. She would be sad when the time came to return home to her parents.

Giselle was aware of her own nipples, of how hard and firm they were. She ran her fingers over them, large and rosy-pink, aching for the touch of Camille's tongue and teeth. She took each of them in turn between her finger and thumb and pinched them, quite hard. The sensation of exquisite feeling, half-pleasure, half-pain, served only to enhance the urgings of her loins, made her push her hips up against Camille's mouth, until she felt the dark girl's tongue pass along the furrow of her labia and gently insert itself into her vagina. She could see her now, wide-mouthed, her hair spilling out on to Giselle's thighs, both girls naked, the radio playing softly in the background. It was the Saturday afternoon chart show. They had taken off each other's clothes when they'd just started the Top Forty and they were still only on number eighteen, which was climbing fast. There was plenty of time to enjoy each other's bodies before they hit the coveted number one spot.

So they lay there on the bed, sometimes changing or reversing position so that Giselle could lick her friend's pussy. They lay together for a while like inverted spoons, each of them tonguing the other's breasts and nipples. It was a delightful feeling, the warmth of the afternoon, the infinite tenderness of touch. As Giselle rolled her friend's firm, brownish nipples between her lips, Camille's hands were between Giselle's thighs, moving in synchronicity, rolling her clitoris with practised ease. Then, quite suddenly, Giselle felt herself aware of a butterfly fluttering deep within her stomach and knew that she was about to climax.

'Lick me out, darling,' she murmured. 'I want to come in your face.'

Camille disentangled herself and slid down the bed. Giselle opened her legs for her, aware of how wet her pussy was. She felt Camille's familiar, expert tongue run along the furrow of her labia, probing and cherishing, seeking out those secret spots that gave her so much pleasure.

'Harder,' she hissed and Camille, who knew her friend's needs, pressed her tongue into her with renewed urgency. It was like a weapon now, a penis, something with which to penetrate her fully, like they did some nights with other means. Giselle wanted her tongue up her, to put her own tongue into Camille, to taste her salty essences, the reality of her pubic bush against her face. And then the flutterings grew imperceptibly into a tremor and she felt herself going over the edge, almost in slow motion, her nipples now absolutely rigid between her knowing fingers, her body arched and expectant as the first wave of orgasm hit her with the impact of a gale-driven sea.

Later, she and Camille lay for a long time in each other's arms. The radio played on, well into the top ten now. For Giselle, it was nice to have come but Camille was happy, for the moment, simply to lie there with her, their arms around each other, a world of little kisses and small words of endearment. Later on, perhaps, they might dry-fuck each other, rubbing their pussies together and murmuring delicious obscenities into each other's ears, but for the moment they were happy with things the way they were. Slowly, imperceptibly, the two of them drifted off into late-afternoon reverie, halfway between quiet contemplation and the mellowness of sleep.

Camille had been talking about the party they were going to have at the college that evening. It was a pity Giselle couldn't be there – she would have enjoyed it. But an engagement was an engagement. Sprawled listlessly on the bed, Giselle had a vision of the orchard of her parents' home and the pears that, every summer, they would gather up. There were quinces too, and apples, until by September the grass would be absolutely littered with them. People from the village were allowed to come and gather the fruit – there was far too much for the Lescarbouras' own use. When she was younger Giselle would not go into the orchard for fear of the wasps that buzzed and crawled around the rotting fruit.

Once someone had come to the house and made them a gift of a bag of supermarket apples. They had lingered on, uneaten, until Giselle's mother – clearing up the kitchen prior to going on holiday – threw them out onto the grass. When they returned from the Ile de Ré a fortnight later the apples were still there, whole and perfect, utterly unblemished. Their own trees fruited, the apples and pears fell and rotted, but still the supermarket apples lay there, looking as if they had been taken from the shelves at the Intermarché that very morning. Giselle went out and picked one up, experimentally. It was as round and green and waxy and whole as it had been in the bowl on the kitchen table. All around her, apples turned to mush and to blackened ruin but these seemed immune to the inevitable processes of decay. Then she went back to school and she never did find what became of the hard green apples. Perhaps they were still there.

Giselle had come to Dunwich specifically to attend the language school. It had an excellent reputation. The fees were extremely high but the class sizes were small and the staff were well respected. There were several such schools in the area but Garfield Hall was undoubtedly the one with the most cachet.

When her parents first announced the scheme to send her to England, she was surprised. She thought her English – learned at the *lycée* with Madame Moscato – was already good enough for her *baccalaureat* but her parents evidently felt differently. She rather wished, at first, that she might have stayed with an English family as she had done when she was younger, but her father had been firm. If only he could have seen what his dear elder daughter was getting up to! It was asking for trouble, to let her loose among a town full of young and attractive people of both sexes. At first she had felt very homesick but now, with three weeks to go before she returned home, she felt very reluctant to leave Dunwich.

Giselle was terribly fond of her father. She loved her mother too, but it was her father who was her particular favourite. She was old enough to begin to wonder if her paternal feelings might not be entirely innocent – for while when she was younger, at the onset of puberty, she had dreamed, sometimes, of being naked with him, even of him penetrating her – but then she had learned that such feelings were quite natural in a girl of her age, and felt relieved. Still, she sensed a little danger there. She still recalled the time she had found her mother and father making love inside the summerhouse, how she had watched from behind in rapt fascination as he entered her. She could see his backside moving backwards and forwards, her mother's legs wrapped around his waist, the bawdy things both of them were quietly whispering to each other.

It was the sounds of their laughter that had first caught her attention. This had helped formulate her whole attitude to sex – it could be many things at many different times but, above all, it was fun. She hadn't felt in the least shocked by what she saw but later, for a while, when she was going through her desperately religious phase at thirteen or fourteen, she wondered if she was going to burn in hell for all time for her sins. She soon grew out of it. The experience helped her grow up a little, taught her that sex was something to be enjoyed by everyone, even when they were as old as her parents. Maman would be thirty-eight that year! Impossible – to be so old and yet still want to make love most nights. Giselle's room was just along the corridor from theirs and, despite the thick walls and heavy wooden doors of their lovely old house, she had a pretty shrewd idea of what was going on.

In three weeks she would be going back to Descarville, to the lovely old house by the river – she hadn't missed the mosquitoes that were an accepted part of life in their district – and her school and her friends. She had about six boyfriends at any given moment, and it would be interesting to see how things would work out when she got back. There were a couple of boys in particular from the village she went with from time to time, both of them of good family, who knew the right places to go to, the right parties to find out about and be invited to. And there was Jean-Paul, whom her parents didn't know about. He was much older, nearly thirty, married but separated. He was the only one who had been fucking her earlier that summer, the others were just for going around with, for teasing. She wondered how things would be with Jean-Paul when she got back.

She didn't know precisely when girls first came into her life. All girls, she knew, went through a period of experimenting but with Giselle, it just stayed with her. It was difficult sometimes to find a girl whom she liked who would actually go to bed with her, but a surprising number of them did. In a little place like Descarville, it paid to be discreet. Every few weeks she and Misette, a girl she knew from school, would go to the discreet little club at La Benoise and see who they could pick up, or be picked up by. Once she had been amazed to find one of her own teachers there, Madame Dupuis, and while both had silently acknowledged the other's presence, nothing was ever said. Descarville was an old-fashioned town and such scandals would not be tolerated. They quite often saw Madame Dupuis at the Pink Pussycat in Gascon-sur-Baines, especially on leather nights.

Giselle's liberality of outlook had its advantages. Her father had given her a generous allowance but it was never quite enough for what a girl of eighteen, alone in a foreign country, might require by way of day-to-day expenses, to say nothing of the occasional luxury she needed to indulge herself with. And so Giselle had found ways of supplementing her income, even in Dunwich. Some of the girls bought and sold a little hash, a little ecstasy, a little speed but Giselle had found something much more interesting and lucrative. There was a discreet house on the coastal road out of town where a great deal of money might be earned in a comparatively short space of time. She would be going there that evening with Brigitte, another girl from the language school. That was why she was catching a few minutes' sleep that afternoon. Those nights at the Laurels tended to be long ones, sometimes not ending until the sun was high in the sky and she would make her way back, a trifle unsteady perhaps, along the cliffs. For a working girl, it didn't do to fall asleep on the job, especially when several hundred pounds could be earned in a couple of hours or so.

She woke up suddenly, pulled from dreams of French summer fields and boys in long waving grass. She felt uncomfortably hot and sticky. The air in the college room was very close, despite the open window. Camille was sitting on the edge of the bed, brushing her long dark hair.

'Come on,' said her friend. 'Let's do something.'

'Just let me sleep,' said Giselle. 'It's so stuffy in here, it makes me drowsy.'

Camille got to her feet and opened the window still further, pulled back the curtains that had hidden what they had been doing together from prying eyes. The sudden inrush of light and air did very little to ease the feeling of heaviness that pervaded Giselle's senses. It was so different from home, these humid English days with scarcely a breath of breeze. At home it got much, much hotter but it didn't feel the same. Somehow there was still a freshness there. Here, on the other hand, the atmosphere was so thick sometimes, it was like being in the sauna.

'Let's go down to the beach,' said Camille, pulling her clothes on. 'There might be someone there.'

'I don't feel like meeting anyone. I'd just like to be by myself. Or just the two of us—'

Camille smiled. She came across and sat next to Giselle, stroking her hair. She was wearing a simple dress of pale yellow cotton. Giselle was still quite naked, her limbs long and lissom in the gentle late-afternoon light.

All of a sudden, Camille bent down and kissed Giselle on the forehead. 'I know,' she said. 'I know just how you feel. But you'll feel better, I can promise you. We can go along past the cliffs, can't we? No one ever goes there.'

'Won't the tide be in?'

'No, not for hours yet. Come on, it will be lovely and cool there, you know you'll like it.'

Giselle raised herself up on her elbows, tousled and heavy lidded. She knew that what Camille was saying was true. It might help wake her up.

'OK,' she said. 'Do you want to go now?'

'We may as well. I'll just go to my room for some things. I'll see you downstairs, shall I, in ten minutes?'

And with that she was gone. Giselle went to the small wardrobe and took out a short summer dress, a pattern of soft greens and reds that went well with her blonde hair. She didn't bother with any underwear, not even pants. She wanted to feel cool and free. She liked it down by the rocks, with the waves from the incoming tide breaking around her. It was a good idea to go there, to feel the sun on their backs, to look out at the ships passing along the coast. She wanted to breathe in the sense of freedom.

The school overlooked the broad green strand that divided Eastern Avenue from the sea. It should have been green but, with the heat, the grass was now parched and brown, dotted with the bodies of recumbent sun-worshippers. There were flower beds, too, that were visibly wilting in the heat. A small green pavilion stood in the middle of the strand, decked with graffiti despite the council's best efforts, a bizarre and stumpy little pagoda. Some of the boys from the college were sprawled out in its shadow, drinking beer from cans although the principal had expressly forbidden it. They called out greetings. Camille and Giselle waved back. It was nice to be popular.

The two girls made their way down the broken concrete paths that wound down to the beach and then walked along the water's edge. Soon they had left the town and its swollen, sunburned summer population behind. The cliffs closed in around them and, when they stepped into their shadow, the could almost feel a chill on their skins. At the foot of the cliffs were rocks, heavy fractured fragments torn out by the endless tides, splashed green and brown with seaweed, limpid pools around them. The broad sandy beach stretched out to sea, a hundred yards away, and yet it was almost deserted. Everyone was up at the other end this afternoon, around the pier.

They walked on, scrambling over the ancient wooden groynes that ran out into the waves and tried to halt the inevitable drifting of the beach. From time to time they paused, like all beach walkers, to look at a shell or pebble that caught their eye. A huge flock of wading birds was standing on a stretch of bare, tide-washed sand, almost all of them facing the same way, looking out to sea. It was like they were frozen there, immobile, but then suddenly they flew off, maybe two or three hundred of them all at once, as Giselle and Camille approached, so close they could feel the beating of their wings. Away in the distance they could see the lighthouse, a white vertical finger in a landscape made up almost exclusively of horizontal lines.

Camille produced a joint and lit it. Dope was an everyday part of the scene at the language school, just as it was at home. It was no big deal to people of Camille's generation. She knew that her parents smoked grass on occasion but there was a discreet and unspoken understanding between them about such things. Slowly, a sense of clearness and calmness began to settle on Giselle. She was glad she had come out to taste the salt tang of the air, to feel the cool breezes on her bare shoulders and arms and legs, instead of dozing heavily in her room, to wake at six with a headache and a feeling of a wasted afternoon.

'Shall we go to the cave?'

Giselle was glad Camille had asked. She liked going there, to the secret spot that they had discovered some weeks earlier, when they had first begun sleeping together. The cave was not theirs exclusively – they knew it was visited because they found cigarette packets and sweet wrappers there – but it was a place to which they could go and not feel they would be disturbed. This was the problem with being so young, Giselle reasoned. Everywhere you went there would be someone to look out for you, someone who wondered where you were, who wanted to keep their eye on you. She couldn't just vanish, take time out for herself. Every minute of her day had to be accounted for, at home as well as at college. When she was older, it would be different. And so the cave became a kind of sanctuary for her, and for Camille. A special place.

They climbed up the rocks, the familiar one they called the cow and calf because that was what it looked like. The cave was just up the cliff, not at all a hard climb, but the cliffs were crumbly, more made up of sandy earth than rock, and it was difficult in some places to find a foothold if you wore shoes. She looked up at Camille who was going ahead of her, wondered how the boys at the language school would have reacted to the view she had of her friend's neat little bum in her neat little white lace knickers. She smiled to herself, involuntarily licked her lips.

A couple of twists and a scramble along a narrow ledge and they were there, twenty or thirty feet above the beach, the sea beneath them gently rolling in. It looked as though no one had been here since they were last there – there was no litter, no mess. Everything looked the same as it always did. The cave was nearly high enough for them to stand up in and it went back about ten feet or so into the darkness. She didn't know if it was a natural cave or whether it was just something that someone had excavated out of the soft and crumbling cliff. There were others like it, all along the coast.

They sat at the entrance on a couple of large rocks, gazing out at the horizon. It was a good place to be. It had a tranquillity that was all its own.

Camille lit another spliff, blew out smoke in a thick cloud. It was a nice time of day to smoke grass, to take you through the early evening in a warm glow. Giselle reached out and took the cigarette from her, drew the smoke deep down into her lungs. Above them a flock of seagulls wheeled in the warm thermal air currents. She could see their eyes, little black eyes looking down at them. She waved. The seagulls flapped their wings in acknowledgement.

When they'd smoked the joint Giselle stood up and took off her dress. Camille did the same. They stood there, at the entrance to the cave, their arms around one another, their nipples almost touching, one pair pink and firm, the other small and brown. Slowly, almost imperceptibly, their mouths and tongues met. The first kiss was slow and long, a gentle indication of pleasures to come. Camille pressed her vulva against Giselle, and was aware of the soft white lace that brushed against her naked skin.

She knelt down, hooked her thumbs around Camille's pants and pulled them down far enough to insinuate her tongue into the gap between Camille's legs. Camille sighed and ran her fingers through Giselle's hair. She always came when Giselle licked her pussy.

Giselle eased the pants down and off, tossed them to one side. Now both girls were completely naked together, there at the mouth of the cave with the tide rolling in beneath them and the sunlight dancing on the waves. There was no hurry. Both of them felt calm and relaxed, though their hearts were fluttering with anticipation. Giselle used her hands to part Camille's legs and then she ran her tongue experimentally around the other girl's lips. She tasted clean and slightly tart.

Still crouching, with her face barely leaving Camille's vulva, Giselle moved around until she found the large flat stone that acted as a seat. She sat down on it and pulled Camille on to her lap until the two girls were face to face, Camille sitting with her legs around her, her pussy already damp against Giselle's thighs.

Giselle reached up and put her arms around her friend's neck, pulling her face down to meet her probing lips. Their tongues played together, breast touching breast in the shadow of the cave, Camille gently rubbing herself against Giselle's lap. Giselle broke off their kiss and applied her lips instead to Camille's breasts, circling the areolae with her tongue, feeling them tense and pucker up beneath her caresses as she gave her attention to each one in turn until they stood up as hard and brown as little acorns.

Then she took each of them into her mouth, sucking deeply, nibbling them with her teeth until Camille shivered and ground her sex against her. 'I want you up me,' she murmured in Giselle's ear, a flourish with her tongue on Giselle's earlobe acting like a signature.

Giselle slid her hand down over Camille's warm, flat belly, feeling the luxuriant pubic hair against the palm of her hand. She knew what her friend wanted, three or four fingers that would give her the feeling of a nice big cock in there, but handled with the sensitivity that only one woman could show to another. Giselle might have liked a cock too, at that moment, but Camille's tongue and fingers would have to do instead. Later, perhaps ... She rubbed her hips expectantly.

Still sucking Camille's breast, Giselle slid her hand into the warm cleft and was surprised at how wet Camille already was. There was an urgency about her now that had been lacking in the afternoon languor of their love-making earlier. She knew what was expected of her. She pushed one, then two fingers into her friend's welcoming sheath, feeling its walls closing over her, the secretions that slowly seeped from her innermost chamber.

Camille gasped, brushed her hands over Giselle's own breasts and kissed her passionately on the lips. At the same time, Giselle slipped a third and then a fourth finger into her, the ball of her hand rubbing against the clitoris that stood out as firm and hard as a little walnut. When she got close to orgasm, Camille became a noisy lover – something that had occasionally disconcerted Giselle in their secret sessions back at the language school. She gasped, and moaned, and whimpered, and Giselle knew she was soon going to shipwreck herself on the reef of her desires.

'Get it up me,' she almost hissed, quite red in the face beneath her summer tan, the words enunciated with surprising clarity.

Giselle withdrew her index finger, rubbed it against the hard button of Camille's clitoris and then, twisting her wrist around, managed to insert its tip into Camille's tight little bum.

'Oh, that's it,' murmured her friend. 'Just give it to me there.'

Afraid that her long nails might hurt her, Giselle merely stroked the outer rim of that second little hole. But it had the desired effect on her lover. Allied to the three fingers tight inside her vagina – Giselle could almost pinch her fingers together through the thin membrane dividing vagina and anus – she quickly brought Camille to a short, shuddering orgasm, their tongues playing little twisting games with each other, their breath coming in ragged gasps until they were still.

After that, Giselle lay down on the cool, flat rock at the mouth of the cave and Camille lay down on top of her. They rubbed their pubic mounds together, aping heterosexual intercourse. Giselle wrapped her long, elegant legs around Camille as, with her heels, she urged their bodies closer together. She wished, in her heart of hearts, that it was a man who was on top of her now, a woman to lick and caress her perhaps but a man to penetrate her ultimately, a man with a long, thick cock that would fill her to the hilt. That, though, would have to wait until later in the evening. And it wouldn't be just one cock either, she told herself wickedly.

Their bodies undulated gently against each other for some while, thigh against thigh, breast against breast, lips against lips. Slowly their movements became more urgent. The grass they had smoked ensured that their skins were becoming one flowing, receptive surface that told of pleasures given and experienced, the stone a hard and cold and pleasurable sensation against their flesh. Above them they could hear the endless call of the gulls, the drone of a passing aircraft. But here, in the mouth of the cave, they were living in a world dedicated solely to the senses of touch and taste, smell and sound. Their eyes for the moment were blind with passion until both had drawn near to the edge of the rapids. Then, having shot over the waterfall, they would feast on each other's nakedness and dress themselves once more, with murmured words of endearment, the quiet acknowledgement of an experience shared, a secret cherished together.

The gorse was in flower all over the heathland as Paul drove the seven-series BMW down the winding roads, its fat tyres humming along the rough country-lane surface. They hadn't been able to get away before four – a couple of phone calls from the States took care of that – and they both wanted dinner and sex. Still, it was a pleasant evening in which to drive, with the roof open and the windows right down. The Scots pines were casting long shadows over the parched, hummocky grass, scored by the predations of a million rabbits. Ahead was the sea and all around them was what seemed like a foreign country, the neat little houses with their walls of brick and flint, the thatched cottages, the big open fields slumbering beneath huge skies that Constable could have painted.

Beside him sat Carole Chivers, his wife, the road map open on her lap. They'd taken a wrong turning a while back, ending up outside some dreadful country pub in a village that didn't even seem to be marked on the *Ordnance Survey Road Atlas of Britain*. The locals drinking beer had seemed curiously unperturbed about being asked for directions by one of the most famous husband-and-wife TV couples in the country but, Carole wondered, perhaps they'd not recognised either of them behind their dark glasses. Which was just as well, in a way. She didn't want anyone putting two and two together.

Anyway, they were on the right road now at last. They didn't need the map any more – Paul knew the way from now on, remembering it from the last time they'd been to Dunwich. She turned round and dumped the road atlas on the back seat, her skirt riding up over her thighs as she did so. Eyes like a hawk, Paul caught a glimpse of his wife's stocking tops and his hand snaked out involuntarily to caress the smooth, silky flesh at the tops of her thighs.

'Can't you wait?' she murmured.

'No,' he replied, 'I can't.'

She felt the same herself. It was only that morning that she and Paul had got up from the tangled bed that they'd shared with a TV weather lady and her partner, and yet she was as hungry for sex as if she'd spent a month alone on a desert island. Still, she had to admit she'd dressed the part, specifically to arouse Paul – the sheer black stockings and high heels, the short skirt, the clingy silk top.

She pulled her skirt up higher for him, revealing the tiny cream silk panties that scarcely covered her sought-after sex, the one that viewers from eight to eighty lusted after five afternoons a week when the Chiverses hosted *The Evening Starts Now*. She took hold of his hand and moved it against her mound, feeling the way the fabric rubbed against her flesh and the tangled pubic hair. She could sense already how damp she was getting – it was something that always excited Paul, the way her knickers got so incredibly wet, the dark stain of her juices spreading from her crotch as she awaited the moment of penetration.

'You're soaking wet,' he said, right on cue.

'I know,' she said. 'I wish we had a vibro in the car. I want to be fucked.'

She had her hands in his lap, squeezing his rock-hard cock as they drove along. Sometimes, she would bring herself off there and then as they drove along. Paul had developed a way of driving on automatic pilot in situations like this which, in their lives at any rate, were not infrequent occurrences. She had sucked him off in a contraflow snarl-up on the M6 only the other week, swallowing down his seed even as the truck in front of them coughed out smoke and began to inch forward. She had once endured an agonising afternoon wondering whether the garage man who was servicing her Porsche had found the large black dildo that she'd forgotten she'd left in the map pocket – he evidently hadn't, when he brought the car back that evening.

Usually, for very obvious reasons in their position, they were very careful not to be seen. At other times they did things that were so wild that the possibility of being seen doing it was a deliberate part of the attraction. Would some truck driver who happened to glance down at the car that had overtaken him on the motorway believe that it was really Carole Chivers at the wheel of that flame-red Porsche, with her skirt hiked up over her hips and her husband beside her in the passenger seat, pushing a large black vibro into her? Driving after dark, fuelled with the best and purest cocaine that money could buy, the sky was the limit for them. Sometimes they'd set off from home just for the hell of it, she often naked in the front seat, or wearing just a PVC basque or a lace catsuit or something similar, and they'd drive around for hours – through town and country lanes alike – wondering if anyone had caught a glimpse of them and wondering what the tall blonde woman was doing with the equally tall, dark, handsome man.

Driving through these endless fields of overripe corn, things were getting pretty desperate.

'Let's do it in the back seat,' said Carole when she couldn't stand it a moment longer.

'Where? There aren't any lay-bys on this road.'

'Don't be so boring, Paul. If you loved me, really loved me, you wouldn't say that.'

He smiled at her, caressed her silky nylon-clad thigh again. 'I'll see if I can stop somewhere,' he said. 'There must be a pull-off we can use, a field or something.'

She pulled her skirt down, hoping she wouldn't stain the expensive upholstery of the car with her secretions. Sure enough, after a mile or two there was a lane leading off just a little way ahead, a narrow path that disappeared into a copse. It was a Godsend. They could do it in there, safe from prying eyes like a couple of teenagers having it off under the pier. Paul pulled up in a cloud of dust and they all but ran down the lane, Carole stumbling along in her four-inch heels.

It was cool and dark among the trees, a welcome change from the blazing late-afternoon heat that hung like a cloud over the rural landscape. The ferns seemed to deaden the noise of their hurried footsteps. High above them birds were chirping as they tore at each other's clothes. She stepped out of skirt and Paul pulled her silken top over her head until the sunlight played on her full, ripe breasts, lighting up the little gold rings she wore in each nipple. She wasn't wearing a bra.

'Fancy a little suck, darling?' she breathed and in a trice he had scooped her in his arms and was licking hungrily at her plump nipples. Carole had extraordinarily sensitive breasts, and their sensitivity had increased after the birth of each of their three children. Now, at the age of thirty-eight, she had breasts that a woman half her age would be proud of. On TV she often liked to wear dresses and tops that showed her cleavage: not too much of course – it was different when she was at home with Paul and their friends – but enough to keep the viewers interested. She used to get all kinds of mail about them, as well as the usual stuff about how much people enjoyed the programme and what was her favourite colour and was it true she had had a crush on Paul McCartney when she was little (it wasn't).

Most of the letters were real wankers' drivel, but one or two of them were a real turn-on. Some guy sent a picture of himself and his wife stark-bollock naked – he was a good-looking guy too, with a hefty old cock on him, and she looked like a young Kim Basinger – and he said he used to wait for the exact moment she would cross her legs before shooting his come all over the twenty-six-inch screen in their living room. His wife, he said, wondered if Paul would like to fuck her bum while she licked Carole's cunt. Carole very nearly wrote back and said, yes she would, and so would Paul. Professional etiquette, however, dictated they remain as silent as Buckingham Palace on the rumours of a royal divorce. She made sure, however, that for the rest of the week she crossed her legs a little more often than usual, and a little more obviously to the camera. She hoped her correspondent was watching; she tried to imagine the moment when he came, almost missing her cue when she thought she'd got the moment right.

Overhead the sky was a deep, almost ultramarine blue, with scarcely a cloud to be seen. She unfastened Paul's belt and got his cock out from his pants, feeling the moisture on the end. Pulling his jeans down to his knees, she knelt down and took the tip of his large, uncircumcised cock between her lips. He moaned and ran his fingers through her expensively coiffured hair.

'You taste good,' she managed to murmur. 'I'm sure I can still taste Krystle's pussy on you.'

'You'd know what Krystle tastes like, wouldn't you?'

'Like *filet mignon*, lightly grilled,' Carole replied and, knowing that kind of thing aroused him, she took him deep inside her mouth, swirling her tongue around the end of his cock. Krystle's quim was indeed very nice to lick and suck, but her partner Kelvin's come was nicer still – and so much of it to swallow at one time, too.

She sucked Paul for a minute or two, liking the feeling of being with him there in the copse, pressed up against a tree. She was wearing nothing now apart from stockings and suspenders and she knew it was driving him nuts, like a photo-spread from one of the better-quality European magazines they enjoyed so much. Once she and Paul and Krystle and Kelvin had, in conditions of great secrecy at the Hotel de Campagne in Paris, had themselves photographed together by one of France's top fashion camera-women. It had cost a fortune, even by their standards, but the results were spectacular. If ever Paul welched on her, or she on him, the existence of those negatives – allied to the insatiable appetites of the tabloid press – was the best banker either of them could ever have hoped for. The negatives were safely stashed away in a New York security vault and the photographs were mounted in a handsome, leather-bound album for the delectation of themselves and, occasionally, of their very closest friends.

He ran his hand over her shoulder. 'Come on,' he said. 'I want to be in you.'

She stood up and automatically helped Paul off with his white Mr B shirt and jeans. 'How shall we do it?' she asked.

'Against this tree,' he said, as surely and confidently as though he'd worked the whole thing out hours in advance.

She turned round and leaned forward, feeling the bark hard and uneven against her naked breasts. She thrust her bum out and could feel him pressing against her, his rock-hard cock against her buttocks. She reached down and, opening her legs wide, guided him into her. He slid straight in, all the way. Everyone said how deliciously tight she was.

'Jesus, you're wet,' he murmured in her ear and then he started to flick her lobes with his tongue, something that was guaranteed to drive her wild. She thrust out her arse at him, her nice womanly arse, and he grasped her round the hips, his hands running wildly over her expensive lacy suspenders, and pushed into her so hard that he went in right to the limit of her vagina's flexibility with every thrust, his cock long and thick and powerful inside her, his balls bursting with semen, and she ground her hips against him and felt, almost immediately, that she was going to explode even before he did.

Later, her pussy absolutely swimming with Paul's pent-up semen and her own abundant juices, she retrieved her panties from a pile of leaves and put her clothes back on. As Paul discreetly buttoned himself up, she wondered why an old married couple like them – it had been over twelve years since they had tied the knot, a long time for a show-business marriage to stay in one piece – could still get it on. Of course each had had many other partners, though with the AIDS scare not so much in recent years, unless they were absolutely sure, but she still fancied Paul and he fancied her like it had been when they first knew each other, when they used to spend whole days at a time in bed together, fucking and sucking each other senseless, morning, noon and night. Perhaps that was the secret, she thought, as she zipped up her skirt and checked that the seams on her stockings were straight. She hoped the little bite mark on her left breast wouldn't show later. If it did, she could always cover it with blemish cream. Twenty years in television had taught her more than most women knew about the art of make-up.

They finished their dressing quickly, aware for the first time of the possibility of discovery. Once, in a riverside meadow near Taunton, they had fucked in full view of an angler on the other bank, but Carole had to be in the mood for that kind of thing, especially as their fame grew and the consequences – and hence the enjoyment of what they were doing – increased proportionally. Still, this little copse seemed as though no one ever used it – there was no litter, no soft-drink cans or cigarette packets or used condoms to show that other people had been there, the familiar detritus of late twentieth-century civilisation.

She noticed, with regret, that one of her stockings was laddered, high up on her thigh. Still, it wouldn't show and she had several pairs with her in her luggage, precisely for that kind of emergency. Carole, ever the pro, was prepared for everything. She fixed her make-up in the car mirror and then, greatly relaxed, she and Paul drove on towards Dunwich.

Sue Browne waited until her mum was busy getting the tea and her dad was watching *Baywatch*. He always pretended it was because he'd switched the telly on to catch the football results, but she knew her old man better than that. He hadn't filled in a coupon for over a year, not since he started buying tickets for the Lottery. She left him pretending not to be looking at the girls in their tight orange swimsuits – well, on anyone else's set they were orange but, even with the colour turned way up on their aged set, it seemed to her to be a lot closer to pink – and made her way upstairs.

She got out clean towels for her bath, found all the bottles and things she needed – hair gel, mousse, spray, all the gear for a Saturday night at the Zero Six. She was looking forward to it, as she always did, even though Billy had to be working that night. Some time or other, during the evening, though, they'd manage to slip away and do it somewhere. There probably wouldn't be time for them to go back to his place, not since her dad had started getting stroppy about what time she got home on a Saturday night or, more likely, a Sunday morning. Still, Sunday afternoon she would go over to his place and, assuming his flatmate Tony wasn't in, they could spend the whole afternoon in bed together.

Billy Brilleaux wasn't the brightest guy she'd ever been with, but he was street smart and besides, he was a genuinely nice guy under all those muscles and tattoos. He'd tried the army but didn't get on with it, all the discipline and things, so he came back to Dunwich where he'd been born and bred. He'd got a job with the Alarming Security Company – she wasn't sure they were called that because of the anti-intruder devices or because of the physical appearance of some of their employees – and that was where she'd met him, when he was on the door at the Zero Six. They'd been going out for three months now and her mum was beginning to wonder if it was getting serious, whatever that meant.

She went back into her room, opened the wardrobe door and spent a long time choosing what to wear before she finally settled on a long, clinging dress in burgundy lycra cotton. It showed her shape off to good advantage and Billy always said she looked good in it. Besides, she'd bought just the shoes to go with it only that morning in Saxone.

She laid the dress out on the bed carefully, smoothing out imaginary creases. Then she went to the top of the steps and listened. She could hear her mum rattling saucepans in the kitchen, music and dialogue booming up from the TV. There was no chance she'd be disturbed now. Her sister Viv, three years younger than her at fifteen, was still round at her friend Di's house and wouldn't be back until much later. Sue had the whole upper floor of the house to herself.

She closed her bedroom door with a quiet click. Normally she would have had a CD or a tape on but she didn't want to be disturbed. She wanted to hear any footsteps on the stairs, even a mouse's. Her heart beating faster than usual, she opened the drawer in which she kept her T-shirts and things and pulled it right out. Everything was where it should be, neatly folded where her mum had lovingly ironed her clothes and put them away for her. Good old Mum – that was one of the things she liked about her, the way she looked after them all. Sue hardly knew how to set the ironing board up, let alone how to use it.

Kneeling down, she reached as far as she could into the drawer, round into the empty space at the back. Her hand slid along the back panel – surely it couldn't have fallen down? Then her hands closed around the plastic bag she had concealed there at the back of the chest of drawers, stuck on with a piece of sellotape in case her mum found it.

In the bag was a pair of black lace crotchless knickers, bought that very morning before she met Billy at the Pier Head Hotel. She was going to wear them that night but she was terrified her mum might find them in the meantime – that was why she'd had to hide them, because she didn't dare think what her mum might say. They still thought she was a virgin, her mum and dad. She didn't dare think about the consequences of discovery. The intentions of a girl who wore black lace crotchless knickers, after all, were pretty unambiguous, especially in a place like Dunwich – and on a Saturday night, too.

She'd bought them because she wanted to give Billy a surprise that night when he fucked her. She knew he'd like them because he'd said something about them once, how that kind of stuff gave him ideas. She liked Billy's ideas and that was a good thing, because he had plenty of them. She wore suspenders and stockings for him, that kind of thing, and sometimes she'd go out with no underwear at all. This was something new for her, for him, for both of them.

Her hands ran over the filmy pants. There was hardly anything to them, just a wisp of material. It seemed a lot of money just to spend on a few square inches of fabric, but she was sure she wouldn't regret it. She found the part line along the crotch and pushed her hand through it.

Unable to contain her excitement, she stepped quickly out of her clothes, the ones she'd been wearing all day. She put the pants on, pulled them up tight around her pussy like they'd be when

Billy saw them later. She studied herself in the long, full-length mirror she'd made her dad fit on the inside of her wardrobe. At first glance they looked just like ordinary pants, if a little on the skimpy side, but when she stood with her legs apart she could see the little pink chink of her pussy lips. She turned round, admiring herself. She'd always thought her bum was quite big but now – especially when she bent forwards a little so that the panties visibly parted around each cheek – it made for one hell of an alluring sight. She studied herself for a good few minutes, sure that she would have the desired bombshell effect.

She took the pants off, put them in the pocket of her bathrobe. Once she was dressed she'd be fine, no one would ever know what she was wearing until later that evening when she and Billy would go up on the roof of the Zero Six or down to the beach by the pier, and his exploring fingers would quickly find out what was in store for him.

Wearing just her bathrobe and a pair of pink fluffy slippers, she went to the head of the stairs.

'I'm just going to start running the bath now,' she called down the stairwell. 'If you want to come in, you'd better come now or it'll be too late.'

Sue always occupied the bathroom for a good hour or more on a Saturday night. It had become something of a family joke. But neither Mum nor Dad made any move and so, secretly relieved, she locked the door and turned on the taps.

Giselle and Camille were walking along Eastern Avenue when the bottle-green BMW passed by them. Something had made the French girl look up and she saw and recognised the handsome couple in a flash, despite their dark glasses.

'Wasn't that—?' said Camille, who had registered the car and

63

its occupants at the same time as Giselle.

'Must have been, I suppose.'

'I wonder what they're doing here? I'd have thought St Tropez was more their scene.'

Their eyes followed the car until it was lost to sight at the far end of the Avenue. Evidently the Chiverses weren't stopping in the town. Giselle had once seen Charlotte Rampling on the Avenue Faubourg but knew that the rich and famous preferred to keep their appearances, off the screen at any rate, to a minimum. She, of course, knew more than most girls of her age the value of discretion.

She felt mellow from the couple of spliffs that she and Camille had smoked. She liked the way the town looked at that time of day, the hard coastal light beginning to soften, the sun way over in the west, backlighting the white buildings that, in some ways, reminded her of home, the south of France. There the similarity ended, however. All around them she could see families making an end to the day, folding up rugs, packing up toys and pushchairs and picnic things, gathering together children and dogs and aged relatives and anything else that might have strayed.

Even so, Giselle thought Dunwich was a nice place to be. It was a little rough at the other end of the town, past the pier, but around here she felt quite comfortable. Giselle was used to affluence, felt secure in its company. And the people who came to the better end of Dunwich were certainly not poor.

She wondered what would be happening at home now. Perhaps friends would be coming for dinner, or her parents might be going out for the evening, to eat at the Vendôme, for instance, or the Cabache or one of their usual places. She had always enjoyed going out to eat with her *maman* and *papa*. The English, they didn't seem to like eating with their children, unless it was at one of those horrible plastic places along the road, Little Thief or whatever they were called, where the food was as tasteless as the decor. She had been to a couple of nice restaurants in Dunwich but she had the impression that children wouldn't have been welcome, let alone teenagers who didn't have much money to throw about, but were intent on spending what little they had on having a good time.

That was one of the things she missed most about home – the way young and old could be together if they wanted to be, the way people of all ages would mingle, the easy atmosphere of the town as it settled down to enjoy itself. In England, everything went dead after ten apart from the drunks and the homeless. She felt a tinge of homesickness and decided she would ring her parents when she got home, even though she normally spoke to them on Sundays.

Even as late as six o'clock, the sun was still baking hot. Since this morning's thunderstorm there had scarcely been a breath of a breeze, even where they were, right on the coast. The two girls were walking arm in arm along the sunbaked patch of grass that separated Eastern Avenue from the sea. From time to time they got strange looks but then, in France at any rate, girls always walked together like this. There were enough foreign people at the language school for the Brits to have got used to it by now.

A couple of middle-aged men in folding chairs gave them the strangest look as they passed, eyes focused on their lissom limbs and jiggling breasts.

'They think we're a couple of lesbians,' Camille whispered, and they both giggled. Giselle squeezed her arm and noticed how nice her friend's breast felt against her. Sometimes she would kiss other women in public, but not here. England was too repressed for that kind of thing. It was bad enough for them to see a boy and girl at it, let alone two pretty girls.

Giselle liked the English but, in many ways, she felt they were a strange lot. They liked to think they were laid-back about things but they weren't, not underneath. She'd heard all about boarding schools and the class system and the strange licensing laws, everything that was designed to stop people having fun. Well, it was the same in France in many ways but at least in France, as in every Catholic country, people knew what really went on.

Only the other week there'd been a big fuss in the London papers – *une scandale enorme* – because some high-ranking politician had admitted once sleeping with his press secretary. The press were baying for his blood and his resignation was expected hourly. The poor man duly appeared on TV with his grimly-smiling wife and two idyllic children, mouthing the usual platitudes about family values and lessons painfully learned.

In France, no one would have given a damn. Everyone knew politicians kept mistresses, and who could blame them? A good salary, a peripatetic lifestyle, the need often to be in two places at once while you were actually somewhere else entirely, preferably in the company of a research assistant with long legs and a short skirt – was it any wonder that a man or woman might find solace in the arms of someone to whom they were not legally joined in marriage? But the English were so prudish, so immediately and universally shockable. There wasn't even a beach for sunbathing *au naturel* in Dunwich, though there were one or two on the south coast. Again no one in Europe thought anything much of it. The *famille* Lescarboura tended towards skiing holidays, but, whenever they had been to Cap du Sud and places, she and Maman and her sister Danielle went around bare-breasted like anyone else. It was no big deal, even for Maman, who got more admiring glances than anyone. She was sure those two old farts in the folding chairs would have had a seizure if she and Camille had walked by them with bare tits.

No, the English needed to calm down a little – a lot, really. They got so uptight about everything but they could never give vent to their feelings. They never shouted and they never touched each other. They never said what they meant, relied instead on silly little codes of behaviour that, to a foreigner, were transparently false. They were too inhibited about too many things. Once, in a restaurant in Dunwich, she had complained that her crêpes were cold. The waiter had seemed genuinely astonished that anyone should have the temerity to criticise the food, let alone an eighteen-year-old girl.

English boys were good-looking and wore nice clothes, but they were just the same as their parents in many ways. She had been in England on this visit for the past three months, and in all that time she had only been out with a couple of English boys. One from the town and another one who had been there on holiday. She had slept with them both but it hadn't been as good as with Camille. There were some nice boys at the language school and she'd gone around for a while with one of them, a Belgian from Antwerp called Pascale, but he'd gone home last week.

By curious coincidence, Camille chose that moment to ask about him. Had she heard from him? Was she going to see him again?

'I think you fancied him,' said Giselle, and Camille – though she was much more interested in girls than boys – didn't deny it.

'What was he like?' the dark-haired girl asked.

'Tall, a bit quiet sometimes, interesting to talk to. He liked the same sort of things as I do.'

'Where did you meet him?'

'At a party. One of his tutors was giving an end-of-exams party and I went with Renate Emderer. She knew one of the boys in his class.'

'You went out together?'

'We went to places, you know, the ones in town like the Zero Six. But mostly it was the usual things, parties and that. It was good.'

'When did you start, you know?'

'Sleeping together? Oh, fairly soon after we knew each other, I guess. It was difficult at first because he shared a room. We had to wait until his room-mate went out or something.'

'Did you spend the night with him?'

'A few times. Once, at the college, Mr Pringle saw him leaving the building in the morning. He knew he couldn't have been one of ours but he didn't say anything.'

'I like Mr Pringle. He has a nice bum.'

'His wife is very nice. She's got a nice bum, too.'

They laughed and walked on a little. Some children were playing with a ball. It rolled towards them and Giselle picked it up and tossed it back to them. She liked little kids. She got the impression that, in England at any rate, they were just about tolerated, but it would have been better for them to have been born as little adults.

'No, it was good with Pascale,' she went on. 'I'm sorry he's gone, I really am.'

'Did you do it a lot, you know?'

'Yes, I guess we did. Belgians can be pretty cold people but not Pascale. He was all over me, arms like an octopus.'

'What was he like?'

'I told you that.'

Camille giggled. 'No, I didn't mean that. You know—'

'Oh *that*. It was pretty good. He really knew how to please a girl, you know.'

'And how was it, his thing—?'

'Huge! He was a very tall man, you know, well over two meters. And he knew what to do with it.'

'What kind of thing?'

'My, you are inquisitive. Why do you want to know?'

'I just like hearing about these things.'

'He liked trying all kinds of different positions. Sometimes I'd get on top of him, and ride him that way. Sometimes, you know, he'd do it in the other—'

'You mean?'

'Yes.'

'Doesn't it hurt?'

'Not if you're careful and go slowly. After you've done it a couple of times it gets easier.'

'I'm not sure I'd like it.'

'That's what I used to think.'

'Did you ever go to the cave?'

'No, that's just for us. I wouldn't go there with a boy. It's too uncomfortable for fucking, anyway.'

'He has really good legs, Pascale.'

'Do you think so?'

'Mmmm. I used to look at them and wish I could stroke them.'

'He'd have gone mad if he'd known. I'm sure he used to fancy you.'

'He didn't?'

'He did.'

'What did he say?'

'He said he thought you had a nice face and he liked your tits.'

69

'I wish you'd told me.'

'You'd have stolen him from me.'

'Well, he wasn't yours exclusively, was he? Besides, we could have shared him if you objected that much.'

'What, he goes out with me one night and you the next?'

'Maybe. Or both of us together.'

It really was outrageous the things Camille was saying. Giselle had never known her talk like this about a boy before.

'You mean, all three of us?'

'Why not? It might be fun.'

'I'm sure it would be. Maybe I should have suggested something.'

'Have you ever done anything like that before?'

'Yes, back home.'

'Tell me about it.'

'There's not a lot to tell, really. I went to a party with this boy I was going out with and we got really drunk, and the next thing I knew we were upstairs and there was this other boy as well who'd been giving me looks all evening.'

'What happened?'

'I'm not sure what was happening. I was too drunk to know much of what was going on.'

'Did you want it to happen? I mean, weren't they taking advantage of you?'

'Oh no, I wasn't that much out of it. They weren't raping me or anything. I wished I'd been more sober so I could have enjoyed it more. I can remember the two of them taking turns to screw me, and then I sucked Jean-Louis – that's the boy I was going out with – while his friend had me from behind. Then they changed places. I had the most awful hangover the following day, I told my mother I was getting flu.'

'Did you do it again?'

'No, that was the only time. Once or twice, me and this girlfriend of mine did it with someone we knew. He liked to watch us having sex together, and then we'd let him fuck us.'

'I like that idea. I wish we were fucking someone right now.'

A handsome bare-chested guy in baggy shorts walked past them at that moment. He raised his can of lager to the two girls and winked. If he'd known that both of them would have been quite happy to have sucked him off there and then, he'd probably have choked on it.

'Maybe we'll find someone to do it with.'

'It's a pity you're not coming to the party tonight. I'm sure we could find someone . . .'

Giselle was aware of how hard her friend's nipples were becoming, brushing against her arm as they walked. Maybe they might have a shower or something together when they got back to the college. They walked on, the sun on their backs, and a hundred eyes followed every shapely step.

Chapter Three

Col was making supper in his tiny, two-up two-down cottage at Crab Bay. The hamlet – though even that was a bit of a misnomer, since Crab Bay consisted of but three houses and a telephone box – was a couple of miles out of Dunwich, past the smart hotels of Northdene, past the cliffs where Richie had walked earlier that afternoon, past the cave where Giselle and Camille had had such fun, past the caravan camp site where, even at that moment, Debbie and Rob were relaxing in bed, past the golf club where men dressed in pimps' trousers were locked in earnest contest, out into a wild, flat no-man's-land of harsh, hummocky grass and drifting dunes.

Once, until the turn of the century, Col's cottage had been home for the Dunwich coastguard. That was a long time ago now, and the nearest coastguard station was fifty miles away, the nearest lifeboat twenty. It wasn't just the sands and the shingle that were shifting along the coast – it was a whole way of life. Col was one of the few left around here who still scratched a living as a fisherman. He shared a boat with a couple of other guys, trawling and line fishing, sometimes setting pots for the crabs. There were no more than about fifteen boats now working out of the tiny wooden jetty at Coxburgh, a mile or so further on, with its ring of tumble-down huts and shacks where they kept their

73

fishing gear. Where once weatherbeaten men in oilskins and uncompromising beards had warmed their sea-chilled limbs by log fires, now its cottages were occupied by people called Arabella and Jamie, who drove gleaming four-wheel drive jeeps down from Highgate every other weekend, loaded to the gunwales with patés and fresh pasta from the Sainsbury's in Camden High Street. On a clear day, there'd be more artists around the place than fishermen. The local pub wised up and now sold gravad lax and vegetarian dishes instead of the thick doorstep cheese-and-onion sandwiches which had done well enough with the local trade for the past seventy years or so.

Col and his colleagues stood out a mile as they wrestled with recalcitrant rigging or sweated over the piston rings on a life-expired Perkins diesel. The parvenues wore lovely thick fishermens' sweaters and waxed jackets that gleamed a dull lovat green under the clear skies of the eastern counties. The fishermen wore thick sweaters in horrible, faded patterns, their elbows patched and the cuffs frayed, their waxed jackets cracked and scuffed and foully fish-smelling. Most of the fish that they caught was sold locally, straight over the side, but they also sold it to local restaurants, the more upmarket kind, who liked to have the real thing on their menus. People liked to buy a crab or two and take it back with them. Thirty years ago the shoals off Coxburgh had provided a good living for fifty or sixty families in the surrounding area. Now, the few survivors drove their salt-caked, rust-ringed Toyotas down to the tiny harbour with a heaviness in their hearts.

Things were definitely getting worse. These past few weeks, there'd hardly been any fish to speak of, even in the deep water off Friar's Point. Numbers had been dwindling steadily over the years as the North Sea neared exhaustion, but everyone knew there was nothing sinister about the missing shoals. No, it was the heat that had done it, bringing the temperature up a little, forcing the fish into deeper waters where they felt more comfortable. When the mercury dropped, the fish would be back. Well, that's what they tried to tell each other, nursing pints in the smoky back bar of the Three Horseshoes, where once they used to play darts and tell foul jokes, while Arabella and Jamie drank Campari and soda and waited for their shrimp creole to arrive.

Col hadn't been out at all for the past ten days – there were just a couple of boats out now, working the shoals. By putting in ridiculously long hours – whatever the health and safety people said, you still had a living to make – they had just about scooped up between them what little fish there were along their stretch of the coast. There was no point in all of them trying to fish the same waters. So Col took the time off, did some work on his roof, did some reading, painted a few pictures. He wasn't that bothered about it, though he could have used the money. There was more to life than that.

Col hadn't always been a fisherman. Ten years ago, he'd been working in a London advertising agency. He was good at it too – as one of the youngest campaign directors in the business, he had a string of awards to his name. He could, they reckoned, have sold ice to the Inuit, sand to the Saudis. It wasn't that he had much of a brain for business, he would admit privately, merely that he had the instincts for the right way to do things at the right time. His ads – on TV as well as on hoardings and in magazines – were widely imitated and he picked up a stack of awards. With bonuses and options and various other elements of his package, Shrive Goldblum McMichael paid him close to a hundred grand a year. Then, one afternoon, not long after the Tories got re-elected for another term and ushered in the phenomenon of 'the eighties', he decided quite spontaneously to pack it all in.

He worked out his three-month period, resisted all offers of consultancy work, and went to live in a retreat in Scotland, where he stayed for upwards of a year till he got his head sorted out. His detox period, he called it later. When he left the community he came briefly back to London, sold the Porsche and his flat in the Barbican, dropped his mobile phone off Waterloo Bridge and burned his Filofax.

He went to India, ending up on the coast of Goa, the former Portuguese colony, mainly because he liked the food. He still had plenty of money – his needs were very simple – but he enjoyed hanging out with the fishermen who worked the coast. Even though he couldn't speak the language, he knew instinctively what they were about. Goanese fisherman are a tightly knit and desperately conservative breed, but they sensed something in Col and, before long, he was out on the boats with them, taking his turn at the oars, setting sail, casting the nets. It was hard work and he was idyllically happy.

A family crisis brought him back to England. When it was sorted out, he realised that he was a lot poorer than he ought, by rights, to have been. It was the kind of situation that he would have panicked about at one time. It didn't really bother him, though, this time – from the Goanese fishermen he had learned to be like the wolf, to adapt to changing circumstances, to recognise that there would be lean times between the killings.

He moved out to the East Anglian coast, partly to escape, partly to paint in the clear blue light – he had been a graduate of the Slade before moving into advertising – and partly to make a living of sorts as a fisherman. He knew that the days of sushi and three-hundred-quid shoes were over and it didn't bother him a bit. That phase of his life was over and done with. He'd enjoyed it while it lasted. Now he was getting closer to the real Col.

So, there in the cottage in the soft early evening light, he stirred the saucepan with its heavy cargo of aubergines, onions and tomatoes, the herbs grown in his own small back garden, a generous slug of wine to give it body. He would serve it cold, with fresh-baked bread and some interesting cheeses, big black olives, a green salad. Ever since he jacked in the advertising agency Col had been a vegetarian, but he felt no qualms about making part of his living as a fisherman. That was what he did, an ancient, traditional vocation. He didn't have to eat the stuff and besides, fish were different to lambs and cows and things – they had faces too but he didn't think they'd have much personality, all that much of a consciousness. One day he might even eat one, but not yet.

He glanced out of the window at the back of the house. Liz was due at eight but he couldn't see her car, even though from his house he could see the coast road stretching away maybe two or three miles. Inside the kitchen, it was getting uncomfortably hot and he longed to get outdoors again into the warm evening air. He stirred the pot again, looking up at the sky. It was still a cloudless blue, perfect for eating out in the garden. Later on they would look through the big reflector telescope that was always set up in the spare bedroom and which, on a clear night, he would take out on to the dunes. The night sky in that part of the world was pitch black. Even the modest glow of Dunwich, only a few miles down the coast, didn't interfere with visibility to any great extent. The skies had been spectacularly clear these last few nights and Saturn would be well within range. It would, he was sure, be a wonderful way to round off the evening before bed.

Liz was a doctor, worked in a hospital about ten miles away. He'd met her at a small exhibition he'd had of his paintings in Coxburgh. He was quite prolific as an artist but his stuff – and the gallery wasn't telling him anything he didn't already know – wasn't spectacularly commercial. Spectacular, yes – those big bold colours and shapes, the suggestion of form and meaning, the overwhelming evocation of powerful forces at work – but it was not the sort of thing many people wanted to buy, even the Arabellas and Jamies. But the gallery owner knew better than to persuade Col to paint neat little estuary scenes or well-wooded landscapes. He could only do things his way. What he didn't know was that Col had a good connection with a London dealer and that was where most of his paintings went, seven or eight of them a year, maybe a thousand pounds a time.

Liz had bought one of his smaller pieces at that exhibition in Coxburgh. He happened to have dropped by the gallery on some pretext or other but really to see how things were going – it was one of those not infrequent periods where his disdain for money was beginning to pinch more than somewhat. It was late one afternoon, just as he and the owner were drinking tea, when she came in. She'd loved the picture on sight and, when he identified himself, had asked him about his work, his influences, what he was saying. She paid in folding stuff, too, which was always welcome – in a cash business like coastal fishing, Col had a very on-off relationship with the Revenue. The pubs were open by then and he asked her for a drink. They got talking, and the drink turned into a meal, and the meal turned into a trip back to Col's house in his huge and rusting Volvo – ideal for carrying nets and canvases – and hurriedly up the stairs to Col's vast bed.

He and Liz had been seeing each other for several months now. She was married but separated, very busy with her career. Seeing Col once a week was an arrangement that suited her fine, and him too – he didn't want any ties, didn't feel his life could support them. He had been married once, very briefly, when he was still making his way at Shrive Goldblum McMichael. It had been a disaster, both of them had been far too young, and he didn't care to repeat the experience. He saw other women besides Liz and he didn't care to ask her what she did on the other six days a week – not a great deal, he got the impression. Her work was too demanding for that. Most nights she came home too knackered for any chandelier-swinging.

He'd just taken the pot off the heat when he heard her car pull up outside. He went out to the back of the house – Col's cottage was back to front, the back facing inland, the front facing the sea so the coastguard could keep a weather eye on things – and found she was just stepping out of her car, looking absolutely ravishing and holding a bottle of something very acceptable indeed.

They kissed their greetings. She was wearing a loose summer dress in a green floral pattern, looked younger than thirty-two years in the warm evening light. Her light blonde hair was freshly washed and caught the sun. Col used to do shampoo ads and this was just how they did it.

'Let me get you a drink,' he said. She was wearing a different perfume to her usual one. He liked this one even more.

She held up her hand. 'Not tonight, I'm afraid. I might have to work.'

He felt a rush of disappointment. 'Not tonight, surely?'

'Well, I don't know. Dr Mahmood is supposed to be doing late duty but he's not been at all well this past couple of days. He thinks it might be a virus. He looked bloody awful when I saw him this morning, anyway. So we fixed things so I'll take over if necessary. I don't need to be there till midnight, though. They'll call me if necessary.'

He shrugged. These things happened. It would be nice to have the evening with her at least. He would enjoy himself all the same, even if she couldn't spend the night with him.

'What can I get you to drink, then?'

'Just bottled water, for me, if you've got it.'

'Very aphrodisiac,' he murmured, but there was irony, not bitterness in his voice. He'd have Evian himself come to that, match her drink for drink as they usually did – he was surprised how much she could put away when they got loose on the old Australian Cabernet Sauvignon.

He looked at her. She smiled, touched him on the arm. They sat down in the garden, talked for a long time until she said she was hungry.

They ate at the table at the front of the house, overlooking the sea. It was nice to be in the shade. Col's garden was interesting but shaggy, needed a lot of work doing to it. He watered it regularly, kept everything from shrivelling up.

The aubergine dish was delicious, and so was the South Australian wine that Liz had brought. He couldn't resist it. He'd put it in the freezer to chill it and it was just at the right temperature. He could only drink so much bottled water.

'A pity you're not having any of this,' said Col, filling his glass.

'Don't worry,' she replied, clinking glasses. 'H_2O is fine for me.'

'Let's hope the phone doesn't go. Then we can get really plastered.'

He'd opened the living room windows so they could hear the music better. Col didn't have much time for contemporary music – he didn't think it had much soul. His record collection stopped dead in the early 1970s. All the music he listened to, pretty well, belonged to the past – from Miles Davis back to medieval plainsong. He regretted this, wishing he could find more fulfilment in the here and now of music as he did in the here and now of other things.

The idea of music as show business filled Col with horror. The stuff they played in clubs these days he couldn't abide, the endless repetition, the heartbeat thump – he wished he could have liked it, if only to stop thinking of himself as an old fart – but he never could, however hard he tried listening to John Peel, not least because he lived not far away. In the end, he gave up and went back to the stuff he liked best. Roots music, he was told it was called. He didn't know if Bix Beiderbecke and Belá Bartók knew they played roots music, but he was sure they'd be flattered if they did.

There was a good atmosphere around the old coastguard's cottage that evening, the warmth and the music and the food and the wine – even if Liz wasn't able to have any, at least until she got the all clear from the hospital. If they hadn't rung by twelve then things would be OK. Col cleared their plates away and brought out a big pot of Haagen Dazs.

'I couldn't be bothered making a pudding,' he said simply. 'Besides, I like ice cream.'

'You should get one of those machines. Our houseman has one – she swears by it.'

'I can't afford one. I've not caught a fish in a fortnight and I haven't sold a painting since July. I'm skint.'

He was, Liz knew, richer than any man she had ever met. She looked around at the garden, the well-tended herbs, the giant sunflowers, the piles of timber carefully stacked and covered, ready for use. At the bottom of the garden was Col's junkyard, all the bits and pieces of ironmongery he'd picked up – an old bedstead, a water pump, that kind of thing. One day, if he found time, he'd do them up not to sell, but for his own use. He had already dug out the well at the other side of the house. He was, Liz reflected, incredibly self-sufficient. Two winters ago he had been snowed up in Crab Bay for nearly a week. The cold had nearly frozen his nuts off but he hadn't minded the isolation in the least. Liz wished she could have been there with him but perhaps that wasn't the point.

By contrast with Col's cottage, the other three houses in Crab Bay – just weekend cottages now – seemed very bland, the neat Laura Ashley curtains, the spruce paintwork. None of them was occupied at the moment although usually there was at least one four-wheel-drive jeep parked there. Col got on well enough with their owners, none of them locals, of course. He kept an eye on their property while they were away, had dinner with them sometimes, but it was hardly a community. Col was, in many ways, a one-off.

He spooned out the ice cream. None of Col's crockery matched and neither did his cutlery but it was all good stuff, picked up for next to nothing at auctions, car boot sales and junk markets. The bowls they were eating out of were Midwinter. Also on the table was a Susie Cooper coffee set, brought at a farm sale for a fiver. He had this ability to find things or rather, as he preferred to put it, the things found him. Last year, being particularly broke after a lean fishing season, he had been wandering along the beach when he found a number of plastic sacks floating lightly in the shallow water. When he dragged them ashore and opened them up, they were filled with marijuana, almost ten grands' worth of it and good stuff too. He kept a little for his own use – Liz said it was the best she had ever smoked – and sold the rest on to a dealer he knew in Norwich, a former commodities broker whom he knew he could just about trust. The money he netted had kept him going through practically the whole of last winter. He'd even paid tax on some of it – described on his returns as profits on the sale of catches, albeit imaginary ones – to avoid suspicion. His accountant had smoked two joints daily for thirty years and knew the way these things worked.

For once, there wasn't much of interest on the beach, that evening, as they walked along it in the yellowing sunshine. In fact, it wasn't much of a beach, just a long stretch of shingle between the two forelands of Friar's Point and Whymark Head, about five miles in all. It was much too bleak and inhospitable to attract the developers, and there were no roads to anywhere, just the long, meandering track that trailed in from the main Dunwich road. Crab Bay was on the road to nowhere and that was why Col liked it so much.

They walked on, hand in hand, barefoot. Though it was not even nine in the evening the water temperature was already dropping significantly, as Liz found when she tentatively dipped in a toe. Still, it was lovely to be out here, the light meal sitting easily on their stomachs. The air was still very warm and soft, just the way she liked it. It would have been nice, had circumstances been different, to have walked all the way out to Friar's Point but they didn't dare stray too far in case the phone went, summoning Liz back to the hospital.

'If I do have to work tonight,' she was saying as they strolled along, 'I'll get the time back next week. Maybe we can have the whole weekend together, if you'd like that.'

He looked at her, his sunburned face red in the glow of the evening light. He had been looking at the sky. To a practised eye like his, you could see quite a lot, even though there was still another hour of daylight left. It would be a good night for observing, he was sure. He had a hunch there might be another thunderstorm in the morning.

'I'd like that a lot,' he said.

'Would you like to go away somewhere?'

83

'Would you?'

'I don't know. We could stay in a hotel.'

'Mr & Mrs Smith?'

'Something like that. Or we could stay here.'

He liked that idea better. She knew he would.

'I could take you out in the boat, if you like. We've never done that really, have we?'

'We went to Southwold once.'

'Yes, but that was all. I wondered about maybe spending the night on board, go up to Yarmouth or Lowestoft maybe.'

'What's there?'

'Bugger all. It's just being on the boat that matters.'

'Won't it be a bit uncomfortable?'

'Not really. The cabin's pretty snug. It smells a bit, as you might expect. I've bunked down there before, loads of times. Once you get used to the smell, it's fine. There's a hot plate so we can have something to eat. She's bigger than you might think, that boat. The engine's good.'

They stopped. Some sixth sense told Col what was happening next. He turned to face Liz and then she was in his arms, her tongue seeking his.

He realised he had not felt so sexually aroused in weeks, months even. A strange kind of exhilaration seemed to surge through him, and he sensed a delicious trembling that appeared to afflict his very nerve-ends. It must have been the wine, he told himself. He'd had the best part of the bottle already, as well as a couple of beers while he was cooking in the kitchen.

He clasped hold of her round the waist, drew her to him. She put a hand on his backside and squeezed. He grunted gently. No words were necessary. He knew what to do.

'Right now,' she whispered. 'I want you right now.'

He looked at her and saw the meaning in her eyes. Through the thin material of her summer dress he could see how hard and firm her nipples had become. Liz had the longest and most pointed nipples he had ever seen on a woman. He could nuzzle them all night long and he frequently did. Heaven only knew what a Freudian would make of that.

They were only a couple of feet from the water's edge, but Liz was in his arms and their tongues were together, hands pushing up under clothes. Their movements alone spoke the language of abandoned passion, of fierce thirsts desperate to be slaked.

'I want you in me, Col,' she murmured. 'Let's do it in the sand.'

He felt the thrill of an unexpected surprise – he'd changed the sheets specially only a couple of hours earlier. He could hardly wait to get home with her but this was something new and exciting. She ruffled his hair and kissed him again. He hoped with all his heart the phone wouldn't ring. Now, of all times.

And then they were pressed together again, their bodies urgent and eager in the softening light of evening. He took her hand and led her up the gently shelving slope of the beach, their bare feet crunching on the shingle away from the lapping of the waves, aware of the erection that was pressing against his jeans, making walking awkward.

In among the sea lavender there was a flattened patch of sparse, thin grass. Here he kissed her really hard for the first time, breathing in the faint musk of her perfume that had been all but undetectable amid the ozone smells of the sea. As though of one accord, they sank to their knees and then he was lying beside her on the grass, one hand under her, the other under her dress, feeling for her breasts. The points were hard with desire.

Her fingers were in his hair, on his neck, across his chest under the buttons of his denim shirt. Liz pulled him over until he was half on top of her.

'Undress me,' she hissed with unexpected urgency. Her hand lightly brushed against his cock through the washed-out denim of his jeans. He undid the buttons at the back of her dress – how soft and cool her neck felt – and eased it over her shoulders. She arched her back to help him. Her tongue was in his ear as she did so.

When he had taken her dress off he stood up and tugged off his shirt and jeans. He looked at her lying there, resting on one elbow, coquettish, marvelling at the fullness of her breasts. She was wearing an elaborate pair of French knickers in oyster satin trimmed heavily with lace, not the kind of lingerie that would be worn normally by a doctor expecting to spend the rest of the night on call. She looked up at him, aware of the way his penis jutted out from his body, his testes heavy and potent. He liked having women look at him like that. It made him feel good, very male, very powerful.

She slipped out of her pants and then he too was naked beside her, his cock pressing hot and hard against her flank, his arms around her. Her breasts were crushed against his bare chest, and he slid down her body, his tongue seeking the nipple. He knew how to excite her in many different ways but this was one of their favourites.

All of a sudden Liz stopped, and looked him full in the face.

'Was that the phone?' she asked.

He stopped what he was doing, not without difficulty. This could be important. Someone's life could be at stake. But there was no sound other than the cry of the distant seabirds and the rustle of a faint breeze through the scrabby grass.

'No, I don't think it was,' he said, and he knew he was right.

He wouldn't have said so just for the sake of it, even though his heart was pounding like the engine on his boat in a heavy swell.

'Must have been my imagination,' Liz soothed him. 'I'm sure it'll be OK. They'd have phoned by now if they wanted me to go in. I just wanted to be sure.'

She felt warm, soft and undeniably female in his arms as she relaxed and her tongue sought his once more. He was squeezing her breasts, aware of how firm they felt, as though the rush of hormones evoked by her desire had somehow changed their texture. Far out to sea, he could see the navigation lights of a tanker making its way along the coast, three or four miles out, close to the horizon. Apart from that, all he was aware of – apart from the raw energy of her desire – was what came through his reeling senses, a delicious cocktail compounded of the coolness of the evening, the alcohol in his bloodstream, the soft breeze against his naked skin and the sand and grass rubbing against their bodies every time they moved. Each sensation added only to the totality of the feeling – in Col's mind there were no such concepts as pleasure and pain any more.

He pushed her on to her back, forcing his knee between her legs. They parted willingly for him. And then he was on top of her, his cock unmistakably there against her groin, urgent, insistent, ready. Liz took hold of it and guided it to her pussy.

'Wait,' she said, aware of his urgency. She moved her hips to accommodate him, this strangely exciting man she had been going with for something like six months and whose personality consistently revealed new facets to her. And yet, in some deep recess of her mind, she felt she had known him all her life.

'Now,' she breathed, but it was not a word, more of a sigh of glad surrender. And then he was inside her, filling her, his breath warm and urgent against her cheek and shoulders. He noticed how she gasped with the release that penetration gave her. God, it had been so long since they'd last done it together, ten days, a fortnight even. Spreading her legs to take more of him in, he looked up and saw the first stars of the evening twinkling in the darkening heavens as he began to push into her with ever-greater passion.

Their lips sought each other once more and Col ground his hips against hers, slowly and rhythmically. She drew up her legs and he inched forwards, even deeper inside her. He looked down at her face, her eyes closed to enjoy her feelings more. She really was quite incredibly good looking, the face framed by the light-blonde bobbed hair, the small nose, the wide, full lips.

He pulled out of her, drew her over until she was on top of him now, her small breasts swinging barely inches from his face, the long pointed nipples just one other symptom of her arousal. She reached hurriedly for his cock, wet and slippery now with their juices, and drew it inside her, then began bobbing up and down, quickly getting her rhythm right, working towards the orgasm that Col knew was coming for both of them. Saturn was quite bright now, he noticed as he peered over her heaving shoulders, and the Seven Sisters were very visible. Then he gave himself up fully to the sensation of being fucked on a deserted beach by a beautiful lady doctor.

Neither of them lasted long, such was the intensity of their feelings. Deep in his loins he could feel something stirring, the irresistible rush that he knew was coming. He pushed his hips up hard under her, almost lifting her off the ground, and in that moment his seed came boiling up out of him, defying gravity, an upward rush that left him breathless. He cried out his joy as he let go and was projected bodily forward, out in to the gazing heavens.

And then, very slowly and quietly, everything came to a swirling halt. There was a great sense of peace around them as they lay there, drawing in air. The world that he had entirely left behind for a few delirious moments was there again in his senses, the sea and the sand and the birds and the grass, the cool night breeze began to make goosebumps on Liz's skin and his own.

She pulled herself off him, sperm seeping from her vagina and running on to his thigh, and he could see a smile on her face. He felt unutterably calm, at one with everything around him. They would go home, drink the rest of the wine, listen to some music. It was going to be an evening to remember, he could feel it in his bones.

He looked up at the sky again, serene and content.

Far away, from the direction of the cottage, a telephone began to ring.

Richie couldn't hear a fucking thing the guy was saying to him. They were facing each other, across the bar, their heads perhaps a foot apart and he couldn't hear sweet FA.

The music was absolutely fucking deafening. It was like real physical pain. You didn't hear it, you felt it, through your feet, in your stomach, in your balls. Almost two months now Richie had been working in the Zero Six and he still hadn't got used to it. Sometimes he used to ask the DJ, Wicked Willy, why it had to be quite so fucking loud.

'It's a wonder I'm not deaf,' he'd said to Rob earlier that evening.

'What?' said Rob, cupping his ear.

'I said, it's a wonder I'm not deaf,' and then he realised Rob was pulling his leg, so he threw a cushion at him and straightened the stupid dickey-bow tie they made all the barmen wear at the club. Then he went for the bus. He felt a real prize wally standing there at the stop. It was absolutely baking hot still and his shirt was sticking to his back already.

By now, having worked behind the bar for an hour, he was positively squelching. Some of the dancers, the sweat was just streaming off them, like footballers at half-time. Usually they turned the volume way up towards the end of the evening but tonight, even though it was only just past nine, almost from the word go they'd had the knobs set at eleven. The dials only went up to ten. There was definitely something in the air that evening, too, a kind of big power that Richie couldn't quite lay his finger on. There was a good feeling about but there was something else, something a bit dark and dangerous.

He tried again with the guy. He was pretty well bellowing at him now, what his order was. Finally Richie caught on – two pints of lager and a campari and fucking soda. Usually he managed to lipread them but this guy, it was like he was a ventriloquist or something, his lips didn't hardly seem to move at all. Richie had learned to lipread from his dad, who could do it effortlessly from across a crowded and noisy bar with no problem at all. He knew how to do it because he'd spent his entire working life in a cacophony of noise. Richie's dad had been a riveter at the shipyard till they laid him off – a real tradesman, served his time and everything and they chucked him on the scrapheap at fifty-two like he was so much non-ferrous scrap. He never had really got over it, the feeling of rejection that lingered long after the redundancy money was all spent. It made you fucking furious, it really did. Now he sat at home all day, reading the *Mirror* and watching the soaps and the racing on Channel 4, as deaf as a fucking post. It made you want to puke, what them Tories had done to Britain. There wouldn't be many voting for them next time round where he lived, that was for sure.

He drew the pints, made *do-you-want-orange-in-your-campari?* movements with his lips. The guy nodded. *At last, we're communicating,* thought Richie. His collar was tight from the bow tie and he was looking forward to his break, so he could have a fag and a cup of strong tea. They weren't allowed to drink on duty but a lot of the guys did. The bastards who owned the Zero Six made you pay for your own drinks – and at bar prices too – which was a bit fucking rich. He didn't drink because he couldn't afford to. The beer was piss anyway, this naff southern stuff, brewed the traditional way for pansies. Give him a Broon or a pint of Fed any day of the week, including Saint Monday. It didn't matter what chemicals they put in it, he liked it. Even the CAMRA guys said Fed was OK.

The place sure was packed tonight. The big square room, on its several different levels, was an explosion of sound and light, lasers spearing the darkness, colours swirling across the walls. In the middle there was a heaving mass of bodies. Mostly the Zero Six played techno, which Wicked Willy liked, with a little deep house which, as far as Richie was concerned, was the same thing anyway. He was more into Zeppelin and Studd, the things his big brother Dave liked. Real bands with real people – I mean, he used to argue, just who the fuck is this Mr B featuring Nicey Nice? Do they exist? Do they shit? What kind of bottled water do they prefer? Nobody ever met anyone called Mr B or Nicey Nice, but a lot of people at home knew the lads who been in the Animals, and they still felt proud of them. That guy from Lindisfarne who died, people remembered him too as one of their own. Mr B could have come from Walker for all anybody knew of him.

The bar ran along almost the whole of one side of the club. The management said it was the longest bar in the east of England, outside London, but Richie didn't believe them. What he did believe was how fucking tight they were, a bar that size with, most of the time, only four guys behind it. He worked his fingers to the fucking bone trying to serve all the punters who were lined up there, waving crisp purple twenties at him. The pay wasn't too bad, though. Five an hour was a lot more than some people got – the other place in town, the Igloo, they only paid their bar staff three-fifty and they had to help clear up afterwards. Working five days a week, Richie could easily end up with a hundred and fifty in folding stuff, no card, no stamps, no questions asked so he could still claim his benefit from back home. Casual labour was a fucking racket and everyone knew it. What did they expect, the way the government had fucked up people's lives? Now the people were fucking them back, with a vengeance. Richie liked that feeling. It gave him a sense of power, that he existed, that he too could make his mark. It beat kicking down bus shelters.

He was aware of an anger in himself that night, born not just out of his frustration at not getting laid for so fucking long but at the money around him, all the trendies with their big wallets and Comme des Garçons clothes, the expensive girls, the idea that everyone was having a good time apart from him. He hated that feeling of being on the outside, cut off behind the bar. He wanted to be over there with the rest of them, having a good time. He bet Rob and Debbie were at it right now.

And still they were piling up two and three deep to get served. Billy Brilleaux's girlfriend Sue came up, buying Bacardi and coke for herself and a lager for her friend. She had her purse open but Richie winked at her and waved it aside. A lot of the staff had friends come in, and when the Malteser brothers who owned the place weren't around – which was usually the case – then it'd be freebie time. Mostly, for the paying punters, it was lager or beer for the blokes and lager or a short for the girls, who got in free before ten so they could afford a bit more for a Cinzano and lemonade or something daft. They didn't do cocktails at the Zero Six, you could get them over the way at Bogart's Bar downstairs at the Pier Head, but that was only open in the evenings. You could charge the fucking earth for them – three-fifty or so for a Double Zombie or a Slamdancer as opposed to two quid for a lager – but they took all day and half the fucking night to make and the management reckoned it wasn't worth it, the staff time they used up. Everything according to the Malteser brothers was down to overheads and margins and that shite, but the punters just wanted to get pissed as quickly as was humanly possible, if not quicker. Besides, Richie said one day when he was bringing crates down, who'd want to be seen dead drinking something that looked like a fucking allotment, it had all them lemon slices and mint leaves and God knows what in it, spilling over the sides. The manager gave him a funny look and Richie remembered something he'd forgotten in the staff room.

There was a lot of E went down in the place too, which was one reason why they'd hiked the bar prices at the start of the summer because people weren't buying booze any longer. So the management, ever alert to an opportunity to chisel the hard-earned stuff from the punters' clinging fingers, brought in this bottled water with the club's name on the label, and they charged them a quid for that even though it wasn't chilled and it probably came out of a tap. Still, the ravers liked it, and it helped cool them down. There had been a few people got in a bad way with the E but never enough to worry the powers that be. A club he and Rob used to go to back home, there were three people had died after going there, two blokes and a girl, and they were trying to get the place closed down which was a shame because it was a great place to pull skirt.

There was a lull in the crush at the bar. Richie looked at his watch. Nine-fifteen, almost time for his half-hour off. Just his fucking luck that the bottom dropped out of the market when it was time for him to have a break. They were quite keen on staff taking a break when they were supposed to and he liked it best when his time off coincided with a real busy period.

There was some good talent in the club tonight. Sometimes, if he wasn't too busy and he could make himself heard above the endless thumping beat, he'd chat to a girl, sometimes just because he was feeling friendly, at other times because he wanted to get into her pants. The week before last, for instance, he'd got talking to a girl who was on holiday from Doncaster with her mates and had ended up going back with her to her place. It was at the big holiday camp outside town which had meant a taxi ride but it had been well worth it for the ride she'd given him that night. She wasn't all that good looking, but she had tits and an arse on her and she knew how to use them. He fucked her on one of the narrow little beds in her chalet – God knew where her mates had got to – and then she'd sucked him off, not minded at all that he came in her mouth, though he was wearing one just in case. It was like playing the piano with boxing gloves on, Rob used to say, but at least it was better than nothing at all if she was one of the careful types. He wondered what it was like to suck someone when they were wearing a fred. It must taste bloody awful, although you could get banana-flavoured ones and stuff. He hated the fucking things, not least because you couldn't get the smell off you for days afterwards. God knows what it was like actually *eating* one of them.

Just when it was his time to sag off, a whole bunch of blokes came surging in and Richie had to help out, pulling pints and slicing lemons. By the time he'd finished it was nearly half-past so he swiped a bottle of coke – he couldn't be bothered going back to the staff room to make tea – and ducked under the bar and made his way out through the emergency exit to the back of the place where they stacked the empties and the management parked their BMWs and Audis. The car park was empty tonight, though, as it often was – the Malteser brothers largely let the place run itself and only dropped by for a few minutes to see how things were going. He hadn't seen neither hide nor hair of them since Wednesday but Billy said they'd be by sooner rather than later.

He heard a noise, a scuffling sound on the fire escape that led from the roof down the back of the building– the club itself was on the first floor, with store rooms and things at street level. He wondered at first if someone was trying to crash the place – it cost a fiver to get in, not that much when it came down to it, but sometimes it didn't come down to it – but then the dark shape turned into Billy the bouncer.

'Thought you were trying to break in,' said Richie, drawing on the ciggie he'd cadged from one of the other barmen.

Billy grinned at him, cracking his knuckles. 'Who the fuck would want to break in there?' he said. 'They got me to contend with, haven't they?'

Billy was a gentle kind of guy if he was on your side, but he could be a holy terror if anybody got on the wrong end of him. He was a big bugger, the size of Robbie Coltrane and just as pretty, but he could get you in an armlock faster than most people could fart, and he had this mean trick with his thumb sticking out from his balled-up fist that had left more than one east-coast heavy flat on his back on the pavement. Above all, Billy commanded respect, not just in Dunwich but all along the coast.

'I seen Sue and her mate,' said Richie. 'Not seen her before.'

'Sue?'

95

A bit slow on the uptake, was Billy. But a heart of gold.

'No, her mate. The one she came in with.'

'What's she like?'

'Not very tall, fancies herself a bit, big frizzy hair.'

'Looks a bit like that woman from *Shortland Street*?'

'That's the one.'

'That's Jacqui. She's at college with her. She usually goes to the Igloo but she's just packed in this guy she was going with and now she's out on the piss. Why, d'you fancy her?'

Richie tried to look non-committal but Billy got the message. Jacqui, eh? Maybe he might see how things were going later. He'd put in a good word for his mate. Richie was all right in Billy's book, a straight-ahead kind of bloke. Billy didn't like wankers.

Billy went off back into the club. Richie finished his cigarette and followed him. The bar was absolutely heaving when he got back.

'Jesus, Richie, where the fuck have you been?' asked Pete, one of the other barmen. Richie ignored him, went straight up to the meanest and angriest-looking punter and took his order. He knocked them off one by one with practised ease, pulling pints and cracking cans. He gave some guy gin and tonic instead of vodka and tonic but the bloke never came back, he forgot the ice in someone else's drink but that was easily sorted. He was running well now, he liked that feeling of when things started to work out. It was really starting to get busy and his ears were ringing but he had the sense of being a working man, doing what he was good at.

There was still that nasty atmosphere, though, like a fart that had got loose in an astronaut suit. Pete was having problems with some half-pissed slob who must have got in when Billy was taking a leak – Ron, the other security guy, wasn't anywhere near so fussy who they let in, even though it was supposed to be smart cash and not too legless – so Richie came over and helped get the situation straightened out. He was just changing the guy's Fosters for a Carling Black Label like he said he wanted when, out of the corner of his eye, he saw a flash of blonde hair and there was the girl again, the same one he'd seen on the beach that afternoon, The Vision. For a few seconds he just stood there until the beer flowed out all over his hand and Pete cried out and Richie came back, with a jolt, to the real world.

It was like someone had tipped a pint down the back of his neck, so great was the shock of it. He tried to keep one eye on his work and one eye on where she'd got to, but it was difficult. He caught a glimpse of her moving through the throng, but then she was lost to sight altogether. One thing was for sure, he hoped she had a thirst on and she'd come to his part of the bar. He tried to beam out mental messages to her, tried to use his brain like a magnet, sending out waves of impulses to her, but it didn't work. It never did. He served his customers without really knowing what he was doing, his heart pounding, his hands noticeably shaking. He caught a glimpse of her again, not thirty feet away from him, and in his confusion gave someone change for twenty when they'd only handed him a couple of fivers. He had to do something.

'I gotta go,' he hissed in Pete's ear.

'Go where? You just had your break. Aw, come on, Richie, there's a queue ten deep.'

'No, I gotta go. Something came up.'

He caught the anger in Pete's eye but couldn't help himself as he ducked through the door at the back of the bar and round the corridor where the empties were stacked, back past a bewildered-looking Billy and back into the club again.

'What's with you, Richie?' the doorman called. 'Your pants on fire or something?'

But Richie, blind to everything except his own raging desires, didn't heed him. He pushed wildly through the crowd, frantically looking for the blonde-haired girl. Just when he thought he'd hallucinated the whole thing he caught a glimpse of her, practically on the same spot where he'd seen her last. She was standing with another girl, dark-haired and pretty, the two of them engaged in animated conversation. Richie pushed closer. Christ, she was a looker all right, tall and blonde and long-legged, a lovely pair on her, dressed simply in tight blue jeans and a t-shirt that had something written on it in French. She must be at the language school, he figured, which might account for the friend as well – she had that Gallic look to her, now he came to think about it.

The two girls weren't dancing, just standing there swaying with the music, occasionally nudging each other and laughing. He saw the blonde one look at her watch and say something to the darker one. Then she disappeared, heading straight for the ladies' loo. A couple of other girls came up now and were talking to the dark girl like they knew her – they must be students too, but they had blokes in tow.

He scuttled back towards the loos, all the time catching enticing glimpses of that divine ass in its tight blue jeans. What was he going to do? Hang around until she came out was the answer, think of something to say and say it quick. He stood there, nervously rehearsing his best come-on lines when the door of the main office opened and Nassar Malteser came out. For a moment their eyes locked.

'What the fuck are you doing?' the manager barked. 'Pete's running the bar practically single handed.'

His heart sinking into his boots like an express lift heading groundwards, Richie could barely think straight.

'I left me wallet in the bog,' he said out blind. 'I got all me money in it.'

He fished in his pocket, pulled it out, waved it in the air like a fool.

'You'd forget your bloody head if it was loose,' said Nassar Malteser. 'We need some more bottled water – it's in the van out the back. Come on, I'll give you a hand.'

Richie turned round, in time to see The Vision come out of the loo and look around her. That bastard Malteser made sure he was busy at the bar, so he didn't see her again that evening. He kept trying to locate her by remote control but his antennae weren't working. He cursed his luck. He was so put out, he even forgot to check out his chances with Jacqui until he saw her pairing off with some guy he vaguely knew from the Pier Head Hotel.

It was the last house of the evening at the bingo and Rob was glad. He'd been at it for almost eight hours, on and off, and he was knackered. In his lime-green suit and dickey-bow tie he looked out at the audience and dragged his rheumy eyes back to the numbers. In half an hour, he hoped, he'd be shagging Debbie.

'Was she worth it?' he intoned. 'Two and six. Potty time, number two. She's under age, sweet sixteen. Getting past it, forty-two.'

He was getting a bit near the knuckle as well. One or two faces looked up from their cards, trying to suss him. He must have got sex on the brain. He tried to change tack.

'Downing Street, number ten.'

'How fast the records go round, forty-five.'

'Naughty naughty, sixty-nine.'

He was off again. Oh Christ, if only he could remember what to say, instead of making it up most of the time. He hadn't a clue what was going on. Smoking a joint just before coming on hadn't helped either. It was amazing stuff – some mate of Richie's from the Zero Six had scored a whole weight in Ipswich. He was sure he was calling some of the numbers wrong but so far they hadn't actually started throwing things at him. He was aware of a distinct murmuring all the same.

He decided to plough on, though every muscle in his body implored him to stop, before it was too late.

'Key of the door, eighteen.'

Thirty four. What the hell was thirty-four?

'Where me aunt Vera lives, thirty-four. Churchill's balls, number three. Early retirement, fifty-five.'

It was the one someone had been waiting for. Thank God, he breathed as the lights flashed and buzzers sounded, and someone could go home a hundred quid better off. He couldn't have gone on a moment longer.

Backstage, having picked up his weekly pay packet from the cash box, he tugged off his shirt and changed quickly into his clothes for the evening – a pair of 501s bought only last week and a Wetback t-shirt, prefaced by a good squirt of deo. Stepping out on to the pier he breathed in great lungfuls of air, a welcome change from the stuffy, fag-smoke atmosphere of the bingo hall. You heard a lot these days about sick building syndrome and that place on the end of the pier was positively pestilent. He felt like throwing up every time he went in it, and as for the headaches . . .

He pushed his way through the thin straggle of bingo players making their way along the pier, the sky blue and pink and orange. He could see the lights of the town winking, the steady flow of traffic along Eastern Avenue. The funfair was still going strong, it was busy until ten every night at the weekend but during the week they closed earlier. He and Richie used to go there sometimes to ride the dodgems. It was supposed to be a quid a time but they knew the guys who worked the ride so they let them crash about for free when their bosses weren't around. Rob would have reciprocated but he didn't think anybody he knew would have wanted to play bingo, least of all on a Saturday night.

At the entrance to the pier Debbie was waiting. She looked really good, a short skirt and a big floppy t-shirt that emphasised rather than hid those eminently suckable tits. He fancied her there and then.

'Hi,' he said. 'Do you want to go get something to eat? I'm starving.'

They went to Pizza Palace, just up the road from the pier. It wasn't very busy, just a few holiday families and a bunch of underage girls who couldn't get served in the pub. Rob had four cheeses, Debbie a mushroom special with double peppers. With over a hundred quid tight in the back pocket of his 501s, he felt like splashing out. He ordered a carafe of the house red. It was going to be a good night.

'Are we going to the Zero Six after?' asked Debbie.

'What do you think?'

'Might as well. Nothing much else to do.'

'Richie's there tonight. We can get in free. He's got a mate on the door. If he's not there, we just ask for Billy.'

He felt pleasantly tired, relaxing with the wine and a girl he was very fond of. They played footsie under the table. It turned him on, he didn't know why, perhaps the way she was smiling at him. They took their time over the house red. It was a bit peppery but it went well with the meal.

The waiters in their red jackets were over at the far end. Rob leaned forward and took Debbie's hand.

'How do you fancy a bit of, you know?'

'Now?'

'No, not right now.'

'Later, then. Back at your place?'

'I mean, once we've finished this.' He indicated the plates with their half-chewed crusts, the almost empty carafe of wine.

'Where? Are you taking me to the Excelsior for the night?' The Excelsior was the glitziest hotel in Dunwich – though the Crown was trying hard to usurp its title – AA/RAC four star and close on a hundred quid a night. There were a lot of big rollers went to those places up on Northdene still.

'Like hell,' said Rob. 'Maybe we could find us somewhere.'

He had in mind a beach hut if they could find one open, or somewhere like that. They'd done it before in the open air darkness, in the municipal gardens for one and round the back of the pavilion on the green. There were plenty of places you could find if you put your mind to it.

'I'll have to think about it, won't I?' she said but he could tell by the smile playing around her eyes that she was game.

She felt his hand on her knee, under the table cloth. Christ, she thought, he wants to have me in the middle of Pizza Palace.

Rob turned and leaned towards her. She parted her legs to make it easier for him. His hand slid up her thighs, on to the tops of her bare legs, feeling how soft and cool she felt despite the heat. Debbie looked up anxiously, but the waiters were still at the other end of the room. Besides, there was a big pillar blocking them from the view of the other diners.

For a couple of minutes or more his fingers delicately brushed across her skin, making it tingle, making her long for him. She wanted his fingers there, his tongue, his penis. She was temporarily lost for conversation.

His fingertips moved higher. She glanced anxiously around the room again. No one could possibly see them, unless they knelt down on the floor and looked up. She felt reassured, and was able to relax. She parted her legs a little more, moved forward in her seat so that his fingers brushed against her sex.

He stroked her delicately, between her legs. He was looking straight into her eyes.

Despite the short skirt she had on, she wasn't wearing any underwear. She could tell how surprised he was. She'd done it specially for him, it made her feel deliciously vulnerable. He'd asked her to do it several times, to come out with him like that, but this was the first time she'd really wanted to. It made her feel more comfortable in the heat.

Now his fingers slid underneath, against the moist lips of her pudenda, the palm of his hand cupping her pubic mound. She had to push herself almost off the edge of the chair so he could reach her and so she was leaning right back. She glanced out of the window and saw people coming and going at the other end of the restaurant, paying their bills, ordering desserts. She poured the last of the wine into their glasses, trying to look nonchalant. She realised her hands were shaking and she nearly dropped the carafe.

Rob's middle finger roved around her labia, probing between the folds, finding at last the entrance and slipping inside her. She had not been particularly wet before but now she felt her juices beginning to flow, easing the passage of another finger and then another, until he had three fingers buried in her, there at their table in Pizza Palace, with people stuffing pasta and ice cream and things only a few feet away.

'Come on, Rob, someone might see,' she heard herself say for form's sake, but she wanted him to go on, to push on into her, to push her over the edge. With the ball of his thumb he found her clitoris and massaged it with infinite gentleness, all the while his fingers twisting and sliding and turning inside her. It was so very different to the rough and uncompromising way most of the boys she'd been out with did it to her, even the more refined ones. Already she was pushing out to meet him, trying to force herself on to him, ready to be penetrated.

She didn't reach a climax, although she was close to it – she felt too inhibited by the other people in the cafe and the waiters hovering around the place. She whimpered and moaned and sighed quietly enough for Rob to think he had brought her off. He withdrew his hand. She felt warm and excited and she wished they could go back to the caravan right now. Her Mini was parked right by the pier.

'Maybe we should go for a walk after all,' she said.

She smiled at him, discreetly adjusting her clothing while he sipped the last of his wine. He looked happy. He liked to give women pleasure. She could see the erection in his trousers.

Rob paid their bill and they made their way out into the night. It was almost dark outside, just a faint trace of colour in the sky. The air was warm and the stars were incredibly bright. Rob knew which one the North Star was and he could just about find the Plough but the rest of it was a big black mystery to him. They held hands as they walked through the Saturday-night throng.

The night was hot and sultry, exaggerating the smells of cooking that came from a dozen restaurants. Maybe this was what it was like in the south of France or somewhere, thought Rob as they walked along, her hand in his. He liked the lights strung up along the front, orange and green and pink and blue. It reminded him of a couple of years back when Uncle Randolph had driven them all the way to Blackpool for the Illuminations in his big old clapped-out Jag. 'Even if it's got a hundred and twenty on the clock, it's better than owt your lot can come up with,' he'd said to Rob's dad, who worked at the Nissan plant.

They ended up under the pier. It was kind of weird down there, with the big iron columns festooned with seaweed and the overpowering smell of water, the distant sound of the waves. She hoiked her top up and he was sucking hungrily at her tits, lovely and round and fleshy with nice plump nipples. Her pussy felt like it was on fire.

'Come on, Rob,' she whispered, stroking his hair as he nuzzled her.

He pressed her against one of the columns, cold and surprisingly rough against their naked flesh. Her short skirt was up around her hips and Rob was busy with his belt. For a second or two they looked at each other in the darkness, the lights of the esplanade playing in their eyes, barely able to see each other's flesh in the gloom under the pier.

And then she stood up high on her toes and parted her legs and he was pushing inside her, hot and eager. She came almost immediately, tongueing him like mad, and then again as he pumped his strong, masculine backside up and down, up and down, his cock seeming to fill her completely until she was oblivious to everything else. When he came into her, it was like a big shuddering spasm for both of them. It seemed to go on and on until finally the feeling subsided and she realised her legs were getting stiff standing like that, and then Rob withdrew and she wiped herself quickly and discreetly with a tissue from her bag. Above them she could hear the sound of people walking along the pier.

105

For some while they stood there, locked in each other's arms, aware of nothing but the crash of waves and the creaking of the ancient iron structure that had sheltered them.

'Come on,' said Rob at length. 'Let's get going. We got a date, remember?'

They climbed the short flight of steps that led to the esplanade. At the top, a bunch of lads were standing around. She knew one of them, a thicko called Maxie. She nodded vaguely at him out of politeness but it wasn't her they were interested in.

The group parted and there, all of a sudden, was Mick Rowlandson. He was glaring right at Rob and looking mean. There was a dark patch under one eye where Rob had dobbed him one earlier.

'Come here, shitface,' he said. 'I want a word with you.'

The other guys were standing around, trying to look tough. Rob vaguely knew some of them and knew they weren't up to much in a scrap, however much they may have ponced about trying to look hard. Still, he couldn't have beaten them all.

'Oh fuck,' he murmured under his breath. Right there at the moment of triumph, and something like that had to happen . . .

Chapter Four

The buffet supper at The Laurels was a quiet, almost subdued affair. The full à la carte menu was available for those who wanted it but most preferred a light meal, a few canapés and a salad, perhaps, or a stuffed pepper or the wild mushrooms in a mint sauce. The wine was good without being exceptional. The hotel bar, of course, was open as usual.

The supper was important, though, as a taster for the evening to come. There was a formal elegance about its conduct, evinced by the candles on the tables and the men, for the most part, in formal evening wear. Paul looked particularly elegant, Carole thought, as they descended the long, winding staircase from their second-floor room. He was wearing a dark evening suit, an Armani shirt. She could see one or two eyes move in his direction and not merely because they recognised him from his television appearances and the photographs in countless magazines.

Carole, too, had dressed with great care for the evening, in high heels and a long, floating black dress from Ghost, whose diaphanous folds did little – for such was her intention – to conceal what she was wearing underneath. With the light falling on her, the dress was almost transparent. Beneath it she wore black seamed stockings, a wasp-waisted corset, a sensationally scooped black uplift bra and tiny black panties that barely concealed her carefully manicured sex. She was aware of eyes lingering as they made their way down the thickly carpeted corridor, of the expressions on people's faces, women as well as men, that registered an interest.

Most of the women in the dining room seemed, in one form or another, to be dressed in black as well. There was a lot of see-through, which slightly disappointed Carole. She glanced at a stunningly tall woman in leather, with long-long legs that didn't know where to stop, encased in wickedly sheer tights with a tiny pelmet of a skirt. She knew her from somewhere. They smiled their greetings. There was another woman she recognised, stately and distinguished. Carole knew she was well into her forties but she had the body and panache of a woman ten years younger, and most of it was on view. Some of the women seemed to have gone completely over the top. They walked by a short and extremely busty blonde lady dressed only in a PVC corselette and black stockings, teetering on four-inch heels with her breasts exposed. The area around her nipples, Carole noted, was powdered and delicately tattooed in a tracery of lines. There was quite a bit of evidence of body decoration – the usual and, to her, rather boring butterflies and dragonflies on shoulders, breasts or inner thigh, contrasting with one tall woman who wore on one arm a long velvet glove while on the other a tattooed snake wound its way down from her elbow to her wrist. There were pierced navels and nipples, heavy earrings and nose studs. These people, it was obvious, meant business.

They helped themselves to wine, were just about to join the queue for the buffet when they spotted old friends. Tom and Melanie Anstruther had been at the last evening at The Laurels and they had spent most of the weekend together – so adequately did they meet each other's needs, there was little need for them to circulate among the various public and private rooms. They had met subsequently, on several occasions, both at their own home and at the Anstruthers'. She found them amusing enough but lightweight. She wished, sometimes, she could meet people who had as much between their ears as they had between their legs.

Tom and Paul shook hands, immediately began talking business. Tom owned a radio station in Scotland, had always wanted to interest the Chiversos in a syndicated talk show. Melanie was a bit of a Barbie type but, at The Laurels at least, that was no great handicap.

'I love your dress,' she said to Carole. 'It's Ghost, isn't it?'

'Full points,' said Carole, but anyone could have told. It was the way she wore it that made it special. Melanie was dressed in a full-length black lace body stocking that revealed every detail of her miraculous figure. On her wrists were silver bangles that tinkled with every gesture she made.

'The Baileys are here,' Melanie added. 'Do you know them? He publishes all those lesbian porno mags but you'd never guess, he's such a gent.'

She nodded at a grey-haired, distinguished-looking man who was sipping wine.

'Surely you know him, if not her,' Melanie went on.

'I don't think I do,' replied Carole, but her eyes were busy scanning the room. Not everyone was dressed to thrill, of course. Some of them hid behind masks – which was probably part of the game for them – but there were quite a few dressed conventionally. Almost everyone, it seemed, was in couples.

She caught someone's eye across the crowded room. Anxious to get away – for Melanie's conversation was already beginning to pall – she made her excuses to Melanie and walked across to some other people she knew. 'I won't be long, darling,' she breathed to Paul. 'I just want a word with someone.'

She'd caught sight of Lynda Cushing, a supermodel who'd been on their show only a few weeks back. Her fabled hair piled up on her head, she was wearing a clinging black lycra dress that revealed her fabulous ass and the cleavage that had turned one well-known make of brassière from an operational loss to a brand leader within six months. She was wearing stockings that, heart stoppingly for most of the men in the room, ended just short of her hemline. It was a deliberate ploy, a little amusement. A lot of girls were dressing that way in discos and clubs. It was very much the height of fashion but, within weeks, it would be gone. Carole began to suspect that even her own see-through might be a little old hat in Lynda's eyes.

They kissed their greetings.

'Hi, Carole,' said Lynda. She was with two guys in their early twenties. 'This is Nick and this is Mark,' she added, introducing them. 'We – how shall I put it? – we have a place together.'

'All three of you?'

'Something like that.'

Good for you, thought Carole. Nick she found very sexy, Mark she wasn't too sure about.

'We always catch your show,' Mark was saying.

'Thanks,' she said, an automatic response. She never knew what to believe when people so obviously courted celebrity. 'You didn't come to the studio when Lynda was on, did you?'

'No, we had to fly to Tokyo.'

'Are you in the fashion business too?'

'We're photographers.'

The penny dropped. So these were Nick and Mark, better known as 231 Pacific – or some such stupid name. They were just about the hottest two snappers in the business right now. They worked together, which was unusual in what was normally a solitary business, and they evidently played together too. *Well, well, well, well, well,* she found herself thinking.

'I'm sorry,' she said. 'I hadn't realised who you were. I love your stuff. Those shots you had in Italian *Vogue* last month were brilliant. I can't remember whose clothes they were, I just looked at the pictures. Where were they taken?'

'Canvey Island,' said Nick, without batting an eyelid. Canvey was a small eyesore community on the Essex coast, noted for its sheer ugliness, its oil refineries and as the birthplace of a whole clutch of well-past-it rock bands whose agents and managers tried, without success, to get airtime for them on Paul and Carole's show.

'You could have fooled me,' she said. 'It looked like Tuscany or somewhere.'

'It's all done on computers,' explained Mark. 'We did the shots on Canvey because we wanted that cold blue early morning light you get around estuaries, and we wanted the water in the background. But the rest of it we did back at the studio on screen. Are you into computers?'

'No, I'm not,' said Carole rather too quickly. 'I have a Powerbook but that's about as far as it goes.'

'Pity,' said Mark. 'That's where everything's going, now. In ten years time everything will be based around the PC. That's where we're investing. We've just got a new system that cost a hundred and twenty grand but we'll get the money back within a year.'

'I'm sure you're right,' she said, made her excuses and went back to Paul.

'That's Lynda Cushing, isn't it?' he said as they moved forward in the queue.

'It is. You remember her, don't you? I'm sure you tried to make a pass at her in the hospitality suite.'

'You're imagining things, my sweet,' he said and leaned over and kissed her on the cheek. 'I only have eyes for you, as the song says. Who are the blokes with her?'

'Nick and Mark. You know, 231 Pacific, the photographers.'

'Major league stuff, eh? Interesting, were they? Maybe we should have them on the show.'

'Mark was about to start boring me into the ground about computers. They don't use cameras much any more, it's all done on computers.'

'Might be the sort of thing we should look at,' he said in his diffident way, but Carole felt differently. She'd already forgotten about Nick and Mark. They had no interest for her, sexually or professionally.

They forked down their food, their eyes roving the room like predatory animals. With such an array of male and female pulchritude on display around them – for here were gathered a hundred or so of the country's most exclusive swingers – it was perhaps ironic that neither of them had, as yet, seen anyone they especially fancied. But then a girl came briefly into the room, her blonde hair piled high on her head, dressed in a skin-tight catsuit exactly like the one Michelle Pfeiffer wore in *Batman Returns*. She looked a bit like her too, that same kind of gamine sensuality. Carole noticed that Paul was staring hard at her too. It was nice for a married couple to have interests in common.

They looked at each other and nodded.

The girl was speaking to a couple near the door. They evidently knew each other well, because they were laughing and chatting quite easily. The girl said something. The man looked at his watch, looked at his partner and nodded. The girl smiled, blew them a kiss and vanished.

'Who was she, then?' Paul breathed to his wife, but before they could begin to find out they were interrupted by Tom and Melanie.

'They're showing movies in the ballroom,' he said. 'It's some Bryonie Levy epic at the moment but after that it's *Marilyn and JFK*. You must have seen it. Or at least heard about it?'

'What's that?' asked Paul. He was well clued-up on movies, especially erotic ones, but this was a new one on him.

'Oh, come on, Paul. I thought you were the expert. Everyone's been talking about it.'

'Well, it seems to have passed us by,' Carole chipped in. 'Tell us all about it.'

'It was made about three years ago,' said Tom, 'but it's never got release clearance. It's about how Kennedy was screwing Marilyn Monroe when he was President, what it led to. The CIA were involved, all that kind of thing.'

He mentioned the names of the stars – some of Carole's favourites. It sounded pretty good to her.

'I've never seen it, but they say the screwing scenes are really good – and there's a lot of them. But the really interesting thing is, they've got some archive footage – or what they say is archive footage – that is supposed to show Marilyn and JFK actually doing it.'

'Who shot it?' asked Carole. 'The CIA?'

'Nobody knows. I know the producer and he isn't saying where it came from. The official line is that it's just some stuff they cleverly recreated in the studio. But I don't believe any of it. I'm convinced this is the real McCoy.'

'How do you know?'

'I don't – it's just a hunch. In one of the scenes there's another woman in bed with them. You can't see her face at any point but I've been told on good authority that that scene was shot in the White House itself.'

'Who was the woman?' asked Paul.

'Jackie O,' said Melanie, triumphantly.

'Allegedly,' added Tom, more cautious.

'We'll have to see for ourselves and decide, won't we?' said Carole. 'Can we take our drinks in with us?'

When they came out of the cinema their mood had changed. They all felt highly charged, ready for anything. Over drinks in the bar they argued vehemently about what they'd seen. It was like all of those shots of so-called flying saucers, that famous footage of the autopsy on the alleged alien they'd found in Kansas or wherever it was. Everything made you say it couldn't possibly be, but a voice said *well, just what if?*

Paul reckoned it was and Tom said it wasn't. Carole and Melanie were undecided but they hadn't either of them realised what a big bum Marilyn had. Still, she had the looks and she could really act when she wanted to, not like some of the platinum popsies who'd tried in later years to usurp her crown.

They went to Tom and Melanie's room to begin with. There was champagne on the table by the door and the lights were turned down low. Paul lay down flat on the bed, still fully clothed in his dinner jacket and bow tie, and Melanie came and knelt over him. She pulled down the top of her lace body-stocking and offered him a breast to suck. Carole was surprised how quickly the nipple became swollen, glistening wet as her husband licked and sucked at it, his tongue alternately tracing delicate little lines around Melanie's areolae.

114

Melanie was rubbing herself against Paul's groin, backwards and forwards, backwards and forwards, while his hands roved up and down her long, elegant thighs. Tom came and stood behind Carole, offered her a glass of champagne. She could feel his erection pressing against her buttocks. She fancied having him in her arse and then for Paul to fuck her pussy, but it was the kind of evening when anything could happen. She knew better than to make plans. After all, she'd been to enough evenings like this over the years. Some turned out to be full of delicious surprises and others – usually the ones from which she expected the most – were about as exciting as a wet Tuesday in Leeds.

Paul kicked off his shoes and somehow managed to struggle out of his trousers with Melanie still on top of him, her bracelets jangling, her tits spilling out. From where Carole stood, with Tom stroking her shoulders, she could see the damp patch between her legs where her pussy was rubbing against the tight nylon. It excited her, the thought of Melanie's arousal. She wanted to kneel there and smell the other woman's secretions, but she knew better than to interrupt them.

Tom's hands were around her waist now and he was nuzzling her neck, his tongue flicking up and down, teasing the soft downy hair and her ultra-sensitive earlobes, bristling with expensive silverware. He reached up and cupped her breasts and she leaned forward so that he could take the full weight of them in his palms, rich and full and so very nice to suck. She rubbed her backside against his cock and she knew he liked that. He murmured something but she didn't catch what he said, intent less on what was happening to her than on what the other woman was doing with her husband.

Melanie slid down the bed and started to suck Paul's cock. This was the moment Carole had been waiting for. She gave Tom's arm a squeeze and quickly crossed the room, kneeling down on the floor behind Melanie. She ran her hands experimentally over her backside and Melanie neatly parted her legs for her. Turning round so she was lying on her back, Carole put her head between Melanie's thighs and pressed her face right up there between her legs. She could smell musk, perfume, the unmistakably heady scent of a woman's arousal. No wonder men were so crazy for it, she thought, after they'd licked a woman out. It was the scent of sex itself.

That little bit of licking and sniffing was all she wanted from Melanie – for the moment, at any rate. She helped the other woman out of the clinging garment and then quickly stepped out of her own Ghost dress and lay down on the bed, still in her underwear, beside her husband. Tom seemed to have undressed remarkably quickly. She slipped her tiny panties over her legs and parted them invitingly for him, and he was on top of her in a moment. Watching the film – could that really have been Marilyn, JFK and Jackie O? – seemed to have dispensed with the need for any foreplay. Carole wanted fucking and Tom was happy to do it for her. She felt very wet and very aroused, very much in the mood for good hard fucking. The artistic stuff could come later.

Tom slid into her as she brought up her legs around him, his cock already thrusting at her. Next to them she could see Melanie bobbing up and down on top of her husband. She was naked now, in all her glory, but he was still in his shirt. She hoped it didn't get creased.

Tom's tongue came slithering up her face and into her mouth. She devoured it greedily, sucking hard at him as she spread her legs even wider. She liked a man who knew how to fuck and Tom certainly had all the prior knowledge for that. It's a pity his wife had shit for brains, she had often thought, it might have been nice to know them better as friends.

Her bra felt tight against her heaving breasts and she somehow managed to reach behind herself and undo the catch. Freed from their constraint, her breasts spilled out. She wanted Tom to suck them while he was still in her but it was awkward the way they were lying, so she stroked her own nipples instead and told him how big his cock was and how much she wanted his creamy come right up her cunt.

Paul and Melanie were doing it doggie-style now and she managed to squirm around so that Melanie's tits were only an inch or so from her face. Melanie wasn't all that keen on doing it with another woman – she'd looked a bit shocked once before when Carole suggested she put a dildo on and fuck her with it – but a bit of necking was all right with her and that extended to tit-sucking too.

So Carole nuzzled up against her and her tongue flickered out and teased the nipples into even further distension, which caused Melanie to gasp and buck and to press her body hard against Paul, who was pushing away at her hammer and tongs, and Carole somehow managed to get her long, black-stockinged legs all the way up round Tom's waist so she could almost move him around in a pincer grip.

He was turned on by her black waspie, she could tell, from the way he kept running his hands over it, the hard satin-finished material, the delicate trim of lace, the tiny red ribbons at the tops of the suspenders. Paul had always liked it too, each time she'd worn it. The seamed stockings were the finishing touch – hard to get, these days, especially ones long enough to fit legs like hers, but she liked the way the pencil-thin line accentuated the curve of her legs. She wore short skirts on TV so it had to be tights –

despite what the viewers probably wanted – but for evening wear, it was almost always stockings.

She could tell that Tom wasn't going to be long now, thrusting into her with increasing vigour, turned on like she was by the sight of their respective partners fucking alongside them. She was well used by now to seeing Paul with another woman, but still it gave her a little frisson of the forbidden, a little tiny tingle of jealousy that only served to sharpen her own prodigious appetite for pleasure.

She stopped sucking Melanie's tits and thrust her tongue deep into Tom's mouth instead. The kiss was long and slow and liquid. When it finished she asked him to fuck her in the bum. For a moment or two it seemed that he was almost going to come at the thought of it but then he quickly pulled out of her and she rolled forward on to her front and presented her rump to him.

Wet with her juices, his prick quickly found the entrance to her rear passage. He went in a little way and then she asked him to stop – it was starting to hurt a little, maybe she wasn't quite ready – but then her muscles relaxed and he slid in all the way and almost immediately she began playing with her clit, the tight little walnut between her fingers, and she squeezed her buttocks and the muscles of her sphincter so that he came off at almost the same time as she did, sinking her head slowly forward on to the pillow as he pulsed four or five times inside her and she felt his come rushing into her bum, everything so much more exaggerated because of the tightness of that little hole.

Almost at the same moment Paul brought Melanie off in a series of short, sharp, squealing gasps. He didn't come himself, just kind of froze while she went into spasm. She lay there, face downwards like Carole, pressed against his shoulders, her eyes closed, her blonde hair all over her face, breathing heavily.

'Fuck me in my bum, like Carole does,' she breathed to Paul, the words hardly audible. Carole could tell how excited he was, could sense the spunk that was building up inside his balls. Kneeling behind her, his breathing harsh and ragged from their exertions, Paul found the spot and pushed. He came almost immediately, his first orgasm of the evening, fluid and abundant.

He'd better be careful, Carole thought as she put her brassière and panties back on. *If he comes too often he'll be no good for later*. She looked at her watch. It was a little before ten. In the next bedroom, incredibly, she heard the *Match of the Day* music.

Later, after a glass of champagne with Tom and Melanie, they went their separate ways around the hotel. Some of the bedroom doors were closed but others were invitingly open. Carole went into one and watched two women going down on another, while a naked man stood by the bed and watched. She came up quietly behind him, put her arms around him – she hadn't a clue who he was, but he had a nice bum and a pony tail, which was two good reasons for her not to feel inhibited – and gently frigged his cock for him. A long, thick jet of semen spurted out over the breasts of the woman who was being licked – she could hear the relief in his breathing.

Carole stepped forward and rubbed the spunk into her tits, which were small but very nicely formed. 'It's good for the skin,' she murmured, 'did you know that?'

She could see the recognition in the woman's eyes but, to spare any possible embarrassment, protocol at The Laurels forbade her from making any formal acknowledgement. Carole bent down and kissed each of the woman's nipples in turn. They were small and dark, hard like little bullets. She nipped them gently with her teeth.

119

In another room a couple were dancing to night-time music – Sade or something – while another couple were necking on a sofa. Both of the men were fully clothed but the woman on the sofa was wearing just a pair of translucent white knickers and a white suspender belt. She had full, heavy breasts and the man was kneading them in his hands like they were dough – not at all the way Carole liked her own breasts to be handled. The other woman was wearing a red lace teddy, red stockings and matching red high-heeled shoes. Both of the women looked like hookers but the guy the second one was dancing with was kind of interesting-looking, like he was an actor or something. She'd got the guy's cock out and it stood out from his black trousers, rubbing between them. It was long and thick and Carole decided she wanted it.

Something about the scene appealed to her. She went into the room and across to the slow-dancing couple. Her hand lingered lightly over the other woman's hips until she got the message and went to join the couple on the sofa. Carole took her place, slipping into the guy's arms and moving across the thickly carpeted floor, a foot one way and back again, just swaying really, in time to the music. She looked up at him – he must have been well over six foot two – and with a start recognised the guy who'd played bass with Eric Clapton at the Albert Hall, a couple of years ago. She'd fancied him at the time and now she was going to get her chance.

As they danced close together, not speaking, she took hold of his cock and rubbed it against the silky fabric of her panties. He murmured something, reaching round behind her and clasping her bum in his hands, squeezing the firm, cool flesh above her stocking tops. His cock seemed to be bulging with desire. She hoped it was for her although from the coked-up look in his eyes he was probably miles away in some private fantasy.

They held on to each other, slowly swaying with the music. He had a terrific sense of rhythm, really erotic. She rubbed herself against him, could almost feel her lips part, was acutely conscious of the hardness of his thighs and of his very obvious erection.

It excited her no end, the heavy atmosphere in the room, the sense of being involved in this way with a total stranger. The next thing she knew, they were necking together, their tongues dancing of their own accord, slow and luscious. The kiss seemed to go on and on.

Finally they broke for breath. Carole turned round, could see the other guy tit-fucking the woman with the big breasts. The other woman was stretched out on the floor. She looked like she was asleep. The guy she was with said something but she didn't quite catch it.

'I said, do you want to do some coke?' the musician asked, looking her in the eyes.

She smiled her assent. Coke would be nice and, if this guy was a musician, it would be good stuff.

Taking a silver phial from his jacket, he emptied a couple of lines on to the bedside table – the other people in the room were too far gone to notice – and took a fifty-pound note from his wallet. He rolled it up into a tube and gave it to her. She reached down, put the tube into her nose and inhaled deeply. The coke numbed her nerve endings but then it hit and she felt herself lifting off, clean out of the room.

'Fuck me,' she said simply, as the guy snorted his own line. Her mind felt clear and diamond sharp, and as dirty as winter slush, all at the same time. It was coke of the very highest quality.

He took her by the hand and laid her down on the bed. Then, as she watched, he took off his clothes until he stood there naked before her. She was seized by an overwhelming desire to suck that big, stiff cock, so she leaned forward and took it deep into her mouth, so big it almost choked her, swirling her tongue round its swollen tip. He tasted fresh and clean – evidently he hadn't fucked yet tonight. *Good*, she thought, *that means he's full of spunk for me*. He was wonderfully hard, too, the way a man is when he's really aroused and hasn't done it for a day or two. She was sure he recognised her, too, and that made it even more exciting.

He was into her very quickly, very strong and powerful, and she knew she was going to enjoy this one. They didn't kiss – well, they'd not been introduced properly, had they – but then she knew that hookers didn't kiss their clients either, and she felt like a hooker, here in a strange room with a strange man and those other people she didn't know from Adam.

She glanced round and the others had stopped what they were doing and were watching her. *All right*, she breathed to herself, *let's give you a show*.

She pushed her hips hard against him. 'Come on, big boy,' she urged. 'I want you up my slit.'

He was stabbing at her with deep, intense thrusts, very male. It was pure fucking now, not at all the way Tom had done it to her earlier. There was something animal about the way he made love and she found it very exciting, devoid of subtlety, just a raw and fierce passion. Coke was like that, very real, very direct.

She felt herself getting wetter and wetter – she was, she realised, still wearing her panties – and she glanced down and could see that big distended cock of his sliding into her, the white area outlined by her stockings and the waspie. She pushed back at him with all her might, squirming and thrusting until it was like they were almost fighting each other. God, it was exhilarating. It was like she was one enormous cunt and he was one enormous cock – that was all there was to it. All she was interested in was his cock and all he wanted from her was that thing between her legs.

'I want you to cream me, you big fucker,' she hissed at him when she knew she was there.

'I got plenty for you, you cunt,' he gasped back at her.

She looked at him, the hair on his chest, the powerful pectoral muscles.

'Well, shoot it up me, then,' she said and in that instant he let fly, flooding her spectacularly and abundantly, and she wrapped her legs in their ruined nylons around him and squeezed and squeezed until she thought she was going to wet herself and then her own orgasm came on, short and fierce at first, but then in one big bursting bubble, and the hard, thrusting movement of her hips subsided at last into a barely perceptible ripple.

At the top of the short flight of steps that led to the esplanade, a confrontation was developing. Mick Rowlandson was glaring right at Rob and looking meaner and angrier by the second. Something in him seemed to be about to explode. His left eye was badly bruised.

'Come here, shitface,' he repeated. 'I owe you one.'

Rob looked around him, a dangerous thing to do in case Mick jumped him.

'You talking to me?' he said.

'No, I'm talking to all the other shitfaces that are standing around. Who the fuck do you think I mean?'

Rob ignored him. He was anxious to get away from the situation. Some of Mick's mates looked well hard and Richie was miles away. He sure as hell didn't want Debbie to get involved.

Mick Rowlandson, though, seemed to have other ideas. He took a couple of steps and stood right next to her.

'Are you coming with me?' he said to her in a tight, angry voice.

'No, I'm not.'

'Why not?'

'Because I'm going with Rob now.'

'That bastard? He's not worth shit.'

'Speak for yourself, Mick. It's Rob I'm with, not you.'

'Just shows you've not got much taste, then, doesn't it?'

'Here mate,' said Rob, a note of steel entering his voice. 'Leave that out, will you? It's between me and you, this is. Debbie, you go on ahead.'

'No, I'm staying with you. I'm not letting that big stupid lunkhead think he can get his own way.'

'Who are you calling names?'

'You, you big dummy. Why don't you just piss off and get out of our way?'

For a minute Rob thought Mick was going to lose it, being insulted like that right in front of his mates, and by a woman as well. He stepped right up to Mick, eyeball to eyeball, ready to clock him one.

For a good thirty seconds they looked daggers at each other. Debbie could see Rob's fists balled up tight like he was ready to thump Mick if he made so much as a move.

'You just fucking back off, and leave us alone,' he said finally.

'You just watch your fucking step,' Mick spat. 'I've got your number, pal, and don't you forget it.' Then he spun on his heel and, followed by his henchmen, walked off a few yards.

'If you think she's so bloody marvellous,' he called back over his shoulder, 'ask her about that time at the Headline Club.'

Then he was gone, swallowed up by the Saturday night crowd.

'What did he mean by that?' he asked Debbie when they'd

gone. He wished he didn't have to ask her but he felt rattled, not quite as sure of himself as he liked to make out.

'He didn't mean anything.' Debbie looked at him hard, squeezed his hand.

'He must have done. Otherwise he wouldn't have said it.'

'It doesn't mean anything, honest. He's just trying to get back at you.'

'But what's it about? What's he saying? If he's going round telling lies about you, I'll ram his front teeth down his throat so hard his stomach'll think it's a bit early for breakfast.'

He stopped, and suddenly it seemed incredibly funny, what he'd just said. He started laughing and Debbie joined in. It must have been all the adrenaline finding an outlet at last.

'Did you get that out of *Viz* or something?'

'No, I just made it up, honest.'

He kissed her, very softly, there by the pier head. He was feeling better already. He knew it wasn't true, but he still had to know.

'Oh, it wasn't anything,' she said when he finally pressed her into an explanation. 'Just one night we went to the Headline – it's closed down now, it's where the Igloo is instead – and everybody got pissed and he got me into the staff cloakroom and was trying it on with me, but nothing ever happened between us. Honest. As soon as I could I got loose, and I never went out with him again. We never did anything, you know. It was never like that, not with me at any rate.'

'That's not what he seems to think.'

'He likes to come on the great seducer.'

'Is he?'

'I don't know, do I? Sharon Surfleet says he couldn't get it up.'

'Did you sleep with him?'

'What do you take me for? No, I just went out with him a couple of times. I wasn't interested in him like that, he was just someone to go out with. He's all right really, he just gets a bit moody sometimes.'

'He seems to think he's got some kind of a hold on you.'

'Well he hasn't, and he never did.' She stopped dead in her tracks, turned round and faced Rob.

'Look, Rob, there really wasn't anything in it, believe me. I don't know what he's going on about. There was never anything in it. He's just a bigmouth, is Mick. It's you I care about. You must see that.'

'Well, if he comes near you again, I'll clock him one. I've just about had it up to here with Mick fucking Rowlandson. Come on, let's go get a drink.'

She looked down and realised his hands were shaking with all the chemicals that were running through his veins. He was about the only person in Dunwich that night who hadn't paid for their excitement.

Paul was amusing himself in different ways to those which appealed to his darling lady wife. He stayed with Tom and Melanie for a while, until the bottle of champagne was finished, and then he dressed and made his way downstairs. It was ironic, he thought, the way the conventions of a swinging party such as this dictated that – in public at any rate – the men should be more or less fully clothed, while the women could do pretty well as they pleased. There was very little nakedness but there were plenty of bared breasts and shaved pussies on view. The fact that they were visible was, perhaps, the whole point. Maybe the men were not so confident of their allure.

Buying himself a drink at the bar – you needed to wear clothes, he reflected, so you had somewhere to carry your change – he was accosted by a woman he had never met before. Her clothing would not have been suitable for Ascot or, for that matter, anywhere much outside the more outré clubs. She was dressed in a shiny PVC corselette that left her breasts bare and cut deep into her crotch, cut so narrow that it barely concealed her sex. Like Carole's, her nipples were pierced and she wore a tiny gold ring in each, linked by a fine chain. She was wearing the obligatory black stockings but her legs were sheathed in long black boots of the same material as her top, ending in wickedly pointed four-inch heels.

When she spoke, it was with a pronounced Midlands accent, sort of kindly and forceful at the same time.

'Would you like to buy me a drink too?' she asked, and he had a momentary flush of hesitation before calling the barman over.

'My name's Candy,' she said. 'What's yours?'

'Paul,' he said. She evidently didn't recognise him. At least he'd given her his real name. Surely nobody was really called Candy, outside page three.

'It's short for Candice,' she said, as if she could read his mind. 'Bit of a mouthful, that, isn't it?'

He nodded.

'I can think of nicer mouthfuls,' she said and laughed, revealing astonishingly perfect white teeth. She sipped her glass of red wine. It evidently wasn't the first she'd had that evening.

'What do you do, Candy?' he asked, intrigued.

'I'm a teacher,' she said. 'Primary school head.'

For a moment, he could hardly speak. He was astonished.

'There weren't any teachers like you when I was at school,' he said simply. 'More's the pity.'

'How do you know that?' she asked, her eyes narrowing. 'You

127

don't really know, do you? I bet you had fantasies about your teachers, all the same.'

'I went to an all-boys school.'

'What about when you were little?'

'Oh, then? I suppose I did, really. Miss Dovey, we had her for my second year at junior school. I suppose I fancied her, even though I was only eight or nine. Yes, of course I did. I caught a glimpse of her bra strap once when we were doing dance drama and I got terribly agitated.'

'There you are, then. And what do you do, Paul, if you don't mind my asking?'

'I'm in television.' She really hadn't sussed him, it seemed. She just smiled and nodded, not as though it wasn't important but as if he'd said he worked for a company that made office furniture.

'Oh yes?' she said, looking at him without an inkling of recognition in her eyes but more than a hint of something else. 'I'm afraid we're in that awful minority that has a set but doesn't watch it.'

'We?'

'My partner, Peter.'

'Is he here?'

'Good heavens, no. He'd rather die than come to something like this. No, this is for me. He goes off at weekends to photograph steam trains.'

'And you do this?' Paul was amazed. It was the sort of thing they ought to have on the show. He could never stop thinking like a television man, even on his weekends off.

'Not every weekend. But we have parties and things, you know.'

'Does Peter go to the parties?'

128

'Some of them, but he's not really that sort. No, he's more concerned with his trains. He's gone to the North Yorkshire Moors this weekend with his mates. Last month they went to Holland for some steam-train run. He's off most weekends.'

'And does he know about this, you know, about what you do?'

'Of course he does. When he gets back he wants to hear all about it.'

It's an interesting arrangement, thought Paul, the S&M schoolteacher and the trainspotter. Maybe the drama department would be interested. He would have to have a word with them, maybe get a treatment going. They had a very good young researcher on the show who was keen to get into scriptwriting.

They sipped their drinks, exchanging smiles. He liked the way her eyes sparkled. He decided he would have her.

'Come on,' he said. 'Let's go somewhere more private.'

'All in good time,' she said, touching him lightly on the arm. 'Have you been in the TV lounge yet?'

'I tend to stay clear of places with televisions in them.'

She looked at him for a moment, puzzled, and then she smiled again with those perfect teeth. 'Of course, I forgot. No, they're not watching *Match of the Day* in there, I can tell you that.'

She took his arm and they walked through the throng. One or two people did a double-take when they saw him but, as ever, discretion spared any embarrassment. Of Carole, Tom and Melanie there was no sign.

The TV lounge had been cleared of chairs and tables. In its place a thoughtful management had placed stocks, a couple of cages, a whipping post. It wasn't anything too heavy – Paul had seen some S&M videos that, for sheer cold-blooded cruelty, rivalled anything the Stasi might have got up to – but it was an area of sexuality that he still found vaguely disturbing. He'd let

Carole tie him to the bed with her stockings and that kind of thing, and she had an outfit at home that was very similar to the one Candy was wearing, but that was about as far as it went between them. What was going on in the TV lounge was a bit closer to the bone. He wasn't too sure he liked it but The Laurels tried to cater for most tastes.

There was a man inside one of the cages, crouching down because there wasn't room for him to stand up in it. He was naked, his penis hanging limply between his legs. A girl in a skin-tight black catsuit was flailing at the cage with a whip. It was the same one he'd seen earlier, the Catwoman look-alike. Paul had to step back to avoid being caught by the backlash.

'You fucker,' the girl was saying in a heavy foreign accent. 'You men are all the same.'

'I'm sorry,' the man whimpered, and then lapsed into sullen silence.

She beat him again, and again, the cruel lashes cutting into his tortured flesh. There was another girl with her, also carrying a whip, a tall and statuesque figure like a young Bardot, the same bee-stung lips and piled-up hair. Paul didn't fancy being beaten but he sure as hell fancied having a crack at the girl in the shiny suit. That accent just had to be fake, no one ever spoke with one so thick. She might have been foreign but he was sure she was hamming it up for all she was worth.

They turned away. Elsewhere in the small, subterranean room other men were tied to walls and posts while they were chastised for their sins, real and imagined. Some of them were hooded. One or two were bound by chains.

'Do you like this?' asked Candy, breathing in his ear. She touched him lightly on his arm and he was aware, without really realising it, that he had an erection.

'I don't know, I'm not really sure.'

'You love it,' she said simply in that kindly but firm voice. 'You know you do, Paul. I bet you'd enjoy it.'

'It's all men, isn't it?' he said to her. 'Why aren't there any women tied up and being beaten?'

'Because women get enough of that in real life,' she replied in her flat, Midlands voice. 'This is a chance for us to get our own back.'

She picked up a short cane that was simply lying there, flexed it between her fingers. 'They used to use these on children, you know,' she said, shaking her head. 'Some teachers must have been absolute sadists.'

They were standing next to a man who was bound hand and foot to a post, a black mask obscuring all of his face except for his mouth. This one, evidently, was one who liked to talk. Those who preferred to suffer in silence were gagged. Another penitent had a pair of white lace knickers stuffed into his mouth and he looked like he was in seventh heaven, despite the bruises on his back.

Most of the people in the TV lounge/S&M parlour were just looking, but Candy evidently seemed keen to take part.

'Gets it out of my system,' she whispered to Paul. 'Men have got a lot to answer for. If they can put one man on the moon, why not the lot of them – sorry, love, that's not intended for you. No, this is just a little light entertainment for me. The real stuff comes later.'

She flexed the cane again and applied it experimentally to the man in the black mask. He flinched.

'And what have you been up to that you shouldn't?' she said in a voice that would have stopped a school assembly dead in its tracks.

'I made half our costings department redundant last week,' he said in a low, steady voice. 'I didn't want to, but I had to.'

'What are you?' she asked.

'Personnel manager,' he said.

'You choose who stays and who goes?'

'Something like that.'

She hit him on the buttocks, not hard. 'How do you decide?'

'Hard to say.'

She hit him again, harder this time. 'I said, how do you decide?'

'Anyone who doesn't play by the company rules. If you're one of us, you're in. If you're not, then your job's on the line.'

She hit him again and again. 'What about women?'

'We don't like having to pay maternity allowances. If we hear a woman's pregnant, we'll see if we can rationalise her out of a job. That kind of thing. We won't renew contracts, we get people to double up if at all possible.'

He told them other things, between sobs of pain. It really pissed Paul off, the cynicism and the lack of care for other people's feelings. They ruined people's lives and they didn't give a toss, they just did the minimum the law dictated and sometimes not even that. At least the guy seemed to feel guilty about it, even if he had a funny way of showing it. It made him feel angry as well as sexually aroused.

'You sod,' said Candy, evidently sharing Paul's feelings, and she didn't spare the rod until his back and buttocks were glowing red.

'Please stop,' the man whispered, but to no avail.

'You must be joking,' she replied. Paul could see genuine anger in her eyes. He was surprised by how aroused he had become, not so much at the sight of the man's humiliation as by the passion it had unleashed in Candy.

She continued to beat him, despite his increasingly vigorous protests, until he called out something that Paul couldn't catch, something like 'butterfly' or 'buttercup' or something. Candy stopped immediately, handed the cane to the girl with the bee-stung Bardot lips and turned to Paul.

'Let's go get another drink,' she said, her face flushed, her impressively bared chest rising and falling. 'I think I got a bit carried away there.'

They went up to her room. There was champagne on ice in all the bedrooms. Paul reckoned he could do with a glass.

'What made you stop?' he asked her as they made their way up the grand staircase, past couples in various stages of undress and amorous embrace.

'He used his code word. When they say "Stop it" and "You're hurting me" and things like that, it's all just part of their game. They might beg you to stop but really, they just want you to carry on. When they really want you to stop, because it's gone too far, then they use a code word.'

'How did you know what the word was?'

'I didn't.' She sipped her champagne and then laughed, warm and disbelieving. 'God, they really are the limit, aren't they, the penitents? The code word? I just guessed. I mean, why else would the little worm suddenly shout out "Butterflies"? It didn't make sense.'

'What if you forget the code word?'

'Then you get a sore botty. But I'm not that into bondage and stuff, I'm really more your straight sex type of person. I just fancied trying some this weekend. How about you?'

'Straight sex, mostly. Other couples, too, that kind of thing.'

'I thought you seemed the normal type,' she said, and closed the door.

They did it, first of all, on the bed. Still in her boots and PVC corselette, she lay down and drew him on top of her. He felt wild and elated, curiously inflamed by the scenes he had witnessed in the TV lounge and a little guilty about it too. He sucked on her bared breasts, the nipples plump and raspberry red, her hand busy with his cock, expertly manipulating it into hardness.

'If only year three could see me now,' she murmured as he slid down the bed and undid the poppers at her crotch. She had her legs wrapped around his neck and shoulders, her suspenders starkly black against the ivory whiteness of her thighs. She was damp and luxuriant, like the dark foliage of a tropical forest and, despite the PVC in which she was clad, an animal warmth seemed to permeate her whole body. He was acutely aware of her various scents and secretions, all the more novel for the strangeness of their circumstances and the novelty of bedding a woman he had only just met and who he would, undoubtedly, never see again after that night. He licked at her with a rare delicacy that soon had her writhing and tossing on the sheets.

'I want you in me now,' she hissed and she all but hauled him bodily into her. Paul's cock felt massively distended; he was more excited than he realised. There was some dark mystery about Candy, something that aroused the inner recesses of his imagination, provided an access into aspects of his psyche that were usually well hidden.

He felt tall and powerful as he pushed into her, noting the way she smiled at him as he went in, her eyes half-closed, dark holes amid all the make-up. She was wearing, he noticed for the first time, gold sun and moon earrings that glistened against her burnished red hair. She was, he knew, a genuine redhead – either that, or she knew the most phenomenally talented colourist. Even her pubic hair had something of that heavy copperish tinge.

She was strong, too, pushing up at him to meet him thrust for thrust. Something in him snapped and he found he was kissing her with wanton abandon, already wanting to pour his seed into her, his lips hard against hers, aware of her tongue and teeth and her saliva mingling with his own. Her fingernails raked his back like a cat's claws, sharp and merciless.

He raised himself up high above her, his palms spread out flat on the sheets. He wanted her to see the powerful chest muscles he had built up over many hours in the gym, the endless working-out with weights that had given him pectorals that were ripe like fruit and an upper-body strength to rival many a professional athlete's. He knew, as Carole had often said as she watched him complete fifty press-ups before climbing into bed with her, where his shagging muscles were.

But her eyes were closed. She was lost in a world of her own making, unknowable, even as his muscles contracted and he felt himself give way to the inevitable, the long pulsing burst of pleasure that signified his release. She opened her eyes and smiled at him while he was still coming into her, surprised and phased, perhaps, by the suddenness with which he had climaxed. He was, as he had often been aware, as turned on by himself as by his partner. He would have given himself a blow-job if he could – autofellation, the ultimate in narcissism.

'Is there anything you'd particularly like?' he asked when he'd got his breath back.

'I can think of plenty. I don't have to come, you know.'

'Whatever. It's just that I really got off then, you know.'

'I know. I could feel it. Your cock felt huge when you were coming. Maybe you should try getting into S&M. It might do you good.'

He lay back and studied the ceiling for a while, then remembered there was a half-full bottle of champagne by the bed.

'There is one thing, you know,' she ventured as she took the glass he offered her.

'What's that? I'm game for anything.'

'You know that girl downstairs, the one in the catsuit?'

'The Catwoman look-alike? The Michelle Pfeiffer fantasy?'

'I could get it on with her, you know. You could too.'

Paul felt a thrill course through his body. There had been something undeniably erotic about the girl. Having her in the company of the equally libidinous Candy would be a double pleasure.

'Maybe she's with someone.'

'So what? No one sticks with their partner here. What about you?'

'I came with my wife. Last time I saw her, she was in bed with some friends of ours.'

'There you are, then. Let's finish the bubbly and then we'll go off and find her.'

It took some searching for them to find Catwoman. Eventually they ran her to ground in the 'quiet room' next to the bar, where people were sitting and talking quietly or, in the case of one near-naked woman, simply lying full-length on the carpet, a Walkman clipped to her suspender belt.

'We were wondering,' said Paul after he had introduced himself and Candy, 'whether you'd like to join us.'

'Perhaps,' said the girl, eyeing him closely. 'Let's go outside, shall we?'

They went through into the bar, the three of them, ordered drinks. Paul was feeling ravenously hungry as he nibbled on the bar snacks.

'The thing is,' the girl said when they were comfortably seated, 'I'm not a guest here.'

136

'I'm sorry?' said Paul. 'I don't understand.' Her accent was nowhere as near as heavy as it had seemed before but he still couldn't make out what she was saying.

'I work here – for tonight, at any rate. If you'd like to be with me, I'm afraid you'll have to pay.'

'You mean?'

She intercepted his glance at Candy.

'It's all right. It's very easy to fix. Just speak to the man with the red cummerbund at the bar. He'll see that it's added to the bill.'

'How much?' asked Candy. 'To do the business. You know, with both of us.'

The girl named a fee. It was more than Paul might have expected but he and Carole were having this weekend on expenses – they would call it 'research' or something, without saying exactly what it was they were researching. The company could look after things like that.

'That's fine,' he said, reassuring, keen to dispel the momentary coolness that bargaining always brought to the pursuit of pleasure.

'We'll go to my room, shall we?' She spoke with quite a refined French accent. She said her name was Danielle but Paul had a strong impression that wasn't what she was christened. She seemed terribly young, too, no more than eighteen or nineteen and yet very well bred, obviously. It was plain she was no ordinary streetwalker, driven into the escort girl racket because she couldn't afford not to be involved. She seemed to be doing it because she wanted to.

'I thought you said you weren't staying here?' asked Candy.

'I'm not. They give me a room to myself. There are some things we might need. They might amuse you, you know.'

Paul and Candy exchanged glances.

Things were certainly warming up at the Zero Six by the time Rob and Debbie arrived and were swallowed up by the crowd. They were hot, like really hot and out of breath. Inside, the temperature was like opening an oven door. There was a lot of heavy drinking going on and the supplies of chilled bottled lager were getting dangerously low. They had plenty round the back in the container but it wasn't cold, and serving people warm lager on an even warmer night was asking for trouble, even with a big thick bastard like Billy to keep an eye on things.

The place was uncomfortably crowded, too. Billy was sure, as he made his way around the heaving throng and the mooching couples, that more people had been let in than should have been. He knew what the capacity of the club was and he wasn't too sure if the Health and Safety guys would have been too pleased if they'd chosen that moment to pay a surprise visit.

He did a couple of rounds of the floor, let a couple of boppers who might be getting over-excited know he was around and had his eye on them, and then it was time for his statutory break. And not before time, too, to get out of that fug of stale air and body heat and perfume and God knows what was being smoked or popped, and take a little time out while the other two guys doing security that night took control for half an hour or so while he had a pee and a smoke. At least that was what he was supposed to be doing, but Billy had other ideas.

Sue was waiting for him by the ladies', at the far end of the bar. She quickly finished her Bacardi and Coke, and then he quickly ushered her through a door marked *Private: Staff Only* and down the long obstacle course of the corridor full of empty beer kegs that ran behind the bar – another risk that was, it was supposed to be kept clear but the drunks only used the kegs as weapons if they left them where they were supposed to, down the side of the club. Fishing out the big, heavy ring of keys that he kept at his hip, he unpadlocked the fire door that the Malteser brothers insisted – against all considerations of safety and basic humanity – be kept locked in case of gatecrashing, and then they slipped out into the cool night air.

There was no one around at the back of the club, in the little compound ringed by wire fences. He took Sue in his arms, kissed her long and deep and slow. She knew what was expected. Taking him by the hand she led him across the stained concrete. Trying not to make too much noise on the rusted steel rungs, they climbed the fire escape and then they were up on the roof of the building, with nothing but the stars above them.

Down below, they could see the lights of the town, could sense rather than hear the low frequency vibrations that passed up from the dance floor beneath. For the past few months people anything up to a mile away – in hotels, in restaurants, in private houses – had complained of 'seismic events' in their neighbourhoods. Candlesticks had rocked on dinner tables, lamps had swung from ceilings, the contents of shelves had vibrated mysteriously. The seismologists from the University of East Anglia had found nothing but then, Billy reckoned, they hadn't come on an evening when the Zero Six was open. Four months ago, ready for the big influx of holiday cash, the Malteser brothers had installed a £160,000 sound system, the most powerful, they said, outside London or Manchester. That was where the shock waves came from, Billy was sure. That big, booming bass sound that the dancers loved created a resonance that he could feel a mile and more away, at home in front of the telly on his nights off.

But Billy and Sue hadn't come up here to check up on sound

139

pollution. Apart from the traffic in the streets below and the occasional, winking lights of a plane passing far overhead, inbound to Stansted, they had the place to themselves. The air felt clearer and fresher somehow, despite the hamburger fumes and the ever-present Saturday night petrol haze. Sue was like putty in his arms and he could tell that she'd been longing for this moment – as he had. He had only half an hour up here with her but in that half-hour he was determined to cram in as much as he could – all seven or eight inches of it, if at all possible.

He shucked off his black jacket with its poncy velvet lapels, undid his clip-on bow tie. Before he could hardly get his shirt off, Sue had his cock out and was down on her knees, sucking at him. God, it was good the way she did it to him, working away with her lips and her tongue until he almost came there and then – not that she would have minded. She'd seen things during stopovers in Bangkok and similar places in the Far East that made even Billy's hair curl. Swallowing a mouthful of come was child's play in comparison. Sue had worked as an air-hostess until the previous year when her company had gone bust and she'd found herself out of a job, going back to the technical college to try and get more qualifications. She was learning word-processing, wanted to get a job as a PA – she was good with people.

She broke for breath, panting, then sucked him again, harder this time, until she nearly did bring him to the edge. His cock felt like it was made of iron or concrete or something, a big solid bone rather than an eight-inch sausage of flesh and blood. He was leaning against the parapet of the building savouring what she was doing to him, the brickwork gritty in his hands, a bunch of pigeons billing and cooing as they hopped around the satellite dish. Tacky it might have been, but where else was there at that time of night and with him due back on duty in less than twenty minutes? He stooped down, hands under her shoulders, and pulled her up to him, his cock still sticking proudly out, showering her with kisses.

'Take your dress off,' he murmured. 'I don't want it to get mucky.'

In the winking red light of the cinema opposite Sue smiled and stepped back a couple of feet. Slowly, tantalisingly slowly, she pulled her dress up over her head.

'Don't look,' she said and so Billy, wondering what all this false modesty was about all of a sudden, turned his head and looked down at the crowds who were streaming out of *Lethal Weapon 3*. When he turned round, Sue was standing with her back to him, her arms and legs spreadeagled against the parapet, a smile playing on her face as he looked at her and she looked back at him.

'What do you think?' she said. His eyes travelled down her body, the long neck, the plump teenaged breasts with their firm young nipples, the pinched-in waist, her buttocks.

Jesus, what was going on? Sue's shapely backside was encased in two filmy black triangles that left the deep cleft of her bum furrow exposed to his astonished gaze. So she'd bought some crotchless knickers after all, like she'd said she might after they saw that Bryonie Levy movie upstairs at the Yacht Club. She must have been wearing them all evening, the thin fabric rubbing against her damp and lecherous lips. His already swollen cock seemed about to burst. Crotchless knickers had always been one of Billy's favourite wet-dream fantasies and now the dream was about to become reality.

'What's that matter, don't you like them?' she laughed. She hooked her hands inside her pants, spread them even wider like a pair of wings and then he was quickly up behind her, his cock begging admittance.

141

'Like them? I love 'em,' he gasped, as she took hold of his bursting dick and guided him into her. She felt wet and slippery, the silky material of her pants slick against his groin. He knew he couldn't hold out very long and neither, from the way she was pushing and shoving at him, could she.

He leaned forward until their bodies were like two spoons curled around one another, slowly rotating his hips as he screwed her. He took hold of her breasts, feeling the nipples hard and excited against his palms. Sue had lovely breasts, he'd always felt. He loved to make himself come all over them, sometimes tit-fucking her for ages while she played with her clitty and they were both ready to come off. But crotchless knickers were something else, especially in the hot night air above the Zero Six, with the sound of revelry coming up at them from the street, the waft of late-night restaurants and the endless shifting sounds of traffic.

'I've been waiting for you to fuck me all evening,' she purred. 'I wanted you so bad, I almost wet myself.'

'You should have said. I could have got off earlier.'

'I bet you didn't know I was wearing these, though, did you?'

The idea of a woman who would do that kind of thing just for him, and for him alone, filled Billy with an overwhelming sense of gratitude. He shot his come into her willing pussy and for the first time that evening the enormous thump of £160,000-worth of sound system faded into obscurity.

Chapter Five

The girl at the bar seemed to have been giving Richie the eye for a good twenty minutes or so. Every so often he'd glance across from what he was doing and there she'd be, perched on her high stool, looking at him. She was with a bunch of mates but it was plain that she'd got the hots for him. She was drinking quite steadily but she always made sure it was him she ordered from.

When she ordered her fifth – or was it sixth – Campari and soda of the evening, he gave her his best smile. That was always a winner, he found.

'Enjoying yourself?' he shouted, above the ceaseless thud of the music.

She nodded in answer, gave him a big smile. She'd been dancing most of the evening with a group of friends but now it seemed she was taking time out to get her breath back, replace some of the bodily fluids she'd lost out there on the dance floor. That was fine by Richie. He'd had his eye on her for the past hour or so. Now she was on her own and he was moving in for the kill.

For once there was a lull in the ceaseless queue of people waiting to be served. The volume levels seemed to have dropped too. It was chill-out time, for a while at least.

'You foreign or something?' he mouthed at her across the counter.

'Yes. I'm from Grenoble. How about you?'

'I'm a foreigner too. I come from Sunderland.'

'Is that in England?'

'No, it's in the North.'

She didn't quite take that one – it was going a bit too fast down the leg side. Grenoble – that was where Linda, his girl from back home, had been on a school skiing trip once. He was sure he'd heard of it before.

'I thought you were foreign too,' she said, laughing. 'Your English is very good, though. Are you at the language school too?'

'No, I'm just working here for the summer. I came down here with a mate 'cos there's no jobs at home. We'll be going back soon, once the season's over.'

She smiled at him. She had lovely teeth, big dark eyes. He fancied her a lot, he was trying to figure out where he'd seen her before. You saw a lot of girls in a club like the Zero Six and it was difficult to pin things down. She could have been here last week or last night, or he'd seen her in Boots or at the pub or on the pier. There was something that rang a bell, though, some distant nagging itch that jogged his memory.

Then he remembered. She was the one who had been with The Vision that afternoon, when he'd seen them on the beach. The friend. The one he always ended up with. Well, it wouldn't be the first time he'd got the friend while Rob or whoever he'd gone out bopping with cleaned up with the main attraction, but this one was fine by him. Usually they were too fat or too thin or whatever – it was Rob who always got to pluck the ripest cherry – but he was perfectly happy to settle this time.

'What's your name?' he mouthed to her.

The music had got loud again. She couldn't hear.

'I said, what's your name?'

Her face furrowed into a frown but then she realised what he was saying.

'Camille,' she said, with a smile.

'Camille, eh? I'm Richie.'

'Richie,' she repeated. She rolled the *r*. 'Richie – it's easy to say, isn't it. Richie.'

'You're doing well,' he said, encouragingly. 'I'll teach you how to sing *The Blaydon Races* next.'

'Listen,' she said after he'd come back from serving some gorilla with a pint of Murphy's. 'We're having a party later, back at the school. Do you want to come?'

He couldn't believe his ears. For a moment it seemed all too much to take in. He'd been close to bursting point all day and then, right out of the fucking blue, he got an invitation like that. It was too good to be true. He may have missed out on The Vision but it was all right, it didn't worry him, nae bother. And, moreover, he'd be paid that night, so he could buy a couple of bottles of something good and take them along. That would impress her, no sweat.

'Sure,' he said, trying not to sound too over-excited. A measure of cool was still called for, as if he'd already got a couple of party invites for that night. 'That'd be great,' he added, real casual but encouraging at the same time.

'Have you got any friends? They're welcome to come along too.'

He wasn't too sure he'd want Rob and Debbie along to play gooseberry, but he decided they were old enough to take care of themselves. He was mostly interested in what he might get out of such an evening for himself.

'That's me mate sitting over there, with the blonde girl,' he said at length. 'He's Rob and she's Debbie.'

Rob and Debbie were at a table nearby, deep in conversation.

'Do you think they'd like to come? There'll be lots of us.'

'I'll ask them. Rob'll go anywhere there's a few bevvies around.'

'You know where the school is? Garfield Hall? Do you know it?'

'Sure I do. But I'll have to finish up here first.'

He looked at his watch. It was almost exactly on the stroke of midnight. The club would be closing in an hour's time, when the licence ran out.

It was as if she could read his mind.

'I'll stick around, with my friends. The night is still young, yes? That's how you say it? The rest of them will have started the party already.'

Embarrassed, Richie wondered if she'd seen him earlier, when he'd been walking along the beach laughing to himself. She didn't appear to have clocked him, but perhaps she wasn't letting on. It was time to try and find out.

'I'd like that very much, Camille,' he said, still with that wide smile. He was absolutely sure about where he'd seen her before. She was definitely the other one, the one who'd been out walking all frigging day with her mate, the blonde bombshell from Planet Sex. Camille, was it? He could grow to like a girl with a name like that. It was a nice name, much better than all the Sharons and Tracys. Her tits were good too. She reminded him very much of that girl in the ads for the Renault Clio, what was her name, Nicole? *Papa? Nicole?* He was sure there was something going on there that Social Services ought to know about.

'That's good,' she said.

'Hey,' he said. 'I saw you earlier. On the beach, and in the town.'

'Did you?' she said. He could see she was trying to remember him but she obviously wasn't getting anywhere. Perhaps that was just as well, seeing he was just as guilty, what with being so totally gobsmacked by The Vision that he hadn't had eyes for anyone else. In a way it made him feel kind of forgettable, but then some guy came up with an order the length of the A1 and when he finally completed it she was gone.

Still, he thought, *I reckon I'll get lucky tonight*. He could usually tell when a girl was going to do it the first time. He'd got it totally wrong with Janice Everley that time at Lefty Wright's party when she'd been all over him until he'd got her upstairs, at which point she went stone cold on him and practically accused him of raping her. But that was a one-off, the slag. Camille was going to be different. Relief mingled with expectation. He had, as always, a packet of three in his wallet and already his cock was beginning to stir at the thought of what he and Camille might get up to back at the college. Students, they were always a randy lot from his experience. He ducked along the bar and grabbed a couple of bottles of something good. He'd pay for them later. He tried to get on with his work but it was a losing battle.

He felt oddly out of tune with his surroundings. Richie had passed a lot of his ill-spent youth in places like this and he knew to recognise the atmosphere in a club. Each one was different, every night was different. This one was no exception, as the clocks ticked over past midnight and he felt something was going to happen. Maybe it was the heat, maybe it was the music, maybe there was some bad stuff around. It was something you could actually sense, a vibe that seemed to be running round the place. Richie had been to some pretty tough places back home where you just got the sense that someone was going to clock you one smack on the beezer, just for breathing. It was like getting stuck with a bunch of Leeds fans in the days when they had both Cantona and Batty, the mad bad days, this air of cold menace ready to erupt. In western movies, this would have been the point where the bartender started taking down the mirrors before they got the chairs hurled through them.

He could see the Malteser brothers off to the side of the bar, talking between themselves and looking more than a shade anxious. Usually they just looked smug.

And still the music went on, louder than ever now. The lights were pulsing like they too were on drugs, like half the dancers, and the whole floor seemed to be shaking. The lasers pierced the air, the big screen was projecting all kinds of weird shit, like one video on top of another.

Whatever was in Richie's personal horoscope, the stars weren't shining any too brightly on the Zero Six that night. Billy and the lads from Alarming Security were much more in evidence than usual. They'd already chucked out a crowd of rugger-bugger types, and some of the boys from the Evenlode Estate looked like they were living up to their guarantee of a spot of bother. One way or another, things were starting to look more than a mite ominous. Richie caught sight of Billy talking to the Maltesers.

The next thing Richie knew, the temperature inside the club had dropped by what seemed like sixty degrees in as many seconds. Huge waves of icy mist drifted across, though that was just cosmetic. The real work was being done by the chiller system, giant industrial-standard machines devised for meat-packing plants. In a comparatively small place like the Zero Six, the big power-driven fans could bring the temperature down to almost freezing inside a minute.

The E-heads in the place, which was about half of them, went absolutely apeshit. Richie could imagine the rush that the chiller gave. It was like passing from the Sahara Desert into the Arctic in one giant step. A gimmick it unquestionably was – and an expensive one at that – but it drew them into the club in droves. They all wanted to see for themselves what happened when your body decides it's going to freeze, while your mind is somewhere up on cloud nine. Some deep-sea diver he'd met, a guy who used to work on the oil rigs off Yarmouth and had seen the world from fifty fathoms down, said it was like being hustled through a decompression chamber at double speed. It was safe, just about – the Health and Safety people wouldn't have permitted it if it wasn't – but what it's long-term effects were no one could be sure. They said the same about E, of course.

Short term, though, everyone got the message. The place began to calm down as well as cool down. As the clouds of dry ice rolled across the place, lit an unearthly green by the ever-probing lasers, people began laughing and giggling, while sweat-strewn dancers were standing close together for warmth, shivering and shaking. The air of menace seemed to have been frozen, for the moment at least. The chiller was like a crack of the whip, a warning shot across the bows. *Any more trouble from you,* it seemed to be saying, *and you'll get another dose.* Maybe this was what the E heads wanted because they were never any trouble, but for the others, the guys tanked up on eight or nine pints of lager, the girls fuelled on Bacardi and Coke, it was a warning to cool things in more senses than one.

'What do you think of that?' he said to Rob when he came up for fresh drinks.

'Fucking amazing, isn't it?'

'You not seen it before?'

'You told me about it.'

'It works every time. Hey, isn't that Mick Rowlandson over there?'

They turned round. At the far end of the bar, sporting the now familiar mark on his forehead, he was with his mates, a different crowd now, mostly skinheads. Mick was looking mean. Whatever effect the chiller might have had on the dancers, it seemed only to have made Mick Rowlandson look angrier and more hostile.

Closing time wouldn't come fast enough, normally. But quite what was to happen when he and Rob got chucked out onto the streets, with nowhere left to run but back to the caravan, was anybody's guess. Things all of a sudden didn't look too good, Camille or no Camille.

Whatever it was she'd swallowed half an hour ago, Carole was sure it wasn't what the guy had said. Her head felt muzzy and her mouth was dry; it was like looking through the wrong end of a telescope. Her head was going round in big crazy circles and both her mind and her body felt like they were glowing. She lay face down on the bed and wondered who she was, where she was and what was going on. In other words, she was blissfully happy.

She was aware that she wasn't alone in the room but she couldn't see anything. She managed to turn her head round to see into the mirror that covered most of the wall beside her.

There was a woman – a girl, really – standing behind her. She was tall and blonde and very pretty and practically naked. She had her hair piled up on top of her head and she was wearing a black brassière, a pair of wickedly high shoes and nothing else. Nothing, that is, apart from the long black dildo that was strapped to her body. Carole had every impression that it was intended for her.

She tried to murmur some words of encouragement but they

wouldn't come – her throat felt dry and constricted. So she smiled and purred and squirmed her backside on the bedcovers, wondering what was going to happen next. She didn't have to wait long.

The girl came and knelt behind her – Carole could see all this in the mirror. She leaned forward and kissed her neck, very softly, little butterfly kisses that showed the tenderness of a woman rather than the urgent passions of a man. Carole had noticed her lips, very pretty with that bee-stung look that the young Brigitte Bardot had. She could feel the black lace of the girl's bra against the sensitive skin of her back.

Carole pushed up with her backside, felt the heavy black dildo against her cheeks. It was warm and firm, like it was alive. It wasn't at all like one of those horrible pink things she'd seen in the back of cheap porno magazines, all knobbly bits and three-speed love action. This was a rich person's sex toy, sleek and elegant, beautifully sculptured for a specific job, a real work of erotic art in itself. Carole was looking forward to having it inside her.

But the girl was not to be rushed. Her tongue flickered out, tracing lines around Carole's neck, along her shoulders, around her ultra-sensitive earlobes. She reached down underneath her and felt for Carole's breasts, the nipples already hard and urgent with expectation. And all the time Carole could see and feel that black thing bobbing there, waiting for the moment to come. She wished she could have rolled over and sucked it.

The blonde girl was saying something but the words weren't forming right in Carole's ears. She got the general drift, though. She could make out words like *sex* and *fuck* and *lick* and *cunt*, the hint of a foreign accent, German maybe. She knew what was going to happen.

'Put that thing up me now,' she managed to say, but the girl seemed determined to take her time, to try and push Carole right to the very edge of desire.

She was aware of how wet her pussy was, the damp secretions that filled her, that went along with the tingling sensation in her loins. God, she felt aroused, even more than she had done earlier when they'd had to stop the car and do it in the woods even before they'd got to Dunwich. She managed to turn her head round just enough to be able to kiss the blonde girl on the cheek, and then their tongues were twisting around each other, their lips barely touching, and she could feel the hard black thing being pressed down hard and unambiguous in the furrow of her backside.

She heard a cough but, try as she might, she couldn't for the life of her see who was in the room with them. She didn't care; all she wanted now was to be fucked and to be fucked hard. She and Paul used dildos and vibros quite a lot at home. She had a strap-on one too, that she sometimes liked to surprise Paul with when he came home late after working in the studio. She would hear his car on the drive and then she'd be waiting for him in the hallway, teetering on her high heels, perhaps in black hold-up stockings or a corset, the black straps of the dildo cutting into her generous flesh. She loved the feeling of power it gave her as she strapped it on, tightening the buckles. It was very different to putting on anything else that she might wear for excitement, like some of her bondage clothes or even just suspenders. Wearing the dildo was an empowering thing for her.

She didn't always use it, either. She fucked Paul a few times with it but sometimes she just liked to wear it, to make him suck it and lick her out and drive her wild until she didn't know what day of the week it was, still less that she would be due in the studio in another seven or eight hours. She liked him to fuck her from behind while she was wearing it, for him to reach round while his cock was embedded deeply in her pussy or her ass and to join her in holding the dildo, even frigging it up and down as though, if it were sufficiently excited by what they were doing and whispering, it might suddenly spurt out its seed all over the bedclothes.

It was a novel sensation, though, for her to be on the receiving end. She and Krystle did it like that, sometimes, taking turns with the black strap-on dildo, wondering what it might be like to be a man. Krystle was very good like that. Once, they'd even gone out for dinner together, just the two of them, Krystle wearing an Armani suit just like a man's and with the dildo already strapped to her. They'd got so excited during the meal that, while they were waiting for their coffees, they'd slipped away and done it there and then in the ladies', standing up, Carole bending forwards over the cistern while Krystle went into her from behind.

There had hardly been room to turn round in that cubicle and they must have made a hell of a noise. But they came out – luckily no one was there – and went back to their table and no one at the adjoining tables could possibly have thought anything of it, just a well known TV presenter and her friend slipping away between courses to powder their noses or – which was more likely in a place with a reputation like Le Gamin to put something up their noses.

The recollected fantasy gave way, gratifyingly, to reality as Carole felt the girl pulling her into position, ready to enter her.

Once more she sought the reflection in the mirror, the sight of her own nakedness and the black-clad girl exciting her. The blonde – she must have been nineteen, twenty at most – was kneeling up behind her, massaging Carole's back muscles. All Carole had to do, it seemed, was to lie there and enjoy herself. Nothing was being asked of her.

She felt hands on her hips, the girl's hands, and she got the message. With an alacrity that surprised her, she pushed her butt up into the sir, presenting her glorious and pampered ass for the delectation of the people in the room. She knew that at least two other people were present besides the girl and herself, because she had heard a man's muffled cough and a woman's sigh. But she couldn't see anything, either in the mirror or by twisting her head around on the pillow. It didn't particularly bother her, because this was what people came to The Laurels for. If it was part of someone's fantasy to watch a beautiful and very sexy television host being fucked by an equally beautiful and sexy girl, then that was what it was all about. Carole loved nothing better than pleasing an audience. This was what made her such a marketable commodity in a fiercely competitive world.

She could feel the dildo now against the entrance of her vagina. She was glad it was to be her pussy, not her butt, because after the session with Tom earlier she didn't think she could take another one that big up there without a lubricant, and there didn't seem to be any around. She pushed back, anxious for the first moment of penetration. She was aware of the delicacy of the blonde girl's perfume and the extreme hardness of her own nipples.

'Fuck me,' she managed to breathe and she seemed to lose consciousness for a few seconds because the next thing she knew, the girl was right up inside her and Carole was on all fours on the bed, still face down, pushing back at her for all she was worth.

It was more difficult to keep in the right position with a dildo because it was held so very securely to the girl's groin by an assortment of straps and buckles. It wasn't quite so flexible as a man's cock, it couldn't swivel in quite the same way. Still, it was a hugely enjoyable experience for her because of the different way the girl fucked her, not the short, stabbing thrusts of the penis with which an over-aroused stranger might screw her, but an altogether more eloquent and sensual rhythm.

She managed to reach round and take a hold of the black dildo as it was pushed in and out of her, feeling it firm and slick with her juices, the smooth girth that seemed to fill her deliciously. She could feel how her lips seemed to close around it, as though kissing it. Her hands moved round and over the harness that was holding it on. It felt like leather or something, cool and smooth and supple, devoid of any decoration, a functional item of clothing.

As her open hand managed to reach and cup the blonde girl's pussy, she felt a hand come round her hips and seek out her own moist, dark places. A finger probed along the outer lips, delicate and teasing. She could see from the mirror that it was the blonde girl, seeking out her clitoris. Carole spread her legs even wider to make it easier for her but it was obvious that the girl knew what she was about.

She traced Carole expertly even as Carole traced her, each of them stroking that super-sensitive little bud with an almost pastoral care, the merest hint of a caress with a fingertip. *Oh God, this is bliss,* Carole thought, burying her face in the pillow and wondering what the view was like in the mirror, *to have this divine creature play with me like that while that wonderful big thing is buried right up to the hilt in me.*

The girl continued to stroke her clitoris with little butterfly touches, rhythmically thrusting in and out of her all the time in synchronisation, and the mists closed in over Carole again as she lost conscious thought and gave way to an abstracted feeling of desire and pleasure all rolled into one, a synthesis of wish and fulfilment, a wondrous one-ness that, for her, was the acme of sexual pleasure. Her own fingers seemed to have a life of their own, soothing and teasing all at the same time.

The girl was hardly touching her now, but Carole's pleasure was increasing with every soft and sticky caress of those fingertips. She gave way utterly, letting the waves of feeling flow through her, aware only occasionally of anything that might constitute rational thought, like the image of a man's cock or the pleasure of sucking a woman's breast, or of being sucked in turn.

She turned her head and gazed at the mirror, but her eyes no longer saw the blonde girl who was draped over her, and her body did not feel the hands that roved over her with such exceptional delicacy of touch, nor the powerful pleasures that filled her loins. She was aware and yet not aware of a mixture of perfumes and sexual smells, of words that were murmured but yet had no meaning, of the taste and texture of flesh. It was like going off to sleep but on the crest of a wave of sheer pleasure, a rolling and powerful motion that carried her along irresistibly to an unknown destination. All Carole had to do was to go with it, unseeing and unquestioning, implicitly trusting, every single nerve ending in her body in perfect harmony. Her mind was one big shimmering sea of purple and she felt, when she finally came, that she had never known such ecstasy in her life.

It was just bad luck, really, Col reckoned. There was no point in getting upset about it – it was part of the deal as far as Liz was concerned. She had a job to do and that was that. True, she couldn't spend the night with him as they'd planned but they'd had a delicious meal together, they'd talked and they'd made love on the beach. That was more than enough but still, somehow, he felt a vague dissatisfaction, as though something was missing.

He took his telescope out on to the patch of scrubby ground

between his house and the sea, on to a rising dune that gave him a superb vista of the heavens. Saturn was already looking incredibly bright and, as one o'clock approached, it was nearing its peak of visibility. The sky was black and the lights from the caravan site barely a mile down the coast were mostly out now, just a few twinkling spots in the darkness.

The air was wonderfully calm and warm, considering it was the middle of the night. All the same, he had a flask of tea with him, there in the holdall with his charts and books, his notepad at the ready in which to record his observations.

He turned and, in the clear moonlit night, he could quite easily see the waves breaking on the shore, almost as far down as Coxburgh where his boat was moored, riding at anchor in the gentle swell. He'd probably go out on Monday morning, walk the half-mile or so along the beach in the early light when he felt at his best. That was, perhaps, why he missed Liz so much – for that early morning feeling of waking up with a woman beside him, the pleasure of intimacy while still half-asleep, the hormones coursing through his body at that hour that always gave him an erection like nothing on earth.

He tried not to think about it, and considered the heavens instead.

It was a very good night for seeing the colours of the different stars, the bluish ones that were comparatively new in the scheme of things, the red ones that were old and dying. There was so much to see, always something new to learn, always new levels of interpretation. He doubted if he personally would ever make any significant discovery but that wasn't the point. He just liked being out there, in tune with the universe.

His body, Liz's body, everybody – they were all made of carbon, the same carbon that the stars were made of. All the carbon in the universe had been made in that same instant, that nanosecond immediately following the Big Bang. It was a thought greater than any orgasm and it never ceased to excite him. Out here in the blackness, looking through his telescope, it was like he was also looking at himself, at his family, hundreds of thousands of light years away. His mind began to reel with the enormity of it all.

He would spend all night out here, as he often did. He wanted in particular to look at Saturn but there were other things of great interest in the sky as well. He didn't just look through the telescope at random. He had a programme of observations to follow, a system, backed up by extensive notes. Back in the cottage his computer carried the full record of all the data he had accumulated since he came to live out here on the coast.

He felt very calm, very relaxed The Milky Way was spectacular tonight, and for a long while he just lay on his back and looked up at it. He wished Liz could have been there to share it with him but there would be other times – she said she could have extra time off in lieu because she had to work that night. And there were compensations – they might have come out here for an hour or so but, the way things panned out, he could have the whole of the night if he wanted it. He'd not done that for a while and he rather welcomed the opportunity.

But still his mind kept going back to thoughts of flesh and pleasure. Liz, her tongue, her pussy, her breasts, the way she moved when she came. He still had a lot of energy in him and he knew that he couldn't entirely work it off out here in the warmth of the night. He poured himself a cup of tea and wondered if it really was true that the Army used to put bromide in it to keep the squaddies' hormones at bay. The way he was feeling at that moment, he could have used some of it himself.

* * *

In the end, they simply slipped away with a crowd of people from Garfield Hall, picked up a taxi from right outside the club. Richie had a word with Billy Brilleaux and Billy made sure he had a little word with Mick while Rob and Debbie and Richie and Camille made a dash for it while trying to look cool, which was quite a tall order. Richie said he'd see him right later, buy him a couple of pints or something. He wondered what it would cost to have Billy put Mick in hospital, but Rob didn't seem at all phased by it.

Richie had been with a girl once from a nurse's home down on Russell Avenue, but this was the first time he'd ever been inside a college other than the local tech back home, which he'd chucked after six weeks because it was fucking obvious he wasn't going to get a job at the end of it.

It was a hell of a lot posher, too. There were carpets on the floors along the long, straight corridors and the paintwork was new and shiny. At the tech, the place looked as if a bunch of Man U fans had just been through it, road-testing assault weapons on the Army's behalf. If the tech had been more like this, he might have stuck it longer.

One wing of the building was where the students lived and it was a lot different to the nurse's home. That had been barest minimum British, lots of ratty old furniture like your granny had, and threadbare carpets and notices sellotaped to the walls. This was more like a hotel, not that Richie had ever been in a hotel as such, just the kind of bed-and-breakfast places where he'd been with his mam and dad as a kid.

They were having a party in this big common room. There were a lot of armchairs that had been pushed back to create an empty space in the middle of the room, and there was a table with drinks and party food, and somebody with quite a creditable sound system was giving it what for. Not your *Greatest Hits* shite, either, but something that sounded like it had been professionally remixed, but which one of the lads at the college had done himself in his college room. *Clever buggers, these foreigners*, he thought.

There was a hell of a lot of crumpet around, too. He didn't see any sign of The Vision, but he knew when to count his blessings, and stuck close to Camille.

They were standing round chatting, just the four of them, Rob and Debbie and him and Camille, and then without realising it they were bopping in time with the music and then just bopping full stretch. Richie wasn't much of a one for dancing but he stuck it out as long as he could, and then leaned across to Camille and said he wanted to get something to eat.

'I've not had owt since tea time,' he said. 'I'm going to pass out.'

'You'll pass out anyway,' said Rob, 'the way you're knocking back the booze.'

Richie glared at him but Camille took him by the arm and they went over to the table where the food was piled, leaving Rob and Debbie to their own devices. There wasn't a hell of a lot left, to be honest, and what there was wasn't the kind of thing that Richie usually liked to eat at do's like this, but he forced down a few things that didn't make him puke and found that some of it he actually quite liked, even if he might have preferred some sausage rolls and a couple of handfuls of cheese and onion. Given time, he reflected, he might try more of this foreign stuff. Pizzas and curries were all right, it was that stuff with garlic in it that he couldn't hack.

It was pretty obvious to him which way Camille's thoughts were heading, and he found it exciting. She was very easy to talk to, for a Swiss, but he wasn't all that smitten on hearing her impressions of English life. He'd lived there for nineteen years and he reckoned he knew the score, he wasn't too interested in anyone else putting their own personal gloss on it. So he nodded and chatted and asked if she'd ever seen AFC Basle – they were Swiss, weren't they?– and it turned out she'd never been to a soccer match in her life, so that was that end of the conversation stitched up.

Music was a better bet and when she said she had the new Simply Red album and would he like to hear it, he literally jumped at the chance. Personally he couldn't stand that blue-eyed albino soul shite but he would do anything to get into Camille's pants as quickly as was decently possible, so he looked really keen and she took him by the arm and led him off.

His heart was fairly racing away – to say nothing of the glowing bulge in his 501s – as they walked down the corridors away from the party. The students were pretty quiet at that time of night, just the odd subdued music coming out of a room. He figured most of them would be at the party and the swots and brown-nosers would be tucked up in bed, dreaming of declining the verb *to be* or whatever foreign language students did. Richie had got grade 3 GCSE English, his best apart from geography, and reckoned it had been bugger all use to him, despite what the teachers said. If there weren't any jobs, what did it matter what grade you got? It was life, not books, taught him what he learned, and his dad, and his grandad before him. People didn't seem to realise that.

They went up a flight of stairs and it was all he could do not to reach out and grab Camille's tight little ass there and then under her short summer skirt, as it went flouncing and swinging ahead of him. Then they were in her room and she'd switched on the little bedside light and was in his arms, kissing him even before he could kiss her, and it was like he was going to explode.

Her body felt lithe and firm and he ran his hands up and down her back, cupping those delectable buttock cheeks. It was so obvious she was going to fuck, he couldn't hardly believe his good fortune. He'd been nearly a fortnight without it and now he was going to break his duck. He knew what they always said about French girls and wondered if it was true of the Swiss as well – they spoke the same language or something, didn't they?

He got busy with her zipper, and then her dress was at her feet and she was stepping out of it, wearing just a pair of tight white panties. She kicked off her shoes and then tugged Richie's t-shirt out from under his belt, still kissing him on the neck, on his cheeks, on his lips. His cock felt like it was going to burst. He hoped he wouldn't spoil things by shooting off too soon.

Then they were on the bed together, both of them naked, and he was acutely aware of his hot, engorged cock pressing against her flank. She didn't seem to resist at all, just let his hands rove over her, across her breasts, down below into that damp little ravine between her legs.

'What are you waiting for?' he heard her breathe and then, without realising it, he had climbed on top and slipped inside her, pumping away for all he was worth. God, she was on heat too – it must have been the night air, still hot and sticky like he imagined it was in New Orleans and in that movie with Marlon Brando, *A Streetcar Named Desire*. Desire, that was a right one, wasn't it? This whole evening had a streak of the exotic running through it, very different to a boozy Saturday night out at home with the puke pancaked in the gutters and the hard men waiting in the shadows.

He knew that he wasn't going to let the side down, that his

cock was big and stiff enough to last out the course without shooting off much too soon. Relieved, he felt himself relax and then he rolled over and pulled Camille on top of him, without taking his cock out of her. She knew exactly what to do now, bouncing up and down on top of him. She slowed things down and took control herself, just like she was giving him a blow-job, only squeezing him with her pussy lips instead. He was surprised how big and full her tits looked from this angle, looking up at her, her eyes closed now as she concentrated on what she was doing, her mouth half-open so she could breathe more easily. She really did look like Nicole from the TV ad, only her hair was darker. He thought she was the most beautiful girl he had ever screwed and he was relieved when she began to murmur and gasp in a very specific way, because he couldn't last much longer himself.

He pushed himself up on his elbows and licked each of those delectable brown nipples in turn, first one, then turning his attentions to the other till it was hard and inviting as a nut. This tongueing certainly seemed to press the button as far as Camille went, because she seemed to get all fired up all of a sudden, bucking up and down on him without once missing a beat, and then she went quiet and looked at him and her eyes seemed to kind of glaze over, and then her pussy gripped him in a vice-like grip such as he had never experienced before, and he felt his come rising up from his balls in an irresistible torrent as he pushed up into her and let fly, his eyes closed, her breasts against his face and his tongue blindly seeking the nipple as they exchanged their rapturous juices. He felt like a whole load had been lifted off his mind.

The second time they did it was wilder still.

'You got great tits, Camille,' Richie said, and he meant it. Away in the distance he could hear the sounds of the party.

163

'You want to suck them for me?' she said. Immediately he slid down the bed, tongueing her gently the way he knew girls liked it, not too hard at all like he was chewing a big wad of gum. Sara Blackmore had told Linda that Rob was like that and he always thought it was funny, but he didn't really believe it, he could tell she liked the way he did it.

'You like having your cock sucked?' she whispered when he was done. The words came out so quietly he hardly knew she'd said anything until the shock waves hit him from below.

'Ah-ha,' he sighed and he wasn't talking about has-been Norwegian pop groups. 'In fact, something tells me you're going to show me right now.'

Camille squirmed round and let her tongue trace a little silvery trail all down Richie's lean, hard body, bronzed a deep colour from all those days in the sun. Not even his long hard nights at the bar could take that away from him. His mates back home would have thought he'd been to Ibiza or something.

'Well, well, well,' she said when she reached his groin. 'It makes me feel hungry just looking at you. You've got a really nice cock.'

She tasted Richie experimentally, like she was a kid on the sea front licking an ice cream cone or something. Then she slid her mouth over the end of his cock and sucked hard at it. She did it totally different to any other girl he'd ever been with, but it felt good all the same. Richie was all for variety, in whatever form it came. He thought Linda was a good little gobbler but Camille was something else.

She was kind of half-kneeling with her biggish boobs hanging down, pear-shaped and heavy, like over-ripe fruit. She'd turned almost halfway round now and she was presenting her gorgeous ass to him. He could see the pink lips of her pussy where his spunk was still glistening, the tight little wrinkled orifice of her bum-hole, and still she went on sucking him, her fingertips playing with his balls and in and among his pubic hair all the while so that it nearly drove him mad. Finally, when he was within an inch of shooting his load right there and then in between those tight lips, she stopped what she was doing and turned round, her hair all tousled.

'You want to fuck me again now, Richie?' she breathed.

He almost pushed her over in his impatience to be inside her. She was over on her front with her lovely bare bum in the air and he came up behind her, his cock feeling heavy and potent despite all the beer he'd drunk since he'd finished work that evening.

Her lips parted for him and he slid effortlessly inside her, right up to the hilt. She was soaking wet down there and there was a musky smell in his nostrils, a cunt smell that he liked a lot. Camille knelt there, rocking back and forth with her eyes closed and pressing her ass against him, fantasising about God knows what, and Richie was making these big vicious shoves into her and gasping out loud with the effort of it all, looking at those dimpled cheeks and her breasts and letting the cunt smell fill his nostrils, feeling like he was some kind of big strong rutting animal.

Neither of them lasted long like this. Camille started grunting and squealing again only louder then before, like he was starting to hurt her or something, and he could see she was beginning to go red in the face. He could feel the urgency in his own loins urging him forward, stabbing his cock into her pudenda, feeling lewd and potent and powerful all at the same time. He was full of spunk, had been for days, and he had gallons of it to spare for anyone who wanted it. *Young, dumb and full of come* was the way he liked to think of himself, but he'd pinched the line from someone else.

He could tell she was coming again because her grunts turned to gasps and she was kind of trying to screw herself sideways around his cock, and in that instant he let fly and could feel the big thick jets of semen coming welling out of him and pouring into her.

With his legs splayed wide apart for so long so he could get into her from behind without slipping out again, his thigh muscles felt weak and kind of trembling. He shifted position to make things more comfortable, and as he did so, his cock kind of fell out of her with an audible plop. It felt huge and distended and slippery and lewd, just the way he liked to feel himself. Camille was lying face down on the bed, breathing heavily. Her eyes were closed and her features seemed so delicate in the soft light of the bedside table. He wondered if she'd let him spend the night with her. He didn't really fancy making the long trek back to the caravan.

They held each other for ages, serene and happy. Eventually Richie's cock began to stir again for the third time. Linda was the only girl he'd ever been able to do it with three times in a row and he wondered if he was going to break his record tonight. Camille slid down the bed and Richie, propped up on the pillows, looked on in fascination as her pink tongue flickered for a moment before she began to lick the tip of his cock, probing the little oval hole in the end. She was holding the shaft in her fist, gently pumping it up and down as she did so. Then she sank her mouth down on to him, wide open, and took all of him in, her tongue swirling around him. She seemed to like eating him just as much as being fucked.

He moved as best he could so he could reach down and run his fingers through her hair and along the smooth skin of her shoulders.

'That's good,' he breathed, aware of little other than the sensations of his body. Lying there on the bed, in this room full of someone else's clothes and pictures and records, he hardly had a care in the world.

Her mouth fitted him like a velvet glove. After a while, it got like she was eating him. He was sure her jaws must have been aching by now but she kept on with her lips and her tongue, teasing and tormenting him, licking him up and down his full length before taking all of him back down deep inside her.

She had a rhythm going now, hypnotic and powerful, and Richie surrendered to it. Images of sex began to fill his mind, various girls he had been to bed with, their tits, hair, lips, pussies – all the women began to blur into one and the focus of that desire was Camille. He didn't know her surname but he knew what his body wanted from her. When he felt he was coming he kind of grunted and touched her shoulder, but she didn't pay any attention, just carried on sucking away at him. Even when he got past the point of no return, when she must have known from the way he writhed and moaned what was going on, she still continued to do him. Now he was fucking her in her mouth the way he'd fucked her earlier in her pussy, strong and sure. And then he couldn't hold back any longer and his stuff came boiling up out of him again. He was excited by coming in her willing mouth and his orgasm was big and prolonged, the spasms amplified, the desire out of control. All he was aware of was that powerful ejection from his body and the feeling of her mouth enclosing him, welcoming him into her, drinking his fluids down, milking him dry, until his body stopped twitching and that tremendous tension was, at last, stilled.

In a room just down the corridor from Richie and Camille, Rob

167

and Debbie were going at it hammer and tongs, he on top of her, she with her legs wrapped tight around his waist so he could hardly move more than an inch either way. An inch, though, was important at a time like this.

'No, don't stop,' she hissed when he made a move to do something different. 'Just keep it like that, OK? Jesus, that feels good.'

She was squirming and writhing around so much, she almost threw Rob off the bed.

He brought her off quickly and expertly. Rob got the feeling that a lot of northern women didn't know too much about eating out and blow-jobs and stuff. Debbie, though, was different. He ran his hands through her expertly pre-tousled hair. Women who were like a wild thing with a dick inside them suddenly became all coy when he tried to get a little lick-action going. Still, once they'd had his tongue in their pussy, they were soon back asking for more.

He climbed on top of her, conscious of his cock bobbing there in front of her eyes, his balls hanging down heavy and full. She was lying back on the pillows with her eyes closed and her mouth half-open, naked as the day she was born. Rob had been surprised how quickly she'd got her clothes off. She'd stepped out of her summer dress just like that, and she was naked underneath. Standing beside her in the room of someone he didn't know, he'd hardly got his shirt cuffs unbuttoned before she was standing there next to him, stark bollock naked and feeling his cock. He knew she'd been waiting for him, building herself up into a peak of anticipation. He liked to know a woman had the hots for him.

So now he was moving back and forth, back and forth, building up the rhythm, using the strength in his arms and legs, feeling her spreading her own legs wider to draw him in until she brought her knees up and then wrapped her legs around him, twisting and turning. They rolled over, still locked together, and then it was her turn to be on top of him, her hair wild and loose, the blonde muff that was almost exactly the same colour – he'd never seen that in a girl before. She had nicely shaped tits and her nipples stood out big and proud and hard. He rolled them between his teeth, nipping and making her gasp as she flaunted herself above him. She was, he knew, entirely at ease with her own body. She didn't have a bikini line around her bum, which was something he had noticed immediately when he first started sleeping with her. She did her sunbathing naked in her back garden. In a place like Dunwich now, that really was daring.

He grabbed hold of that firm, nineteen-year-old ass and squeezed the cheeks hard. She moaned and, leaning forward, bit him hard on the neck, so hard it hurt. *Hell*, he suddenly thought, *I hope that won't leave a mark*. Shocked, he pulled her ass down onto him, feeling his cock burying itself right up inside almost to the end of her vagina, and then he could feel it coming, that irresistible urge deep inside himself. He carried on thrusting, sharp, vicious stabs now, but he was well on his way. With one last effort he pushed up at her, lifting her whole body clean off the bed and up into the air, and then he was shooting his seed into her, on and on into the night, and then she too seemed to tense up and squirm and gasp, even while his cock was still hard inside her.

She lit a cigarette after for each of them, lay back on the bed smoking. Rob had one hand resting on her thigh, brushing those blonde curls, wet and matted now from his sperm and her juices. Feeling confident, the way he usually did when he'd just taken a woman, he slipped a finger inside her, then two. She made no move to stop him, just lay back on the pillows, blowing out smoke. After a while she stubbed out her cigarette and turned her head to face him.

'You really are one hell of a sexy sod, you know,' she said to him.

'Oh yeah?' he said. 'What makes you say that?'

'Just the way you do it, that's all. That's the way I've always felt about you.'

'I love you, you know.' There, he'd said it. The words had just popped out of his mouth.

She smiled, kissed him gently on the cheek. There was a big poster of a Harley Davidson on the wall, he noticed. He wondered what sort it was.

'I love you too,' she said.

When Carole came round she was alone. Her head felt surprisingly light and clear, though her memories of the past few hours were more than a shade hazy. She looked at her watch, two-thirty almost. She got to her feet, found her dress which was draped over an armchair but could find none of her underwear. She couldn't think where she might have lost it – in any one of a number of places over the past few hours.

She slipped the dress on, aware that every detail of her body was revealed through its transparent folds. The thought didn't bother her – that was what The Laurels was all about, that was why she had worn it that evening. There was some champagne still left in a bottle on the dresser and she poured herself a glass, let the bubbles weave their accustomed magic as they rose to her head. Champagne or coke – it was a difficult choice, but Carole was rich enough not to have to make it. She could have both if she wanted to, and she often did. What she'd taken earlier, though, she had no idea. She assumed it must have been some kind of mild hallucinogenic to make her head go off sideways like that.

She found her shoes and stepped out into the corridor. She was, she realised, on the same floor as the room she and Paul had taken. She had no idea where he might have disappeared to, but when she opened their bedroom door she soon found out.

The scene was like something out of the last days of the Roman Empire. There was a chain of people, perhaps five or six at least, sprawled in attitudes of wild abandon among a litter of empty bottles. Paul was stretched out on the bed with some dark-haired girl while some other woman, a blonde, was tongueing her out. Kneeling at the side of the bed, she was being screwed from behind by a naked guy.

'Jesus,' Carole involuntarily murmured to herself as her disbelieving eyes took in the scene. Underneath the naked guy, spreadeagled on the floor, another blonde was lying, playing with his balls with her tongue. It was like a scene from a movie like the ones they were showing downstairs.

Two girls were lying together on the rug, eating each other out, at the feet of a fully clothed man who was smoking a small cigar and looking utterly nonchalant as the world fell apart all around him. He looked up and caught Carole's eye, and smiled. She noticed how dark his eyes were.

'Come and join us,' he called in a quiet voice. 'I think I saw your husband somewhere over there.' He waved in the general direction of the tangled heap of bodies on the bed.

Carole smiled and came over, perched on the side of the big armchair.

'I'm Jamie,' he said. 'Paul and I used to be at Central Television.'

Realisation dawned. So this was Jamie, the guy whose exploits

171

had filled in many a gap around the Chivers's breakfast and dinner tables. He was a legend in his own lunchtime, a twentieth-century Lothario, the cocksman with the surest touch. They said he'd screwed someone in a London restaurant, and he was even more good-looking than she had been led to believe. She'd seen him in photos but in the flesh he was quite ravishing, with an almost perfect symmetry to his face and dark, mysterious eyes.

'You just missed seeing Paul and that other guy screwing these two,' he went on, indicating the two girls at his feet. 'One of them was up her bum, the other in her pussy. I don't think I've ever seen it done before.'

Carole said she had. She'd had it done to her, in fact, but she wasn't going to say so. It had, after all, been with a member of the Royal Household, and she was intensely loyal to the Crown. But she was taken, nevertheless, by the idea of having Jamie in her while someone – Paul for preference – took her in the rear. She felt ready for anything and her pussy didn't feel in the least bit sore, although she'd had several partners that night, with the prospect of more to come.

Jamie seemed to get the message. He reached out and pulled her down on to him, right there in the armchair. Soon they were necking like a couple of teenagers while, all around them, people licked and screwed and sucked.

'You're a lovely kisser,' Carole murmured in his ear.

'I could say the same about you. Let's hope the other things are just as nice.'

She could feel how hard his cock was through his trousers.

'How come you're fully dressed?' she asked him.

'I only just got here,' he replied. 'I bumped into Paul in the corridor and came right in. I wasn't expecting this.' He nodded at the room around them, a mass of heaving, twisted bodies.

She gave his cock an exploratory squeeze.

'I bet you've got lots of lovely spunk, then,' she said. But he seemed entirely nonplussed, and only held her closer.

'We'll have to see about that, won't we?' he replied.

There was a pause between them.

'Would you like to go to my room?' he said, as if reading her thoughts.

'There's no room on the bed, is there? And I'm much too old to do it on the floor.' Which was a complete lie, of course.

She opened the door. Across the way, she saw a well known *Daily Mail* columnist disappearing into a bedroom with a Labour MP. It was that kind of an evening, she reflected. Earlier on, someone had shown her photographs of an Oscar-nominated actress in the earlier, less consciously artistic stages of her career. She had had half a lifetime of professionally knowing about the lives of the rich and famous and it never ceased to amaze her what people who should have known better seemed to get up to. She half expected to see Princess Di being chased naked down the corridor by the Brigade of Guards.

Jamie's room was on the floor below. The two of them quickly undressed. She was taken by the size of Jamie's cock – his reputation, for once, seemed to be borne out by the reality, and certainly he knew how to use it. She was down on her knees in an instant, licking and sucking it. She liked the way it hung, big and heavy. She wanted to suck it more later but for now, all she wanted was to have it in her as quickly as possible. She was in a very genital mood that evening.

She looked up at him with a soft and wanton stare that bordered on insolence, her tongue playing with the big purple-tipped glans. He looked back at her levelly, then turned and lay down flat on the bed.

'Here,' he said softly. 'Come and sit on my prick. You look like you're dying to fuck me.'

Again their eyes met – there was an undeniable chemistry between them. She came and straddled over him, made him lick her pussy for a little while – she was aware that she was starting to feel a little dry down there – but that seemed to get her going.

His cock, when it was inside her, was every bit as good as she had been led to believe. He knew how to use it too, powerful and yet gentle at the same time. She threw her head back and squeezed him with her vaginal muscles alone, gently bobbing up and down with just the tip of his penis inside her until her passions got the better of her and she pushed hard down on to him, feeling him slide right up inside her, long and incredibly hard and filling, and then she raised herself up again, her hands pressing down on the already tangled sheets.

With the light of pure lust in her eyes she rocked up and down, spitted on him, her senses attuned to the incredible feeling of penetration that he evoked in her. He pumped into her from underneath so she could feel the animal force of his muscles, that strong back, the powerful thighs. She wanted very much to have him and Paul together, if Paul would agree – he was a bit funny sometimes about doing it with her and another guy, but to have her in bed with another woman was absolutely fine by him.

Rapidly losing control, she squeezed hard with her vaginal walls, grinding her backside hard down on to his thighs, aware of the wetness that seemed to spill everywhere from her. That must have been the fourth or fifth time she'd fucked that evening and yet she was still ready for more, still wanted the kind of novelty that only screwing someone new could bring.

They were both of them fairly far gone now.

'You know what?' she said as she battled for breath.

'What's that?'

'I want you to fuck my tits. You like my tits?'

'I think you've got great tits, Carole. Always have.'

They slowed down, and she gently eased off him, lay down by his side, took his cock in her hand. It felt hot and stiff and sticky, nice to lick. She did so and he tasted good, her own juices rich and tangy.

Then she pressed his cock against her breasts, smothered it in the deep channel of her cleavage.

'That's good,' he murmured. 'I always knew you had good tits.'

'Do you fantasise about them?'

'Sure.'

'Does Paul talk about me? About bed and things?'

'No, he doesn't. At least, not to me.'

That was good. She didn't talk about Paul either. They were very loyal, in a way, to one another.

'What do you do when you fantasise?'

'Just the usual things.'

'And you think about my tits?'

'Sometimes. And other things.'

She pulled him over on to his side, squashing her breasts against him and trapping his cock in her cleavage. She was aware of how hard and plump her nipples were, the little golden rings that pierced them, as she played with them between her fingers. With her other hand she was delicately caressing her clitoris.

'Would it excite you to know that I sometimes wear clamps on my nipples?'

'Yes. When do you do that?'

'On TV, sometimes. It hurts at first but then you get this wonderful glow. I was wearing them that time I interviewed Hugh Grant and I nearly came there and then talking to the camera.'

175

'You didn't show any signs.'

'A real pro, you see. Other times, I might have something up my cunt. I think the viewers would go wild, wouldn't they, if they knew?'

'I bet they fantasise about these things.'

'I bet they do, too. I know I do.'

She took hold of his cock, formed her fingers into an O-shape and frigged him up and down. Far sooner than she had anticipated, she was aware of a sudden change in his breathing and then he suddenly shot a perfect arc of come all over her breasts, from her chin almost down to her navel, thick and creamy and abundant.

It was good to feel wanted. She liked that more than anything in the world.

Chapter Six

They were ready for Rob when he came out of the party. One minute he and Debbie were standing outside the language school, as if not quite believing what had happened to them, the next he was set upon by a bunch of headcases.

Richie had come out with them. A sixth sense had told him something like this might happen. Rob quickly pushed Debbie through the door to get her out of the way, before turning to face his aggressors. Sure enough, it was Mick Rowlandson again, only this time he'd come armed with a baseball bat and half a dozen assorted heavies. Big sods, they were too, with shaven heads, National Front by the look of things.

'You wanker,' Mick hissed which, to Richie, seemed a little unfortunate, all things considered and given the events of the last few hours.

Rob experienced a sinking feeling. He really wasn't in the mood for this kind of shite, tonight of all nights. Did he really have to play the knight in shining armour role, defending Debbie's honour against the marauding savages? He felt quite tired, one way and another. It had been a long day and this was no way to bring it to a close. All he wanted to do was get away, find a cab if they could, and make their way back to the caravan site.

'Aw, just fuck off, will you?' Richie interjected before Rob could get a word out.

'I'm not speaking to you, sunshine,' spat Mick. 'I'm looking for your mate here.'

'Yeah well, me and him go together, right? If you've got an argument with him, shiteface, you've got one with me an' all.'

Mick looked at one and then the other. *Christ*, thought Rob, *he's a mean-looking bugger*. He wasn't that bad to look at, you could see why the girls went for him, but there was something else about him, a kind of wounded aggression that made him dangerous. Perhaps the girls didn't see that side of him until it was too late. He still couldn't understand why Debbie had gone out with him, but he could see why she'd packed him in so quickly.

They were standing in the car park at the side of the language school. Traffic was passing not fifty yards away, along Eastern Avenue. Even at that late hour there were people around but not so many that it would inhibit Mick from what he had in mind. They were in for it now, it seemed. There were a couple of big sodium lamps above them and Rob and Richie were careful to stay well within the pool of light. If they got lured into the shadows, heaven only knew what might happen to them. They were outnumbered by three to one and, while both of them were pretty good scrappers, neither of them fancied their chances much. Especially not against a baseball bat and whatever those shaven-headed goons had got stashed in their pockets, bottles and bricks and mostly a knife or two.

What to do? Should they try and bluff it out, make a dash for it, wade in with fists swinging or wait for the cavalry to arrive? It wasn't much of a choice. It was time to stand up and be counted and neither Rob nor Richie was going to duck it.

Mick Rowlandson was building up a fresh head of steam. He

came right up to Rob and thrust his chin in his face.

'I'm just about fucking pig sick of you,' he said. 'You're getting on my fucking nerves.'

'Mind your language, sunbeam,' said Richie, unable to resist. He nodded in the direction of Mick's bevy of beauties. 'There's ladies present.'

'I told you to shut the fuck up.'

'The girls won't like it.'

'Don't you try and cheek me, you bastard.'

'Nobody tells me to do anything. Nobody at all.'

'Especially not a prat like you, Rowlandson.'

Those words from Rob started it. One of the heavies, a guy with a swastika tattooed on his forearm, made a lunge for Richie and grabbed him by the wrist. Richie tried to head-butt him just like Duncan Ferguson did that time, but only caught him on the side of the head. Mick Rowlandson swung one on Rob but Rob ducked out of the way, grabbed him by the waist and tried to upend him. Driving in like a rugby league player, he got him off balance and the two of them went over. They were wrestling on the floor and a couple of Mick's lot were trying to get a kick in on Rob, but Richie was too close so they started kicking him on the shins instead, even while he was grappling with the guy who'd headbutted him.

Mick was still clutching his baseball bat. Knowing you could do a lot of damage with something like that, Richie managed to stamp on his wrist but Mick still clung on to it, trying to swing it round even while he was still down on the floor with his arms round Rob's neck. He caught Rob a fair old swipe one-handed, smack on the elbow, and Richie could see his mate wince at the sudden onrush of pain.

There were two of the heavies had hold of Richie now, one

with his arms around his shoulders, trying to pin his arms to his sides, and the other round his legs. He knew they were getting the better of him, no matter how hard he struggled and tried to lash out. He was swearing fit to bust – in fact all of them were shouting at the tops of their voices. He hoped that it would just be fists and knees and stuff, that there wouldn't be any knives or anything – he still remembered that lad down Gallowgate Road who'd got cut up one night after a fight outside the chinky.

Rob was swearing and lashing out and he seemed to be getting the better of Mick Rowlandson until he got a kick in the side of the head from a size twelve DM, which seemed to stun him for long enough for Mick to roll him round and get him pinned against the tarmac, still warm from the weeks of summer sunshine. Two guys had Richie's arms pinned now and the blows and kicks were starting to come in on him, no matter how hard he tried to shy out of the way.

Then the unbelievable happened. All of a sudden there were cries and a whole bunch of people from the college came spilling out. Richie caught a glimpse of Debbie and Camille, and then these big strong Italian-looking lads were wading in like the Juventus supporters they probably were. One of them, only a little guy but he seemed to have the strength of ten, caught Mick Rowlandson with a smacker right in the solar plexus before dragging him off Rob and wrestling the baseball bat from his grasp.

Everyone was shouting and Richie could understand most of it, without looking for subtitles. *Bâtarde! Scheisskopf!* It meant the same in any language. There was a lot of racist stuff coming out from the lads with the number-two cuts but this seemed only to fire up the boys from the language school. The one with the bat caught Mick Rowlandson a cracker right across the knees and then on the elbow. Richie could tell he really felt it, but he had problems enough of his own. He managed to get his knee in on the guy who'd been trying to pull his left arm out of its socket, and then all of a sudden it went quiet, everyone panting for breath, Mick Rowlandson and his lot just standing there, looking angry and cowed and outnumbered. He had a cut on his lip and his jeans were torn and he looked beaten, for the moment at least.

They stood there for what seemed like a couple of minutes, in the harsh orange glare of the sodium lamps, and then he squared up to Rob one last time.

'Don't think you got away with this,' he managed to say through his rapidly swelling lips. 'We'll be back. And you won't have all these fucking puffs to protect you. Next time, pal, it'll be just you and me.'

Rob looked him smack in the eye. 'Oh yeah,' he said. 'If you're so tough, how come you need a baseball fucking bat and half a dozen goons to help you out? Come off it, Mick, you couldn't do your granny over even if she had her hands tied behind her back. You're soft, you know that? Soft as bleeding shite. Soft as bleeding shite.'

Mick Rowlandson looked furious but didn't say anything. One of his mates, though, came up to Richie and looked him up and down.

'I know where you live, son,' he said quietly and simply so no one else could hear, and there was an air of cold menace in his voice. Then the whole bunch of them ambled off, trying to look well hard. Someone picked up a can or something and threw it after them, but by then lights were beginning to come on in the college rooms above them and it was time to split.

The cold, pre-dawn air was helping to clear Carole's head. She had got back to her room, found it deserted apart from a few used condoms, a pile of bottles and the odd stray item of someone else's underwear. Of her husband there was no sign.

She changed into something more suitable for the outdoors than high-heeled shoes and a transparent dress. The hotel was very quiet as she made her way along the corridors and through the lobby, although the party was still going strong in the dining room. Odd people – individuals, couples, larger combinations – were sprawled on chairs and sofas, for the most part dead to the world. Near the reception desk a man in a dinner jacket was performing oral sex on a very large and jolly-looking lady who looked at Carole with unseeing, kohl-rimmed eyes as she walked past and stepped out onto the front steps.

The stars were still bright in the sky. It had been an exceptionally clear night and Carole, despite her sweatshirt, could feel the diamond chill of the air. It was a little before four, and the first greyish lightening of the sky was visible in the east.

She made her way out of the hotel grounds, the trees dark against the heavily watered lawns. She stepped across the wide main road – deserted at that hour of a Sunday morning – and made her way down the narrow concreted track that led to the beach, past the boarded and shuttered cafeteria and the public lavatories discreetly tucked away behind the sunken garden. At the last minute the path plunged down through a cleft in the cliffs and there, before her, were the sea and the waves, a dark grey, crashing presence in the stillness.

She walked down on to the beach, aware of the incredible freshness of the air, in contrast to the heavily sensual miasma that had seemed to hang over The Laurels. For a few minutes she simply stood there, feeling the air on her face and her over-taxed body. She remembered the breathing exercises the lady on their show had taught her and stood there for a few minutes, feeling the world slowly beginning to slow down as the oxygen reached her brain. Then she kicked off her shoes and felt the sand on her feet, clean and cold as she walked down to the water's edge.

Instinct told her to turn left, northwards along the coast. She had no idea where she was going, splashing through the shallow surf while, a hundred yards away, the great North Sea breakers rolled and crashed. She could hear the rush of pebbles as the sea tugged them back down the shore. Everything around here was the same deep blue-grey, tending to black – the cliffs, the sea, the sky.

It was very isolated down here on the beach at this time of the morning and yet she did not feel in the least bit vulnerable. If anything, she felt that she had found a safe haven, a place of peace after all the divine madness of those last few hours. God, they had made a night of it, all right. Thank goodness they had come to The Laurels for only one evening this time. The last occasion they were here, it had been for a whole weekend and she'd hardly been able to get up to do the Monday afternoon show.

The sound of the surf was almost deafening. Here she was, a woman used to spending almost every minute of the day and night in the company of others, being watched over by producers, publicity women, fans, security guards, and for a few moments at least it was rapturous to enjoy the sensation of being completely on her own, with no one knowing where she was or where she was going, least of all herself. The sense of peace and freedom was almost overwhelming.

Her mind was already beginning to empty itself of everything that had happened back at The Laurels. Sure, she and Paul would pick over the pieces later, in the car going back home and, on and off, for the next few weeks, until the next occasion presented itself. She had left it behind like she had sloughed a skin, like she had shed her transparent dress and her stockings and replaced them with simple jeans and a sweatshirt. It was a sight more comfortable and natural to walk in bare feet that in strappy black patent sandals with five-inch heels.

She wasn't really thinking at all – she was just experiencing, alive to the possibilities of this morning, the potential that lay hidden behind the slate-grey cliffs, beneath the black sea flecked with white. Despite the hour she felt wide awake – perhaps it was the drugs she had taken or, more likely, it was the natural chemistry of the early morning air. She breathed in deeply and gratefully, great lungfuls of air, and felt its oxygen slowly permeating her bloodstream and rising to her head. She was higher than she had been all night, and that was really saying something.

She didn't feel like stopping anywhere in particular so she just carried on walking, the sky getting a little less dark, the stars beginning to lose some of their brightness. She saw strange outlines on the top of the cliff but then she realised it was just the low roofs of caravans, dozens and dozens of them, lined up along the coast, silent and watchful. It was a different world entirely to the one she and Paul lived in but here were her audience, asleep on their thin, narrow mattresses, dreaming of the kind of life that only people like the Chiverses really knew.

She could see a little more of where she was walking now, the faint phosphorescence of her footsteps in the wet sand, the thin coating of pebbles and shells that the sea had brought in. For a while she walked on the shingle at the foot of the cliffs but it hurt her bare feet and slowed down her progress, so she walked along instead ankle-deep in the cold water that rolled around her and wiped away her footprints as soon as she had made them. For a second, a single rash second, she thought of walking off and never coming back but there was too much at stake, too much to give up now. She valued herself too highly.

On an instinct she turned round and she could see the red light at the end of the pier winking on and off, a steady pulse like a heartbeat. It was like a back-marker for her. Dunwich itself was hidden behind the curving outline of the coast, but she was aware of the faint glow of its streetlights in the night sky. When she next turned round even the light had disappeared and she was completely on her own now, unshepherded and unheralded. She liked the feeling of total isolation it gave her.

She must have been walking for half an hour or more – she'd left her watch behind at the hotel – when she came to a little bay set into the coast. It wasn't a cove like you might find in Cornwall or Devon, just a place where the sea went a little further inland and the cliffs gave way to coastal dunes. There were a few houses there, dark and silent, no lights showing. She wondered if it might be time to turn back but then a movement in the dunes above her caught her eye.

She froze, motionless. There was a man there, she was sure. She heard a cough and then the sound of a zip being pulled up.

'Hello,' said a voice, deep and friendly. 'Not many people about at this time of the morning.'

'No,' she said in the direction she thought the voice had come from. 'No, I don't suppose there are.'

She heard a rustling and then she could see someone's outline against the sky, between herself and the dunes.

'Feels like it's going to be another nice day, though,' said the voice, closer this time.

And then he was beside her. She jumped, involuntarily.

'I'm sorry,' he said. 'I didn't mean to startle you.'

'I guess I got used to being on my own. I was surprised to hear another voice.'

'Out for a walk, were you?' He sounded very friendly, no threat at all.

'Yes. How about you?'

'Looking at the stars,' he said. 'I've been out all night, observing. I live just down the way there, that last house on the right. Here, do you want to have a look through my telescope? I was just about to pack up.'

What an extraordinary turn-up, she thought. There she was, getting in tune with the wonders of nature, and up pops a man who offers to reveal to her the secret of the universe.

He was tall, very tall, dressed in jeans and a heavy sweater. He had on one of those fisherman's jackets with lots of pockets, not the kind worn by people who drove too-shiny FWD vehicles but the real thing, stained and work-used. Beside him was a telescope, a very big one, so heavy it was mounted on a solid-looking tripod. It looked like the real thing, a scientific instrument rather than a hobbyist's toy. At his feet was a big canvas holdall, unzipped.

'Have some tea, if you like. I've got a flask. I was going to have a cup myself.'

Suddenly it seemed like the most marvellous idea in the world. A cup of tea, a good old-fashioned English cup of tea. At that moment, she would have given anything for it, and she said so.

'My name's Col,' he said as he handed her the plastic cup. 'I'm sorry there's not much left.'

'That's all right,' she said. 'Just a sip is fine.'

'I live in the end cottage over there,' he said again. He indicated, with a broad sweep of his arm, the group of black, silhouetted shapes behind them.

'I'm Carole,' she said, and offered him her hand. His skin felt rough but it was firm and warm – a nice handshake.

'Are you on holiday, then?'

'Something like that.' He didn't seem the type who would understand about places like The Laurels.

'Nice weather for it.'

'Isn't it just?'

'How's the tea?'

'Very refreshing.'

When she'd finished her cup – actually it was getting a bit cold, tasted a bit stewed – he swung the telescope round, busied himself at the eyepiece.

'Here,' he said. 'Take a look at this. Tell me what you see.'

Intrigued, she looked through the lens. At first she could see nothing, only blackness, but then she got closer to it and she could see this blob, an orange blob that seemed to shimmer gently in the blackness.

'Do you know what it is?' he said when she described what she saw. Carole could tell the Plough and the Seven Sisters but that was about as far as her grasp of fundamental astronomy went.

'No, I don't,' she said simply.

'What do you see to either side of it?'

She peered intently through the eyepiece. She could just see a faint line that seemed to run through the blob, right through the middle, like a pencil stroke.

'There's like a line passing through it, from one side to the other.'

'That's Saturn,' he said. 'What you're looking at are the rings, seen sideways on.'

She turned back, scarcely able to believe her eyes. Sure enough, she could see the rings now, just the edge. It was awesome.

'Why is it orange?' she asked.

'That's the planet's atmosphere. We can't see the surface, it's always hidden by clouds.'

It was absolutely amazing, a revelation. She wished he could have shown her everything in the sky.

'Can you see anything to the left of Saturn, spreading out in line with the rings?'

She studied the eyepiece again. It was hard to see through it. It wasn't like taking a picture with a camera, you had to be sure of just where you were looking.

'There's another little blob, very faint. And another one— no, two more. Maybe three.'

'Those are the moons of Saturn. The big one is Titan. If you look closely you can just about make out another three of them – Thetys, Diane and Rhea. Saturn is very low in the sky now, very bright. Just about the brightest thing in the sky at the moment. You must have seen it, even if you didn't know what you were seeing.'

It seemed the most natural thing in the world to accept Col's offer to come into his cottage with him for what he called a 'proper cup of tea'. He packed up his telescope, took down the tripod with its heavy telescopic legs. She carried the big holdall for him herself. It seemed to be full of books and charts and things, a torch and a flask. On the way across the dunes he pointed out the Milky Way, so bright even in the rapidly lightening sky that she wondered why she had never noticed it before.

Because you have never looked for such things, an inner voice told her.

The first grey fingers of dawn were stealing through the windows of Billy Brilleaux's flat. Sue closed the bedroom door, went through into the bathroom and cleaned her teeth. Then she unzipped her black sheath dress – not without a certain difficulty, because they'd all had a lot to drink that night – and stepped out of it. She heard Billy's tread on the stairs and glanced in the full-length mirror on the clothes cupboard door, a girl in her late teens dressed in black crotchless knickers, with high heels, her hair piled high on her head in an elegant chignon.

'That's a sight to awaken the dead,' said Billy as he came into the room and swept her into his arms. She could feel his erection against her hip. She could sense how aroused he had been for the past hour or more, while he got the last of the late-night revellers out of the club and closed the place down. They'd gone on afterwards to a place on the Norwich road where nobody bothered too much about the licencing laws and then, when they couldn't wait for each other, had gone back to Billy's place. She'd told her mum and dad she was staying the night with Jacqui, which was fine because Jacqui's parents were away for the weekend and there wouldn't be any problems about corroborating the story.

They went at each other's bodies hungrily, Billy still in his shirt and clip-on security man's bow tie, Sue soon naked apart from her pants, her bra tossed carelessly aside after he had all but torn it off her in his haste. They scrambled into bed and his penis slid massively and immediately inside her and the shock made her gasp. There were none of the usual preliminaries. Those crotchless knickers seemed to drive Billy wild. She must remember to buy some more – they looked liked being her meal ticket.

Their bed was soft and wide and low and Sue welcomed him into her like a long-lost friend, her nerve-ends alive to every last nuance of sensation. She rubbed her skimpy, silky briefs against him. She sensed at once how fired up he was, how she needed to do little more than lie back and let the urgent, remorseless waves of his passion sweep over her, carrying her away in their wash. His immediacy surprised her – she had scarcely guessed how much he had been holding back his pent-up feelings.

He powered into her with short, sharp thrusts, his hands under her backside, pulling her hips up towards him. His big body was heavy on hers, but she let herself go with the tide and came almost immediately, alive with sensation, scarcely noticing even the shuddering sequence of convulsions with which he climaxed inside her. She felt wanted, desirable. She felt safe with Billy, could let her own emotions out without a leash. In the outside world things were different.

The flutterings ceased inside her. His powerful shoulders were stilled, and he sank down beside her, his fingers trailing through her hair, delicately looping the strands. She loved the contrast between his violence and the extreme tenderness he showed on occasion. His breathing, like hers, was short and ragged with all the exertion of their love-making. She could feel his chest rising and falling against hers, felt his penis slip out of her and trail wetly and plumply across her thigh. She opened her eyes and looked at the ceiling, the subdued wall lights over their heads.

Billy rolled over on to his back and sat up.

'Jesus,' he said. 'I thought I was going to explode.'

She was aware of his come seeping out of her vagina. He put his arm around her shoulders and stroked her hair. She knew his appetites were not yet slaked. In a few minutes she reached down and took hold of his penis. It felt sticky and heavy and yet it stiffened perceptibly under her touch. She could feel it rising and hardening under her expert touch, filling with expectancy. Billy could easily do it twice in half an hour.

'Did you see those lads looking for Rob?' she said as she took his penis into her mouth.

'Oh yes?' said Billy. He didn't seem especially concerned. 'Where was this?'

'Back at the club.'

'Rob can look after himself.'

'You must have seen something.'

'Ah, it was just Mick Rowlandson throwing his weight about.'

'Couldn't you do something? Before things got too heavy?'

She licked him expertly. She could taste her own secretions mingling with his sperm.

'I did. I had a quiet word with Mick. He said he'd be a good boy.'

'Rob seemed to disappear pretty sharpish after that. I wondered where he'd gone to.'

'You don't fancy him, do you?'

She grunted *no*.

'I didn't think so,' he murmured absently, and that was all. She half-turned towards him, arching her back and pressing her pubic hair against his hard masculine thigh. She began to rub herself against him in a slow, sensual, unambiguous movement. His penis, she noticed, was already stiff and ready for her.

Still she prolonged the movement, building up not just a rhythm but a mood, a strange kind of dance. His arms reached out for her and his hands were against her breasts, taking their full weight, feeling the hardness of their tips. With surprising delicacy for such a big man he wriggled down the bed and pulled her panties off. They were absolutely soaked with their mingled juices. Now she was as naked as he was.

She kissed him, still grinding her hips against him. And then, without dropping a beat, she rolled over lithely on to her front, moving like a snake, and knelt up on all fours. He moved around behind her, familiar with her desires. Parting her legs as far as she could, she pressed her backside against him, aware of the bouncing, jiggling movements of her breasts as she did so. She felt like a bitch on heat – lewd and sexually demanding. Billy was powerless to resist her allure. He was a man who liked to look. Some men preferred to do it with their eyes closed and the lights out. They were wimps.

'What are you waiting for?' she breathed, and then she dropped forward on to her elbows.

She could feel the sweat on his body, very male beneath the aftershave he wore, could smell her own desire for him. He moved around behind her and she could feel his hands on her back, his body probing hers, sliding down the furrow between her cheeks, and then he was against the entrance to her castle and she had taken him in one hand and almost pulled him into her.

He pushed hard and was almost instantly swallowed up inside her, his strong hands steadying himself on her hips. She squeezed her tight, muscular walls around him and she felt full, satiated with him. But still he pushed on, deeper into her, forcing her head down into the pillow until she felt he must be buried into her right up to the root.

She came again, not quite as quickly as before, shuddering into delirium even as he came inside her for the second time in twenty minutes.

And then they lay back on the pillows together, their bodies filmed with sweat and the hypnotic scents of their coupling mingling in the night air. Sue, her breasts rising and falling in a heavy rhythm, looked around her at the scattered clothes, the jewellery spilled over the dressing table, the discarded undergarments. Her passion spent, she felt strangely empty. She looked at Billy for the last time before she switched off the bedside light, but he was already asleep.

* * *

Camille persuaded Richie – not that he needed much persuading – to stay the night with her in her room at the language school. Rob and Debbie, however, elected to go back to the caravan for what was left of the night. It would have been a long walk back, but they managed to get a cab on Eastern Avenue. The guy wanted to charge them three quid extra but Rob beat him down and they got the fare for a fiver, which was lucky because that was all the money he had left.

What a fucking night that was, thought Rob as he pushed the door open and the familiar stale smell greeted them. The adrenaline was still pumping through him and, though he'd long stopped shaking, he felt amazingly strong and potent. Like an old-time conquering hero, or whatever the song said.

Debbie made them both a cup of coffee, and then they got into bed. As their mouths melted together in their first healing kiss, he quickly forgot about everything that had happened in the last few hours. It just flew away like a cloud of poison gas in a strong breeze, scattered into minute particles and rendered harmless. He could wallop Mick Rowlandson any time he wanted to. True, he'd not exactly flattened him there in the car park, but he was sure as hell getting the upper hand on him when all the kids from the language school came spilling out and put a stop to it.

Her tongue felt firm and strong as Debbie played around his lips (he liked a girl who was a good kisser, right back from the days when necking was about all there was, unless you were lucky enough to cop a feel inside, and such things were significant). He breathed in her perfume, soft and fruity, with a sensual hint of musk. Sex, he had come to realise, wasn't just about touch and stuff – the way your body felt when it did things and things got done to it – but a whole lot of other things besides. One of them psychologists he'd done for GCSE – Freud was it, or maybe Engels – said everything came down to sex in the end. *Too fucking right, mate*, he thought as he rolled Debbie over on to her back.

He clasped her closely, a brilliant eruption of desire coursing its way through him like a lightning flash. Using just the very tips of his fingers, he played with her shoulders and the soft bare flesh of her upper arms. His tongue roved over her face, her neck, her ears. He could feel the way that her breasts were crushed heavily against him, the nipples hard with desire in the cool night air. He hadn't a fucking clue what time it was but he guessed it must have been at least four. Outside, it was starting to get light.

He could feel the warmth rising from her body, bringing with it a deeper, more sensual edge to her perfume. The bed began to feel comfortable and snug, even though it was a ratty little narrow thing. He was amazed at how soft and curly Debbie's hair was as he played with it, their lips pressed together still, their tongues weaving and intertwining like the adders that once, up on the heath beyond the caravan site, he had caught a glimpse of. Debbie hardly ever smoked, and one of the things that had first struck him about her was what incredibly sweet breath she had. It was like it had a perfume all of her own. And she loved him, she'd said so. He breathed that in as well.

She murmured softly and squirmed a little in his arms, pressing her thighs against his, flesh against flesh. She reached for his hand and placed it on her breast. Its point was hard and full. He took the weight of her breast as she leaned forward slightly to kiss him full on the lips again and it seemed to spill over into the palm of his hand. He stroked her, pressing against her flesh, squeezing and cupping, persistently amazed at how soft and warm her body was. He returned her kiss with passion and his tongue again sought hers. He noticed almost incidentally how incredibly stiff his penis seemed to have become all of a sudden and, with her body lying half on top of him, it felt horribly uncomfortable, like a spring trying desperately to uncoil itself.

She had lain her hand across his chest, running her fingers through the covering of dark hair. She raked her long, carefully manicured fingernails across his nipples and bit his earlobe. 'Come on, lover,' she breathed. 'Let's see what you've got for me.'

She was still playing her hands across over his body, cupping his pectorals as though they were female breasts. She dipped her head and took his nipples in her mouth by turn. As she did so, he opened his eyes and looked down at the bump their bodies made under the bedcover. He pulled it back a shade and gently moved her over towards the cold, formica-clad wall of the caravan, ready to roll her on to her back again and climb on top of her. Her breasts, uncovered now, wobbled noticeably as she did so. They were magnificent, large and full, tantalising. She caught his gaze and smiled, kissed him on the neck. Then she wriggled around in the confined space and pushed her superb bosom towards him until she had almost pressed them into his face.

'Fancy them, Rob?' she breathed in a husky whisper.

He reached down, clasping those marvellously pneumatic tits. They were heavy and pear-shaped, the nipples a delicate raspberry pink, long and inviting. He licked each one in turn, eyes closed in rapture, like a baby at the breast, and then with an audible sigh he took as much as he could deep into his mouth.

His tongue swirled around her nipple just as Debbie's had with his, nipping and teasing, caressing and cajoling. She threw her head back at the sheer pleasure of the sensation, her hands playing with his hair, running through it, feeling the individual strands. Rob took a lot of care of it, always used the right shampoos and stuff. For a bloke, he had very fine hair.

He released the nipple from his mouth and saw it glistening and swollen to twice the size of the other one. She looked down at him through her mane of blonde hair and smiled encouragingly.

'The other one,' she murmured. She had the devil in her tonight, sure enough.

He repeated the exercise, licking and lapping, feeling with his hands how strong her back muscles were as she pushed her chest forward towards him. She seemed to be pulling him up and on to her breast like a mother with her baby, urging him to suck, offering him not just pleasure but life itself. He noticed the marks on her skin where her brassière had held her flesh at bay.

They rolled over to lie side by side on the bed. All the while her tongue and lips and hands had been hungrily seeking his body. His own hand slid between her legs. She moved slightly to accommodate him and then he could feel the soft, crinkly fur of her pubic mound and touch the lips that gaped so invitingly. He closed his eyes, alive only to the experience of his exploring fingers, the different textures, the hot and cool, the wet and dry.

She was incredibly aroused – he had noticed how her pants were soaked right through when she slipped them off and tossed them on to the floor. The first time he had ever slipped his fingers inside her he had noticed that special kind of wetness and yet her pussy was as tight as a glove, no slack in there at all. It was all her natural hormones, or something, the way those juices flowed. She was so wet that he wondered – and, knowing Debbie, it wasn't beyond the bounds of possibility – if she had already come. He ran a finger experimentally along the warm, slippery groove of her vagina. She moaned softly, and spread her legs wider for him. He stroked her gently, his fingers delicately exploring the sensitive folds that he knew so well by now, his knuckle brushing against the erect clitoris that he knew exactly where to find.

He opened his eyes and saw she was looking at him again, willing him on. *So that's what love looks like*, he told himself, and kissed her gently on the forehead. He pushed a finger deep into her vagina, and then a second one, and her gaze never faltered. Her tongue snaked out and sought his, one arm wrapped casually and affectionately around his shoulder, the other lying between his thighs, loosely cradling his cock. His hips moved slowly and easily against hers, like a long, low, loping blues rhythm, sensuous and easy. She matched him, note for note, lick for lick. He felt good.

When she came, with his fingers still wriggling inside her, it was without obvious display of fire or fury. She sighed, drew in her breath, held him tightly and stopped moving altogether. Her eyes, for the first time, were tight closed. Then she let out a great, shuddering exhalation of breath and flopped back against the pillow, a gentle smile playing around her lips.

They lay together, soundlessly, for several minutes before he climbed on top of her. Her pussy, when he entered her, was tight and welcoming. He felt enveloped and embraced at the same time, as though she were urging him ever deeper inside her. Debbie hiked her legs up over his own, spilling the bedclothes all over the floor, and it seemed to draw him in even further. Slowly he began to move inside her, swaying and sliding, an inaudible beat pulsing through his blood like it had been earlier that evening in the club, something you couldn't hear, only sense. It all seemed so long ago now, fucking under the pier, the fight, the party. This must have been the fourth time he and Debbie had fucked that day – incredible. And still, it seemed, she was hungry for more.

She matched his every move, pushing up against him when he pushed against her and then, with perfect synchronisation, drawing away again. As he felt himself drifting away, her hips

197

pressing up to meet his every urgent thrust, he drew his penis out almost to the glans and then, with deliberate slowness, slid it all the way back in again.

She cried out. 'Oh yes,' she hissed in his ear. 'Do it like that.'

He pulled out again, and in, each thrust like another new entry into her virgin vagina. The sense of excitement that he experienced was incredible. This wasn't fucking any more – this must be what they meant by making love. She raked her fingers across his back, more than playfully – it inflicted a sharp and momentary pain on him that only served to heighten his awareness of the sensations that were running riot through his body.

Slowly, consciousness of everything else began to ebb away. The caravan, the tangled bedcovers, even the early-morning breeze that had played through the open window – all slowly drifted away, unheeded and forgotten, until there was only the two of them, lost in a world of muscle and flesh, of fluid and feelings, wandering alone through the darkened realm of the senses.

His body seemed possessed of a gentle, inordinate strength. He powered himself up from his elbows, taking the full weight of his torso on to his wrists, and thrust hard into her. She squealed – really squealed this time – but he was almost heedless, driven by his own biological urgency, his senses aflame. Their rhythm built up in intensity, each in turn adding a new twist, a different way of pushing, one's tongue from time to time seeking the other's and then pulling away, trailing across cheek or shoulder, soft wet trails of saliva invisibly mingling with body sweat.

Until, finally, he threw himself forward over the edge of the cliff, aware only fleetingly of the tumult in his loins, the pressing urgency, the contractions and spasms and pulsing outburst of

198

energy that preceded that great and final stillness. And he realised, without knowing why, that he was weeping.

Camille and Richie went back upstairs once all the fuss was over. They'd been lucky – another half an hour or so and the party would have finished. As it was, Debbie had come rushing inside, all panicked and flustered, and got help.

The college was settling down for the night – doors closing, people saying goodnight in a half-dozen different languages. With so many people milling about, Camille was able to smuggle him in without any difficulty.

She took him to her room. He tried to kiss her even while she was closing the door behind them but she resisted. He couldn't see why, but when he turned and looked around the room he could understand.

Kneeling up on the bed, wearing bra and pants and nothing else, was a girl he'd seen at the party. She smiled at him.

'Say hello to Richie, Françoise.'

'Hello Richie.' She pronounced it *Ree-shee*, in an accent so thick you could have cut slices off it and served it with the Sunday roast. It was obvious she'd not been at the language school long, or they'd have done something about it.

Richie felt like he was going to faint clean away. There was a rushing in his head. None of this was real. Was it some kind of gag, a set-up? He half expected Rob or, worse still, Jeremy Beadle to come leaping out from behind a cupboard door.

Camille nudged him and brought him back to earth.

'Hello, Françoise,' was all he managed to say. His throat was dry and his heart was ready to pump a hole right through the front of his chest.

Camille produced a bottle of wine and some paper cups. So,

the party was going to continue, was it? Sex and violence, that was what this evening was all about, like a really good night on the telly. This was turning into something else, sure enough. He was only halfway through his first drink and tugging on the joint that Camille had passed him when Françoise was snuggling up to him.

'Camille says you have a nice big dick and you know how to use it,' she breathed in his ear. She pronounced every word separately, as if there was a big space around it, but the meaning was clear.

'Does she now?' replied Richie. 'And something tells me you're anxious to find out if it's true.'

He didn't think the French girl – he assumed she was French, with a name like that – could understand all that much of what he was saying but he reckoned they were still speaking a common language all the same. He had certainly liked the look of her when he'd seen her at the party earlier – short cropped blonde hair, big cornflower blue eyes and nice-looking tits. She wasn't very tall, but then neither was he for that matter. He usually, when in waggish mode, put it down to malnutrition in the slums and a poor diet during the war, but he didn't reckon Françoise was up to that. Instead he kissed her very gently on the side of the cheek. The dope he'd just smoked was incredibly strong too – there was a rushing in his ears to add to his palpitations, and his skin seemed to come out in pinpricks.

Camille slipped out of her clothes, came and sat next to them on the bed. She looked ravishing in the dim light of the room, just a couple of candles burning and a bedside lamp. And she was into double-diddling too. Maybe, who could know, she might even have a lesbo scene going with Françoise. It was all getting a bit too much for Richie to take in. He was sure he'd wake up any minute and find the sheets sticky with sperm.

Now Richie was the only one wearing clothes, but not for long. They took them off him one by one, the two of them acting like a team, and he could feel his heart racing. When they eased his pants off he was glad he had an absolute whopper to show them, as stiff as a board and twice as tasty, and that made him feel even better. *Big is beautiful*, he used to like to say. He reckoned Françoise could just about manage that, whichever end she chose to have him in first.

Acutely aware of the presence of Camille, who was stroking his thighs with one hand while, with the other, she ran her fingers through his hair, he could only groan with pleasure as Françoise covered his face with hot, wet kisses. *Christ*, he thought, *this is just absolutely fucking unbelievable*. It was like the sort of thing you read about in girlie magazines – usually it's two blokes who get picked up by these two bored housewives, or the guy who comes home one afternoon and finds his wife in bed with the next door neighbour. He'd always been a bit turned on by that kind of thing but he never in a million years ever reckoned it might happen to him, still less in a foreign fucking language school with a couple of girls who could hardly speak English. *Well*, he reflected, *neither can I*.

Camille gently began stroking his bursting cock even while he was necking with Françoise. It couldn't be more than an hour or so since he'd screwed her, but he was already worried that he was going to come too soon, so great was the feeling inside him. She was frigging him up and down now and he was scared nearly shitless that he was going to come all over her hand, especially now that he was squeezing Françoise's tits and getting quite a tidy scene going with her as well.

Think of something really boring, he told himself to try and stop the urge within his balls. *Think of something so dull it would send even John Major to sleep.* His mind raced; he wasn't going to have any more of that stuff, it was making his head spin. So he thought, and thought hard. Cardboard boxes. Ryvitas. A motorway service area. Youth programmes on TV. Any Channel 4 film. Pink Floyd. Janet Street-Porter. Chinese food. *Eastenders.* *Carry On* films. Barbara Windsor's boobs – oh God, no, think of something boring, anything but sex. He tried to summon up imagery from within himself – history lessons at school, the Open University, *Blue Peter*, DIY superstores, electrical showrooms, WH Smiths, Our Price Records, shopping malls, car parks, Ford Mondeos, caravans – he wondered where Debbie and Rob had got to. It would be different from now on with them going at it behind the curtain. And then back to the boring thoughts, even as Camille took his cock into her mouth and began to suck, oh so slowly and oh so sensually.

Liverpool's away strip. The entire Arsenal team. A nil-nil midweek at Elland Road. Stan Collymore. El fucking Tel. The guy from the Football Association who was always on the news. Turnip fucking Taylor – do I not like that?

Oh Christ, he was thinking about men – did that mean he was gay or something? But the treatment seemed to be working. He didn't feel any more like he was going to shoot his load. He could relax, enjoy himself, go with the flow. He began to calm down, didn't feel quite so hot and sweaty. The first rush of dope was beginning to wear off, thank God.

Next thing he knew, Camille had climbed on to his lap and spitted herself slowly on him. For a minute or two they more or less just stayed there, hardly moving, but then they began a slow, insidious, unmistakable rhythm. Richie felt a sudden rush of excitement, ground his hips in time to the way she was moving.

This time, it was the chemicals produced by his own body that went racing round his bloodstream, not the ones that were grown under lamps in a huge shed near Rotterdam.

'No, lie still,' ordered Camille. He did as he was told. She raised herself up until only the head of his penis was still enfolded in her vagina. And then, using her pussy muscles alone, she squeezed him as hard as she could.

'There,' she said. 'Can you feel that?'

'Of course I can. That's amazing. How do you do it?'

'That's my little secret,' she said. 'Do you like it?'

He lay back on the bed, oblivious now to anything but the sensations that came from his groin. She squeezed him again, and again. The sensation was divine. Then she would slide her hips down until his penis was fully swallowed up within her before once more pulling herself up, her luscious backside poised in mid-air.

Richie could see how his cock slipped inside her, felt the rich covering of fur as it brushed against his balls. All the time she was doing this alternate pushing and teasing, the delicious squeezing of the most sensitive parts of his anatomy.

'OK,' said Camille. 'Now it's Françoise's turn. We've got all night for each other. We don't want to tire each other out too soon, do we?'

No chance of that, thought Richie as, with elegant grace, Camille slid off him and he was able to quickly shed his remaining clothes. After a fortnight or more without, he reckoned he could keep going for days on end now. He was sure he'd not be fit for anything in the morning. Christ, it was the morning, he noticed from the clock on the bedside table. It was nearly five o'clock and he could hear the birds beginning to twitter outside.

Françoise quickly took her friend's place. She had taken off her bra and pants and stood there naked before him. Richie, wanting to have her just as she was, reached out to her and pulled her to him, on top of him, his heart pounding with lust. His hands reached around her waist and grasped her plump bum-cheeks, squeezing them even as he began greedily to tongue her luscious pink nipples.

She moaned, her tongue seeking his. There was no need to say anything. Their bodies did all the communicating that was necessary.

She wasn't perhaps quite as tight as Camille or, maybe it was the excessive lubrication that filled her pussy, fuelled by desire, fired up by her having just watched Richie and Camille making love. Richie felt his penis thrust up deep inside her and then the two of them were pushing away at each other, the hardness of his cock contrasting with her pliant wetness of her pussy, her legs parted around his hips, their thighs together. She must only be seventeen or eighteen, thought Richie, and he fancied her like fuck. If he hadn't have already been with Camille, he'd have made a bee-line for her.

'Why aren't there girls like you where I live?' he gasped between thrusts. Girls who looked like Camille and Françoise certainly existed in the North East, but they could have come from another planet. He saw them from time to time, shopping in the Metro Centre, driving past in smart white cars with big spoilers on the back. He never felt he'd be in bed with two of them at the same time, smoking their dope and squeezing their tits.

'Why aren't there boys like you where we live?' said Camille. 'They're so boring – all they're interested in is football and how many beers they can drink.'

Richie didn't feel that was a million miles off the mark but he kept quiet. He was becoming very tactful in his old age.

'And what's so special about me?' he said, as the first intimations of his inevitable and irresistible orgasm began to fill his loins.

'Because you know what a girl wants—'

'Which is?'

'To be fucked senseless. Come on, Richie, screw her hard. And then you can fuck me all over again.'

With his tongue Col tasted the smooth flesh at the top of Carole's thighs, ran it along through her belly so he could smell the scent of her sex, warm and musky and unquestionably waiting for him. Through her dark bush he could see the pouting pussy lips, pink and swollen. He buried her face between her thighs, seeking out the hidden folds and recesses, and she moved herself to press her pussy against his face, her legs over his shoulders.

They were in his living room still. They'd not been able to make it up to the bedroom in time. And yet the curious thing was that, even as she came inside and he put the kettle on to make her the cup of tea he'd promised her, he'd not intended going to bed with her. Neither, he thought, had she. It had just happened, the way it so often did.

Col loved to go down on women, to find their secret places, to give them the pleasure they craved – it was one of his great strengths as a lover. The flesh of Carole's vagina was smooth and firm to the touch and, as Col licked her out with the discerning appetite and appreciation of a carnal gourmet, he was aware of her excitement at what he was doing to her and the finesse with which his tongue did its work. He tortured her and teased her, withholding his darting, probing tongue for long, agonising seconds before it came flickering out again. And then he was subtle and tender, breathing gently on her pussy to bring out the

205

full range of sensual experience that was open to her.

He wondered why he'd felt so incredibly aroused. Was it, perhaps, because he'd felt in some way frustrated because Liz had been called away, denying him the wild night of passion that he'd been looking forward to? No, he didn't think it was that. That suggested he was in some way angry or frustrated with Liz and he didn't feel like that at all. No, this thing here with Carole, a woman he'd never seen in his life before, had simply happened because it was meant to happen.

When she came, she almost crushed his upper vertebrae, so hard did she clamp his head between her thighs. She let out a great, shuddering sigh and Col could feel the ripples running through her, as irresistible and forceful as the waves breaking on the beach a couple of hundred yards away. Only very slowly did her muscles begin to relax and then, not without a certain difficulty, Col managed to extricate himself.

'I'll get that cup of tea now,' he said, but when he looked down on her, sprawled in an attitude of abandon with her legs still spread apart, still wearing her rucked up sweatshirt, he realised she was actually asleep. There was something strangely familiar about her face but he couldn't quite place it. These days, he hardly saw anybody new from one week's end to the next but in the past, there had been a lot of people in a lot of places. It obviously didn't matter much who she was or where she came from, or he'd have remembered.

Meeting Carole was like finding something wonderful on the beach. His whole house was groaning with all the different kinds of pebbles he'd picked up – jet and amber among the more familiar quartz and flint. There were some that, by rights, shouldn't have been in that part of the world at all, brought there by who knew what currents across the fathomless seas.

Almost every day he would find something interesting. On Saturday morning, just yesterday, he'd found a coconut, perfectly fresh. The week before, a silver thimble, the top badly dented but a silver thimble still. It was hallmarked and Liz was going to look it up in a book. It was very old. She had wondered, when he'd shown it to her, if it might have come from a wreck off the coast but whatever there was out there, was already well enough charted. Sunken treasure and things was just dreams, really. Still, he would have liked to have known how that silver thimble happened to be there, just sitting on the edge of the water, lapped by the tide, waiting for him to discover it. It was still sitting on the kitchen window sill in front of him as he waited for the kettle to boil.

'This is the most amazing place,' said Carole as he came back into the living room with two steaming mugs.

'Thank you,' he said. What else could he say? Compliment her on her excellent taste?

'I love these paintings.' She pointed to a couple on the wall, one with a woman's hand resting on a vase, the other a very tiny landscape that, nevertheless, seemed to contain the essence of the enormous open countryside around them.

'Who are they by?' she went on. 'They seem familiar.'

He looked at her. Standing by the fireplace with her back to him, she was naked from the waist down. She had a nice bum on her, sure enough.

'I painted them,' he said simply. 'A few years back.'

'You're a painter?'

'Some of the time. I'm a fisherman too.'

'A little bit of everything,' she murmured as she took the mug from him.

Later, they went upstairs to his room. She kept stopping to look

207

at things, the shelves full of objects, the stuff hanging from the walls and ceilings. There were maps, telescopes, obscure instruments. There were a lot of flowers, too, and paintings. Very few photographs, she noticed, apart from a few in the tiny kitchen, which were obviously of friends. Not married, she could tell at a glance. Might have been once but not any longer. But he seems to have got his act together.

She knew he would have a bed like this – big and old, almost filling the room, covered by a patchwork quilt that was very faded but well cared for nevertheless. There was some good furniture, a Georgian dresser that could easily have fetched four or five at auction and the fireplace was a gem, obviously original. It would have been a lovely room to have spent time in, looking out over the sea, the broad window sill with its collection of shells and starfish. The floorboards were bare and scrubbed almost bleach-white but there were thick rugs on them and the room was warm and inviting, like a sheikh's inner sanctum. It had a nice smell to it too – a man smell that had nothing to do with aftershave or sportswear, but something much subtler, far less tangible. She could tell he was her kind of guy just from the way he undressed her.

He fucked her long and slow. She loved the feeling, lying there in that big comfortable bed, with the seagulls wheeling about outside the window, their cries harsh in the early morning air. She came very quickly again, just as intensely as before, and before she drifted off to sleep in his arms she felt like she had, at last, come home.

Chapter Seven

Richie had rather thought and hoped he'd get to spend the night with Camille and Françoise but, at six-thirty in the morning, they chucked him out. Smack on to the street.

It was a bit of an earwicker, that one. There he'd been, lying snug as a bug between the two of them, with his worn-out, semi-flaccid willy pressed up into the furrow of Camille's bum while Françoise was curled around his back, her boobs pressing nicely against his shoulder blades. Paradise, that was. Still, he told himself philosophically as his feet beat the pavement, all good things must come to an end one day. Their winning streak last season, the long and seemingly unending spell of hot weather, his own job prospects – all of it, sooner or later, bit the dust. Wallop.

He'd thought, sure as sixpence, that they'd let him stay. But Camille had nudged him awake and kissed him on the forehead and told him they weren't allowed all-night visitors at Garfield Hall.

There's not a lot of the night worth arguing about, he'd murmured as he struggled sleepily and unwillingly into his clothes, but it wasn't worth making a fuss about it. They seemed as disappointed as he was. He was sure he was good enough for one last crack before he got stuck into a big fried Sunday breakfast.

He kissed both of them goodbye, said he'd give Camille a ring, made his way silently down the corridors and, as he had been told, out of the rear exit by the car park, away from the night security man's office. Where he'd got to when they had their dust-up with Mick Rowlandson, God alone knew, but they'd come out of it all right and a good three points up into the bargain.

He looked back at the college, at the curtained windows festooned with stickers for roadshows and discos and animal rights. He was reminded, for no apparent reason, of what he'd heard about the residences at Durham University – or was it Newcastle? Women were allowed in the students' rooms until midnight but they had to keep one foot on the ground at all times.

He liked that, once he'd figured it out. It was his brother Dave who told him that. He'd told him another one, a true story allegedly, about some guy who was sitting his finals in law at Oxford, and halfway through the exam he'd put his pen down and stuck up his hand. The invigilator said he'd have to be escorted to the lav and back but the guy said that wasn't what he wanted.

He wanted a pint.

The invigilator thought he'd gone mad but the guy stuck it out and said *no, I want a pint of beer and I have a right to have it*. So the invigilator spoke to the other invigilator – all the pens had stopped scratching by this stage – and they sent for the Dean, and they all put their heads together and got out the college book of statutes and there it was, in very small print in an ordnance of 1583, that gentlemen were entitled to bread and ale during their examinations. It had last been empowered in 1690 but no one had thought to remove it from the statute book.

I'm not bothered about the bread, your man kindly interjected. *It's just the beer I want. Beck's, if you have it.*

He'd obviously done his homework and there was not much

210

else they could do about it. So they sent down to the refectory and got him a bottle and a glass and he knocked it back with great relish and burped it back up again and then finished his paper while the Dean and the invigilators huddled in a corner.

As the guy came out of the building, the Provost intercepted him, asked if he'd enjoyed his beer and, on receiving an affirmative reply, promptly fined him one silver sovereign for failing to wear a ceremonial sword.

He sniggered quietly to himself. He didn't want people to see him laughing in the street, but that was the way he felt. It was the first time Richie had ever been out in the town at that impossibly early hour, especially on a Sunday when he should have been back at the caravan sleeping off last night's beer. His ears were still ringing from the disco and his eyes, bleary with lack of sleep, felt like they were full of sand, but he was on top of the world all the same.

His mind kept going back to all the things they'd got up to in that room with Camille and Françoise. He reckoned he must have come five or six times, and his balls fairly ached to prove it. He couldn't wait to tell Rob, not to boast openly about it, of course, but just to drop a little hint here and a little hint there, nothing too obvious at first, like dangling a baited line off the end of the pier until finally he hooked it. And then he'd let him have it, the full story, exclusive on page 3. *My naughty night with sex-crazed students. Funboy Richie says 'Entente cordiale? Not 'alf, mate'. My nude romps with lingo lovelies.*

There was hardly any traffic about at that time of the morning. A prowl car came by and the flat-tops peered across and gave him the once-over, but he looked like he had a home to go to so they gave him no bother.

It was an incredible feeling, really, being out there at that time of day. The sun was bright already but the air was still crisp and fresh, not a cloud in the sky. There was a perfection in his heart as well, a feeling of satisfaction, of something laid to rest.

He was walking along Eastern Avenue, grinning to himself, just the way he'd been when he'd first clapped eyes on Camille and her mate. He wondered where she'd been last night. After glimpsing her down the Zero Six, she'd vanished. She certainly hadn't been at the party, or he'd have pointed her out to Rob, just to prove she existed.

It was funny, that. Still, he reckoned, he'd got better things to worry about. Now he wanted nothing more than to get back to the caravan and get some breakfast inside and then some good hard kip.

Giselle was in her room, alone at last. She took off the skin-tight PVC catsuit that she'd worn, mostly on but sometimes off, for the whole of the previous night. It felt nice on but it felt nice off, peeling it away like a second skin.

She looked in the big bathroom mirror at herself. That was one of the things she liked about working these occasional weekends at The Laurels. She had the chance to relax in real luxury, to pamper herself in a way that was all but impossible at Garfield Hall. Shared bathrooms, communal rooms, the general lack of privacy – how she wished sometimes that things could be different.

She'd give the clothes and her money – five hundred pounds, nearly four thousand francs, not bad for a night's work – to Brigitte, who was getting a mini-cab back to college. She wanted to be alone for a while, to collect her thoughts, maybe to take a walk along the cliffs or something.

What a night it had been. She stood there naked as the bath

taps ran, absently stroking the thick, luxuriant towels.

She had been with various people during the course of the evening. A couple from London who said they were on the board of Asprey's, the royal jewellers; a woman from the Foreign Office, very crisp and businesslike to talk to but between the sheets, she was an absolute tigress on heat; two gay men – or perhaps they were bi – who were fashion photographers. They just wanted her to lie there and pose for them – no cameras, of course, they weren't allowed at The Laurels – while they wanked each other off. That kind of thing was easy money for her.

Best of all had been that nice but strict woman in the bondage gear and the guy she was with. She got the impression they'd only just met. He said he was in television and she recognised him immediately. She was sure now that he was the guy she'd seen the previous afternoon driving along Eastern Avenue when she was coming back from her walk with Camille. Afternoon television would never be the same again, she wryly reflected.

Giselle rarely did penetrative sex on evenings like this. It wasn't her decision, it was what her customers seemed to want. So she would suck and touch and watch and feel, whatever they asked her to do or she felt like doing herself. It was odd that, the way she rarely got fucked. It didn't enormously bother her. There were other ways of enjoying herself.

It seemed to be her presence that excited them most, this tall blonde French girl in the skin-tight, shiny suit, the wickedly high heels, the pony tail. That Barbarella stuff was old hat even in the sixties but it had always been big in France and Giselle had the flair and panache to pull it off, to make it different, to make it hers and hers alone. She managed to look both alluring and dangerous at the same time and, for men as well as women, that was a powerful aphrodisiac.

Paul and the woman – what was her name now, Mandy? Candy? A real swinger's name but all but forgotten now, barely hours afterwards – had quickly initiated her into their little games.

Both of them were naked and they took it in turns to lie with her on the bed in her room, the same room she always had every month. They must have liked the feeling of her PVC next to their skins – a lot of people did, she reckoned, especially the English. There were quite a few foreign guests at The Laurels as well but they didn't seem to go quite so much for that kind of thing. Brigitte did very well with them, though – straight sex and French, mostly, because Brigitte had an exceptionally tight pussy which was a marketable commodity in the flesh business.

Paul had unzipped her and was playing with her tits while Candy – yes, of course that was her name, how could she forget so soon? – while Candy watched, touching herself down there all the while. She had a nice bush of auburn hair. Giselle had offered to lick her there and then but the woman declined, politely but firmly. Later, she said. Something about her told her she was a schoolteacher.

The next thing was, Paul had got into Candy from behind while Giselle was invited to watch. She had seen quite a few people doing it by now – it had started many years ago when she had first seen her parents at it in the summer house, and she had added to her experience considerably in the past few months – but she very much liked what she saw. He seemed very strong and elegant, very muscular, very much as she had fantasised about him from watching him on television. She had a slow, sensuous burn to her, a woman who took her pleasures voluptuously. She was sure she was into S&M in one form or another but the woman didn't ask for anything so maybe it was just a fantasy with her.

She'd thought that was what they wanted her for, because Giselle had all the things she needed in her room and she said so, but Candy just nodded and she knew better than to press her further.

Paul had a very large, very thick cock and Giselle had no difficulty imagining what his wife and co-presenter would look like with it in her mouth, in her pussy, up her bum. She was sure they would be up to anything, those two, even long before she had ever imagined meeting them in the flesh, so to speak, still less being in this kind of intimacy. Brigitte had told her she'd seen Carole Chivers in the dining room dressed in see-through black.

She stretched out in the bath water, chin-deep in suds, and breathed in the aroma of the expensive oils. She felt very good, very content. She liked what she did and she liked making money from it. She liked the class of customer The Laurels attracted. Mr Begbie, the man who arranged these little soirees, had asked if she would be interested in a little extra work, mostly in London on the well-paid diplomatic circuit, but she had always said no. It didn't really appeal to her and besides, she'd heard some unhappy stories about what really went on in the hotels around Park Lane. There was one place off Kensington High Street that was notorious. Sometimes girls ended up in hospital.

Her fingers strayed quite naturally to her pussy as she recalled what had happened next. Paul hadn't come in Candy but instead, he'd asked her to lie on the bed and unzip her PVC all the way down. She'd thought he would just want to pull himself off over her bare breasts but no, the next thing she knew was Candy had straddled over her and offered Giselle her pussy to be licked.

Of course, she'd jumped at the chance, that luscious auburn mound with the pouting pink lips pushing through the luxuriant dark cleft. Candy tasted as good as she looked, too, just like eating candy should be. Her tongue had snaked out and into Candy's forbidden places without any further bidding.

The next thing she was aware of was Paul's rampant cock pushing against them. He was crouched right over them now and it was obvious he wanted to fuck Candy while Giselle licked her out. It was a bit awkward at first – it always was – till they got themselves sorted out and comfortably settled on the bed and then they went at it.

Giselle was running her tongue along Candy's rich-tasting, swollen cleft and then along the length of Paul's cock. Sometimes he'd pull it out almost all the way and hold still so she could lick it right along its considerable length, from his big purple glans to his heavy balls. That was great, doing it like that. Although Candy's thighs got in the way she could see most of what the two of them were doing to her and it was terrifically exciting to watch. It didn't bother her that there wasn't much in it for her – that was why she was playing with herself now, in the bath, making up for it. She didn't always come when she was with someone like that, she never knew why.

Anyway, the juice had been practically flowing out of Candy's pussy and all over Giselle's chin, and Paul was on top of her, his thighs – he had nice legs, she noticed – on either side of her head. And then all of a sudden she could see his cock twitch and his breathing changed.

He pulled back and then, with considerable force, pushed himself right up inside Candy's pussy. Giselle opened her mouth and managed to get one of his balls between her lips and she could feel it contract immediately as his climax came on. She sucked and sucked and she could feel him pushing, the come positively shooting up that wonderful thick shaft of his and into Candy's welcoming pussy, and she could really feel his balls contracting as he did so. Candy was pushing and wriggling too, and squealing softly, and Giselle opened her eyes and had this wonderful vision of her pinky-wet slit with that cock jammed right up into her, her lips parted wide to take it all in and the hair matted with her juices and perspiration and come, and it wouldn't have taken more than the merest touch of a fingertip against her own clitoris for Giselle to have come herself, instead of waiting for now and the moment, that wonderfully rich moment, when she could finally let go, there in the warm bath, serene in luxurious and wanton privacy, at one with herself and her body.

Far away in the twisted landscape of his dreams, Billy Brilleaux walked naked across the dance floor of the Zero Six. He was surrounded by equally naked women, fervent in their admiration. At the far end of the room, surrounded by pulsing lasers and lights, was a windmill he had never seen before, in front of which stood Sue, her legs apart, waiting for him, her pouting pussy lips protruding prettily from those wickedly sheer panties.

Billy knelt before her, obedient. The women were clapping him now. He leaned forward, his tongue extended, and bestowed that first, slow, teasing, significant lick. His cock protruded massively from below his stomach, an animal of great power and potency. The sails of the windmill turned round and round.

He awoke quite suddenly, and was immediately aware of his erection, of the aching stiffness of it all, the early-morning hormones running riot. He blinked his eyes, unaccustomed to the clear white light of morning. The red digits on his bedside clock said 6:45. He had never noticed before the way that the : seemed to pulse. It puzzled him. He could feel a good solid early-morning fart coming on.

Once he'd got rid of it as discreetly as possible – he didn't want to show disrespect to Sue, who he always felt was a rung or two up the social ladder from himself – he felt a lot more comfortable. He was warm and snug and content. His eyelids began to droop again. He closed his eyes, trying to recall his dream, aware still of that monstrous erection between his legs.

The room, he could see it now, the people all around him, Sue in her black crotchless knickers. Everyone seemed to like him. Everyone smiled in acknowledgment. Half-dreaming, half-imagining, he resumed what he'd been doing to Sue's pussy, more reverently than ever.

It was incredibly real, like it was all happening to him. He knew it wasn't real, of course, but he was happy for it to go on that way.

Once more he knelt before her, once more she parted her legs invitingly for him, the scrap of sheer black knicker that stood between himself and the moment of ecstasy. Greedily his mouth and lips closed over that coral-tinged oyster, and his tongue flickered out.

The clock flipped over, unseen. 6:45. 6:46. 6:47. 6:48. All the time the : pulsed like a little heartbeat but Billy, lost in his reverie, no longer saw it.

He pressed himself against Sue, her bum warm against his body. She sighed, and stirred, and rolled obligingly over on to her back. She opened her eyes and looked at the clock. It said 6:50. She could feel Billy's big erection hard against her thigh, his arms thrown protectively around her shoulders. She could see her clothes, his clothes, scattered around the untidy room, the stacks of tapes, the magazines.

She turned around, wide awake, and reached down to Billy's groin.

But Billy had gone back to his dreams.

* * *

218

Richie went back along the clifftop path, looking down at the grey waves as they rolled in and out, and ducked through the twisted wire fence that marked the edge of the caravan site. He hoped Rob and Debbie were there, rather than at her place – he realised he'd forgotten his key, and he'd nowhere else to go, short of knocking up Billy Brilleaux who would probably be on the job again with Sue and hardly likely to welcome him with open arms.

It was not quite a quarter to eight, but the sun was already high in the china-blue cloudless sky. The tide was going out fast, leaving the beach clean and scoured for the holidaymakers who, freshly dressed and breakfasted, would start making their way down to the beach in an hour or so. For now, an absolute silence hung over the site. Even the gulls were high overhead and made no sound. He walked down the long rows of tin shacks, all of them in the same boring colours, cream or beige or silver relieved only by paintwork in the kind of dull-as-ditchwater pastel colours you only encountered at Social Security offices.

What a place to come for a holiday, he told himself, to sit for a week inside a tin box with your neighbours shitting and farting not ten feet away, the kids squabbling over who got what, across a narrow little track where the cars were pulled up, the Sierras and Cavaliers and Montegos, conformist cars for conformist people. You never saw anything like a Xantia or one of the souped-up Peugeots here. That was what Richie would have, given the choice and enough money. He was beginning to feel quite French already and he'd known Camille for no more than seven or eight hours. Once more those lewd thoughts started to flow through his mind.

He caught a glimpse of Mick Rowlandson and a couple of other guys in leather jackets about a second before they would have glimpsed him. They were coming along the top road, trying to look nonchalant but he knew where they were heading. Quite what they had in mind was another matter but he knew damn well it wasn't to knock Rob up to say *how do* and would he like a cup of tea in bed.

His heart sank into his boots with the speed of an express lift. Here was trouble and no mistake. One of the guys with Mick was even wearing a Chelsea scarf.

Quick and quiet as he could, he ducked down and scurried along the next line of caravans. He knew he hadn't much time. He had been almost home when he saw Mick and his bunch of heavies but they still had to go through the main gate and along the main avenue. He had two minutes, if that, to get whoever was in the caravan out. There was no point in trying to tough it out this time. After his humiliation at Rob's hand, Mick would be thirsting for revenge.

Richie doubled around the back of the caravan, tapped furiously on the end window where the fold-down bunk Rob slept in was. There was no response. He wondered, for one glorious moment, if Rob might not be there at all, might have gone back to Debbie's place, but he didn't think it likely. Her flatmate's parents were down for the weekend.

He tapped again, harder this time. Wake up for God's sake, you dozy bugger. Still no reply. The panic was rising in him fast. He wanted to run and hide, to get out of the way of whatever was coming. They couldn't try and barricade themselves in. The door was so loose, a child of ten could have pulled it off its hinges. Caresaway Holidays offered what they called 'no frills bargain breaks' and the no frills seemed to extend to things like routine maintenance and basic security.

A footstep made him turn round. It was Rob, holding the News of the Screws. He must have been up to the camp shop – it opened on seven on Sunday – to get the paper, check the football results.

His expression of alarm must have registered on Rob.

'What's up mate?' he said, a look of anxiety passing quickly over his face.

'Mick Rowlandson's here,' said Richie. 'I just saw him on the top road.'

'Where's he now?' said Rob and made to look down the line of caravans – the daft sod – but Richie grabbed him by the arm.

'No time for that. We got to get out of here. He means business.'

Then he remembered Debbie.

'We've got to get her out,' he said, panic-stricken.

'Who?'

'Debbie.'

'Debbie's gone back home,' said Rob. 'She left her car here. She went off about half an hour ago. She goes to the sauna on Sunday morning. It's cheaper before eight.'

Richie felt an indefinable surge of relief. It was as great, in its way, as the aftermath of his first orgasm of the night.

'Don't tell me your life history, mate,' he hissed. 'Let's get out of here.'

They ran off down the line of caravans, away from the direction Mick Rowlandson and his henchmen were approaching from, towards the sea. There was a narrow defile led partway down the cliff and they'd just about reached it when they heard a shout from behind them. They turned, and there were the three of them.

'Come here, you fucker,' called out Mick, shattering the peace of the Sunday-morning caravans.

Rob and Richie didn't stand around. They were off down that ravine like a couple of startled rabbits, kicking up dust and loose stones which went bouncing and dancing past them as they scrambled down towards the beach.

'Shall we split up?' said Richie when they reached the bottom. They could see their pursuers coming down after them, maybe a couple of hundred yards behind. One of them picked up a rock and lobbed it at them.

'No, best not,' said Rob. 'At least we'll be two against three. If we split up and they get one of us, they'll damn near kill us.'

They shot off along the beach, towards Crab Bay. Richie was tired and hungry and shagged out but he ran faster than he'd ever done in his life. The way he flew along the wet sand, he could have given that black guy who played for Wigan a run for his money.

Rob was no slouch either. He'd been quite a runner when they were in school, middle-distance stuff. They legged it as fast as they possibly could.

They turned round just once. Mick Rowlandson and his cronies were a long way back but they were still there, thundering along. Mick they knew they could take but those others were big bastards, they'd seen them the night before in the car park at Garfield Hall and they knew how to ride a punch in the gut.

'Where are we going?' panted Rob and all of a sudden Richie hadn't a clue what to do next. They should have gone the other way, back towards the town. Out here there was bugger all, just dunes and inlets and mud. They'd walked right into it.

But they carried on nevertheless. There was no point in turning round to face their inevitable fate.

Richie's heart was really hurting now and it was painful to breathe. He had a big stitch low down on his left side and the laces on one of his trainers had come undone. Rob was up ahead a ways, sprinting still with his head back.

All of a sudden he stopped dead. There was a boat up on the shingle, a little pale-blue fibreglass thing, not much bigger than a plastic stacker box but a boat just the same. It was the kind of thing the crabbers used for punting about just off-shore.

Richie ran up. Miracle of miracles, there were a couple of oars in the boat, stowed away down the side away from prying eyes.

'Do you know how to sail one of these? You used to go sailing.' Rob was yelling at him, wide eyed, his breath coming in great racking gasps.

'That was kayaks. We used to go out on Kielder dam when I was at the youth club. You wouldn't come, remember, you were too busy shagging Sharon Peters. Or at least you said you were.'

'What do you mean by that?'

'Lefty Wright said he knobbed her at Kevin Coiley's party and he was the first. That was long after she'd finished with you.'

'What's Sharon fucking Peters got to do with it? For God's fucking sake, man, what does it matter now?'

He looked around, furious. The others weren't more than a hundred yards away, toiling along in their heavy boots.

For such a little thing, the boat was surprisingly heavy, but Rob and Richie somehow managed to manhandle it down the gently shelving shingle. The tide was going out quite fast now, but that would be to their advantage. If they could just get the bloody thing to float, it would help carry them away from their pursuers.

In the distance Richie heard a deep boom, and then another. Sometimes the RAF did practise bombing runs along the coast but never this close to Dunwich. He looked ahead, out to sea. Black clouds were building up along the horizon. There was thunder in the air.

Their feet were splashing water now but still that boat was bumping along the bottom. Mick Rowlandson and company were close enough for them to see the anger in their faces, the veins standing out livid. And then, buoyed up at last, the boat floated.

'Get in,' ordered Richie, 'and get fucking paddling.'

He continued to push from the stern, up to his knees now, while Rob lashed out furiously with the oar. For a sudden anxious second Richie felt his leg giving way and realised he'd reached the steep shelf where the beach suddenly dipped down, where the safe bathing limits were strung up all along the coast. In their blind panic he'd all but missed the signs.

Instinctively he reached out and grabbed the back of the boat. They were starting to make way now. With one last effort torn from his tortured lungs and muscles he pushed himself out of the swirling tide and hauled himself into the boat.

Pure adrenaline kept him going, made him pick up the other paddle and get to work. He looked back and there was Mick, up to his waist in water, shouting, making violent gestures at them. The other guys were standing at the edge of the water, like big cissies afraid of getting their feet wet.

Rob and Richie got the hang of it pretty quickly. It was different from Sunday afternoons on the pond in the park with your favourite uncle. Then, there wasn't someone standing on the shore waiting to kick your fucking head in. So they pulled and sculled like they'd seen it done every April on the Boat Race and before they realised it Mick Rowlandson looked like an angry little toy soldier standing there at the water's edge, still shouting at them.

The rain was starting to come down now, hot and heavy summer rain just like it had done yesterday, but Richie didn't care. Not even when a great boom of thunder made him jump. He was soaking wet already, from the sea and from all the running, but at least he was alive and so was Rob. He pulled his paddle out of the water and turned to face his mate.

'Rob,' he said quietly.

Rob turned to look at him. He looked exhausted, his hair plastered down over his forehead. The rain was streaming down his face.

'Is it true?'

There was a pause.

'Is what true?' said Rob as the tide took them further away to safety.

'About Sharon Peters? Did you really shag her?'

A clap of thunder woke Carole. One minute she was on a boat sailing down the Nile, watching the circus on the river bank, the next she was looking at the broad back of the man sleeping next to her. The room, the antique bed, the pictures – none of it made any sense until she remembered, in a flash of intuition, where she was and who she was with.

She didn't seem to have her watch with her. Propping herself up on her elbow, she half-climbed over Col, whose watch was on the bedside table.

He stirred and opened his eyes.

'Hello, Carole,' he said, softly smiling. He had lovely bedroom eyes. 'What time is it?'

'Jesus, it's nearly eight,' she said, scarcely believing the evidence of her own eyes. She felt like a guilty adulteress who'd overslept.

'You have to be somewhere?' asked Col, sitting up.

She smiled, a fast cold smile that gave nothing away.

'You're with somebody?' he said, intuitively knowing the answer.

'Well,' she began. 'It's not quite like that, but—'

'You have to be going?'

'I'm afraid I must.'

There was another huge boom of thunder, this time almost overhead. It made the house shake, and it made Carole jump. She could hear the rain battering against the window.

'Can I get you any breakfast?'

'Nothing, thanks. But coffee would be nice.'

He got out of bed, looking ravishing to her even in her anxious state, and pulled on an old dressing gown.

'I'll go see about it,' he said as he pulled the door to. 'The bathroom's just along here.'

She dressed quickly in last night's clothes, splashed water over her face. Her make-up didn't look too bad but could benefit soon from some major remedial work. By the time Col called to her from the foot of the stairs, she felt just about ready to face the world.

It seemed ironic that she, a woman who appeared before four or five million faces most afternoons, almost all of them strangers, should feel so anxious about meeting her husband again.

She went downstairs. He had coffee waiting for her in the tiny living room.

'Lovely cups,' she said as she sipped. 'And nice coffee too.'

He smiled. It was like the ads. He'd left that world behind, a long time ago. What lovely eyes he had, she thought. They looked so balanced and yet so sensitive at the same time.

She went to the window.

'Who lives in the houses over there?' she asked.

'People from London, mostly. They come down for the weekend. One of them's for sale.'

'Are you from London?'

'I lived there once. I live here now.'

'You don't miss it?'

'Not in the least.'

She looked around at the books and the paintings and decided he was probably right.

'I'll give you a lift back, if you like.'

'That would be kind,' she said. She didn't want to bother with the farrago of demurring. It was tipping down outside and she was only wearing a sweatshirt.

Their eyes met. There was, she noticed, no sign of a television in the room.

'You really don't know who I am, do you?' she said.

He turned the question round on her.

'Do you?' he answered simply.

Later, he drove her back towards Dunwich in his salt-rusted Volvo. It was still coming down cats and dogs.

'Shall I see you again?' he said when they reached the main coast road.

'Would you like to?'

He laughed, a gentle laugh. 'Yes, I think I would. How about you?'

She had already made a note of his telephone number, copied it down on a scrap of paper when he wasn't looking.

'I've written down the number of my mobile on the pad by the phone. Call me whenever you like. If I'm busy, you can leave a message.'

She recognised The Laurels up ahead. There was no sign of life behind the dark trees that screened it from the road. The rain was still streaming down.

'You can drop me here, if you like,' she said to him.

He pulled the Volvo into the side of the road. Again he looked at her with those quiet, knowing eyes, the half-smile playing on his lips.

'I'll call you,' she said as she opened the door, and then she kissed him lightly on the cheek. There was a brilliant flash of lightning. He told her to take care.

He watched her shapely ass as she crossed the road – still almost bereft of traffic, even at that hour of Sunday morning – and disappeared down the drive. The Laurels, he knew, was one of the most expensive hotels along the whole stretch of the coast. Still, she looked like the type who could afford it. She was married, definitely, had been anxious the whole journey back, wondering what she would say to her husband. She had media written all over her – a journalist perhaps? *Daily Mail? Hello?* Not his type, really, despite the fact that he had her number.

Put it down as a one-night stand, he said to himself, and then he turned the old car round and sped off back to Crab Bay. Big puddles had formed all over the road.

It was really coming down now, just as it had done yesterday. The wipers could hardly cope with it, so solid was the sheet of water through which he was driving. The windows were starting to mist up. He had almost reached the turn-off, his eyes instinctively glancing out to sea, when through the drifting gusts of rain he caught sight of a small boat bobbing up and down in the waves. It was quite a way out but there looked to be two people in it.

Spontaneously he winced. They shouldn't be out there, in that kind of weather, in an open boat. It looked like one of the crabmen's dinghies, but none of the regulars would be out there at that time on a Sunday, even in fine weather, let alone with the sky looming black and the wind gusting like billy-oh. It was a couple of kids, most likely, and if he didn't get a move on they'd be in big trouble.

What to do for the best? For the first time in years, he regretted not having a mobile phone. He could go home and phone the emergency number from there, or he could drive to Coxburgh and use the call box by the tiny jetty. It was about the same distance.

He decided on Coxburgh and put his foot down. He realised, as soon as he made the call, that it might already be too late, that they would probably be shipping water. His only course, given the time it would take for the rescue services to get their act together, was to put to sea himself.

He ran along the ramshackle wooden jetty to where the *Erica B* was tied up. Even in the comparative shelter of Coxburgh Creek she was riding uneasily on the rising sea. He jumped aboard, unlocked the cabin, set about starting her up. It usually took a few minutes of caressing her before she was turning over nicely but this morning, bless her, her ageing Perkins diesel coughed out the black stuff almost straight away and she was soon running like a train.

He knew, even as he cast off and swung her cautiously round in the shallow waters around the harbour, that it would be difficult to keep to the channel at such a low tide. He was also worried that the engine might fail on him. She was pumping out plenty of revs but there was a curious knocking, as if one of the big ends needed a rebore – it was only six months since they'd had to strip her down the last time.

He passed the lines of pleasure boats riding languidly at anchor, creating more of a wash than he'd ever made in his life. As he cleared the end of the long spit that separated Coxburgh from Crab Bay, he radioed the coastguard station, let them know what he was doing. Then he swung the *Erica B* around to starboard and headed off down the coast, about two hundred yards out to sea where he knew the water was deep and the currents favourable. The wind hit him almost immediately and he had to fight the wheel to keep from keeling over. He could see nothing ahead of him except a stormy sea and the endlessly driving rain.

Carole was just cutting into her grapefruit when she caught sight of Paul making his way, a trifle unsteadily, across the dining room towards her.

'Hi!' she called brightly. 'How d'you fancy a kipper? Or perhaps you'd like poached eggs?'

He sat down opposite her at their table by the window. The rain was easing up now and the sun was poking through clouds that were speeding away eastwards. Already, as her mother used to say, you could see enough blue sky to make a pair of sailor's trousers.

Paul's face, though, was as grey as the clouds. His eyes looked like beetles swimming in tomato soup. At the idea of food his body visibly recoiled.

'I was absolutely ravenous, but you were still sound asleep. So I came down to breakfast on my own. I hope you don't mind—'

All Paul wanted was to be left alone in a corner to die quietly. Somehow he managed to force a sip or two of black coffee between his ashen lips but he averted his eyes when Carole tucked lustily into the big plate of bacon, sausage, egg, mushrooms, tomatoes, sautéed potatoes and fried bread that the waiter had brought.

'Would you like to order now, sir?' he asked solicitously, but Paul merely shook his head and tried to will his hands to stop shaking.

The dining room was almost deserted. It could accommodate forty or fifty covers easily but only a dozen or so were occupied at that time. Most of the guests at The Laurels were probably sleeping it off after their exertions of the previous night. A few die-hards, quite possibly, were still living it up, with other people's wives, other people's husbands, expensive machinery and expensive whores.

Gradually, consciousness returned to Paul. He persuaded the waiter to bring him a large Bloody Mary, for which he tipped him handsomely. He was still resisting solid food but he just about managed to nibble a few nibbles on a piece of toast.

The atmosphere in the dining room was quite unbelievable. After nine it started to fill up, but it was still very much as it would have been in any one of the hotels along Eastern Avenue and Northdene, the respectable ABC1s with their *Telegraphs* and *Sunday Times*, making jovial but inconsequential remarks to their fellow guests about the weather.

Barely minutes ago, hours at most, these people had been screwing each other senseless. They had ejaculated into willing mouths, penetrated every manner of orifice, enjoyed bodily sensations of all kind. There had been captains of industry with pierced penises in bed with two-hundred-pound hookers, while at least one titled lady – a regular in *Country Life* and *Tatler* – had been enjoying the indubitable pleasures of the lash at the hands of a demure French girl. Men who had spent the night crouching alone and cowering inside an iron cage, to be periodically lashed by thigh-booted Amazons with rouged nipples, now anxiously scanned the cricket scores, to see how well Middlesex or Northamptonshire were doing. It was a scene so English as to bring delight to the heart. Where inhibition had been so wildly abandoned, now every repression was safely and properly back in place. Only the odd tremble of the hand or reddening of the eye told of a night of recherché eroticism.

'I've been thinking, you know,' said Carole, as she tucked into toast and marmalade, 'I'd love to buy a little cottage around here for weekends. What do you think?'

Paul fixed her with a baleful eye.

'It's a long way to come for a weekend.'

'No, but a long weekend. You know, go on Thursday and come back on Monday.'

'What about the weather?' He nodded at the window and the heavy grey clouds. 'What about the show?'

'We could do it easily. If we set off straight away, it would be no problem. We could even get them to send a chopper. They'd do it. Just ask Barney.'

'I'm not so sure. It gets bloody cold up here, especially in the winter. I don't really want to, to be honest.'

There was a long pause.

'Would you mind if I did, then?'

'Did what?'

'Bought a cottage. I'd love to have a place of my own like that.'

'Do what you like. But what's wrong with the place in the Algarve? Or the flat in town?'

'It's not the same. It's not like having a place of your own, though.'

'Do what you like. It's your money.'

'There's a place called Crab Bay which is meant to be really nice. And also Coxburgh. We could have a look in there on the way home.'

'Maybe,' he said. 'Is there any more of that marmalade? Or have you scoffed the bloody lot?'

Giselle was sitting in the mouth of the cave in the cliffs, soaked to the skin and shivering, but her attention was given over entirely to the drama that was unfolding before her.

After the long night at The Laurels, she felt she needed a walk to clear her head. She didn't want to go straight back to college. There was nothing to do at that time on a Sunday morning anyway, and there'd be no one about. Camille and her other friends rarely got up much before eleven, if then.

So she gave her money and the bag with her clothes and sexy little knick-knacks to Brigitte, who would look after it for her, and went down to the beach. She loved it at that time of day. It reminded her very much of the Ile de Ré, the sheltered spot on the south-west corner of France where she and her family had often holidayed. Once she got past the cliffs, out towards Crab Bay, there were the same dunes, the same open beaches, the same open miles of nothingness apart from a few fishermens' cottages and ramshackle jetties where they moored their boats.

It had been a glorious summer morning when she had skipped down the winding path, past the municipal gardens and the pavilion. The sun was already high in the sky and the heat was beginning to build up. She was wearing only a t-shirt and a pair of shorts – anything else would have been hot and uncomfortable.

The freshness of the salt-sprayed air down by the sea hid from her a growing heaviness in the atmosphere. Looking down at the prints her bare feet made in the wet sand, pausing from time to time to pick up a shell or a pebble – she found a starfish, already dry and stiff – she did not notice the dark clouds building up on the horizon, the way the gentle breeze suddenly dropped.

The storm, when it hit her, took her almost completely by surprise. One minute she was walking along in the sunshine, the next it had suddenly grown quite dark. Before she knew it, cold fat drops of rain were falling quite heavily, at first in a shower, then in a downpour. Within thirty seconds she was soaked to the skin.

There was no shelter for her, out on the beach. The rain was coming in from seawards so she couldn't take refuge at the foot of the cliffs. It seemed like she'd have to make a dash for it, to race the mile or so back to The Laurels. She felt a wave of total despair – she really didn't know what to do.

The first bolt of lightning shocked her into action. She knew it was dangerous to be out in an electrical storm. One of the men from her village, a farm worker, had been badly burned only last year when a lightning bolt hit his tractor. But where could she go? What shelter was there from the storm?

It was then that she remembered the cave. It was only a couple of hundred yards away, a mad scrambling dash across the sand and shingle and then over the slippery rocks at the foot of the cliffs. The climb was harder than ever, she found it difficult to maintain her footing and the rain seemed determined to blow her back, but somehow she made it.

She sat in the mouth of the cave, panting for breath. How very different the circumstances had been when she was last here, with Camille. Her situation now was almost a mockery. What a fool of fortune she was! But, at the very least, she was safe. She looked out to sea, at the rain that drifted around like mist, at the waves that were being whipped up with sudden violence.

If she had not been so cold and wet, she would have enjoyed it. She loved storms, waterfalls, blizzards – anything that brought out the elemental in her. But she preferred to experience it in comfort, from the safety of her house or the warmth of a car, the windscreen wipers slapping away at the pouring waters, the way the lights smeared and blurred through the rain. Alone in a cave, high up on a cliff, brought her uncomfortably close to nature.

She'd only had a croissant and coffee for breakfast, very early, and she felt hungry, but there was nothing she could do about it.

She could see the lightning flashes, could observe the way the storm slowly began to move inland. To the north, the sky was a pale grey; to the south, and the heart of the storm, it was almost black. She rubbed her arms against the cold and shivered. She wished she was back in her bath again at The Laurels. There was nothing she could do but to settle down and wait for the storm to pass.

She had been sitting on that cold, damp slab at the mouth of the cave when a movement caught her eye. Down below, maybe a quarter of a mile away, a little boat seemed to be bobbing on the water. It didn't appear to be going anywhere, just surging backwards and forwards, this way and that. It was a small open boat, a dinghy, the kind everyone used to have fun on the river, not the sort of thing in which you would set out to sea in a storm. It was too far away for her to see if there was anyone in the boat. Common sense said there wouldn't be – it had presumably broken loose from its moorings.

Once, twice, the boat was tossed high in the air and crashed down again. She remembered, with a shudder, how sick she'd felt on the cross-Channel ferry. She was relieved there was no one in the boat. At times, too, the waves seemed to engulf it, breaking all around it in a vicious cloud of spray. It was certainly an awesome sight, and one that held her attention for many minutes.

Then, as the boat drifted helplessly towards her, she noticed a movement. An arm, a leg, she couldn't tell what it was. Then, even more incredibly, she saw another boat round the spit past Crab Bay and come crashing through the waves. It was one of the little fishing boats like they had at Coxburgh. It seemed to be hugging the coast, looking for something specific. Perhaps it was looking for the dinghy – she hoped so.

The storm seemed to be building to a peak, and she took

shelter further back in the cave – she felt intimidated by the display of elemental force. But still she could not keep her eyes from the drama that was being acted out in front of her. The fishing boat seemed to be moving towards the dinghy and her heart skipped but then, tragedy, it seemed to be going in the wrong direction altogether, and the expanse of water between them grew greater almost by the second. Watching it tore her emotions to shreds but it was as compelling to watch as anything she had seen in a movie.

A sudden clap of thunder made her duck and when she looked next, the boats seemed to have vanished. She looked out across the sea, through the rain, and all she could see were boiling, empty waves, the slate-grey surface broken in to a million jagged ripples. Of the fishing boat and the dinghy, there was no sign.

But no, there it was. She caught sight of the tip of its mast, the pennant flying there like a beacon. And then it appeared almost broadside, low-hulled in the swell, and she could see the wheel house and even the lifebelt lashed to the side. She looked around and not a hundred yards away was the dinghy, two figures – not one – still gamely clinging to its sides.

The next minute, the fishing boat had come alongside. It was bucking and rolling in the heavy sea but she could see the man come from the wheelhouse and stand in the bows. He had something in his hands – a rope, it had to be – and he was trying to throw it to the dinghy. Once, twice, he almost made it but then another big wave came in and the boats were hauled apart.

Again the fishing boat circled round, came alongside, tried to hold steady. The two figures in the boat were trying to stand up but it was very difficult for them, she could see. She was afraid that at any moment they would be pitched out into the waves.

She was standing up in the mouth of the cave now, urging them on. She hadn't realised it but she was shouting, clapping her hands, trying to will the rescue to take place. Again the man – he seemed, incredibly, to be the only one on board – threw the rope and at the fourth or fifth attempt one of the figures in the little boat caught it and held it fast. The other one scrambled forward to help him and then she could see both of them clinging to it for dear life.

For maybe ten minutes she watched that scene before her. The storm passed on. The rain was passing away from her now. But still out there they were fighting that heavy sea.

She emerged from the cave, made her slippery way down to the beach. Running along it, she kept losing sight of the boats. They were only a couple of hundred yards out to sea but she knew the waters out there were deep and treacherous. The principal at Garfield Hall had told them, very early on, of the dangers of the currents, and to heed the warning signs.

She drew level with the scene. The sky was getting visibly brighter now and she could see every detail, sparklingly clear. Despite the way her soaking wet clothes clung to her, she felt a curious elation – surely, nothing could go wrong now?

She could see the man in the fishing boat – very tall, very strong-looking – making the line fast and then beginning the slow business of hauling the dinghy towards the stern of his boat. All of a sudden a shaft of rich, brilliantly clear sunshine lit up the scene, the boats rising and falling in the swell, the two figures in the dinghy poised ready to jump.

The two boats rode together for some minutes and then, like the stars coming into conjunction on an astrology chart, the moment seemed to be right – she could sense it. One second the boats were ten or twenty feet apart, the next they were abreast of each other and the two people in the dinghy were scrambling over the side. Close to, they looked like boys, no older than she was.

There was a chattering overhead which grew nearer and then all the considerable sound of the sea was drowned out by a big yellow helicopter that passed right over where she was. It had been flying along the line of the coast and now it just hung in the air over the two boats, the down draft from its rotor blades flattening the waves.

She could see the man on the fishing boat making gestures to the chopper, and then a big hatch door opening in the side of the helicopter. A man in a bright orange helmet appeared, shouting something through a megaphone. Some sort of negotiating seemed to be going on, although the noise from the engine was deafening.

The next thing she could see, a line had been dropped from the chopper on to the tiny deck of the fishing boat. A man came abseiling down it, then another. Nothing happened for quite some while but then, just when she thought she couldn't stand the noise a moment longer, the two helicopter crew and the boys from the dinghy were winched one by one up into the sky.

Giselle had to shield her eyes from the glare now, the sun was so bright on the yellow paintwork of the chopper. They didn't even bother to close the hatch door before the helicopter wheeled around and set off back along the coast. The whole thing – she looked at her watch to check it – couldn't have taken more than twenty minutes, from the moment the man in the boat made his line fast to the completion of the rescue.

She felt exhilarated, standing there at the edge of the waves. She could see the man on the boat, coiling up his rope, the boat riding gently at anchor as though nothing untoward had happened. He looked up, and saw her standing on the shore. He waved. She waved back. She was aware, for the first time in an hour or more, of the warmth of the sun on her body.

Richie had never been in a chopper before. It was noisy and basic, a far cry from the jets on which he and Rob had flown off on holiday each year until they had no money to do so with. It was more like a flying jeep than anything else.

There was no point in bullshitting these guys. Clutching a hot drink – he couldn't tell whether it was tea or coffee, but it didn't matter – he and Rob told them what had happened in every detail. They said about Mick Rowlandson and his mates, about being chased along the beach, of resigning themselves to getting on the receiving end of a good kicking until they'd spotted the boat and somehow got it to sea in the nick of time.

The weather had been fine until then, that must have been when the storm came on. All of a sudden they found themselves drifting helplessly out to sea. They'd lost one of the paddles and the other was almost useless. They kept losing sight of the land. Water kept coming over the sides and they used a plastic bucket to try and chuck it back, but it was a losing battle. They tried to stand up and wave for help but they couldn't keep their feet for more than a couple of seconds at a time and besides, there would be no one about in all that stuff to see them.

'We just felt we had to do something,' explained Rob. The crewmen were kind and considerate but they looked as though they'd heard it all before. This single operation alone would cost them the best part of four grand and they were way down on budget already. They flew directly over the caravan site, over the cottages of Crab Bay and then tree-hopped across the flat countryside, heading for the nearest hospital.

Richie was still shaking and not just from the cold. He huddled inside the big thermal blanket they'd wrapped him up in. He'd been so scared out there, he'd actually pissed himself. He was never, ever going to go to sea again. All he wanted was to get back home – and he didn't mean the caravan.

'Rob,' he said after a while, when he'd begun to thaw out a little.

'What?'

'I'm not sure I can stick it much longer, down here.'

Rob looked thoughtful.

'Do you mean you want to chuck it?' he said eventually.

'Something like that. How about you?'

He didn't say anything. Not right away, at any rate.

'I was thinking maybe we should think about going back.'

'We're supposed to stay to the end of next month.'

'Aye, but what's to keep us? The money's shite and what happens after that?'

'What about Debbie?'

Rob took so long to answer that one that Richie thought he'd said the wrong thing. Maybe they'd had a bust-up or something. Maybe that was the real reason she wasn't at the caravan that morning.

'Well,' he said at inordinate length. 'It's funny you should mention that.'

'How's that?'

'You know she was offered a place at Bristol? To do English?'

'That's right. I thought she was dead set on going there.'

'Well, she's been offered a place at Newcastle as well. Starting next month.'

It took a long while for that to sink in, while the rotor blades hammered through the sky and the chopper tried, unsuccessfully, to shake both itself and its human cargo to bits.

'Do you think she'll take it?'

'She might. She only told us this morning, like. It was a surprise, I can tell you.'

'So she might come up there to live?'

'Better then that. We might move in together.'

'What'll you do for money?'

'She gets a grant. I'll get a job.'

'What fucking job?'

'How do I know? Or I'll just stay on the dole. What do you think?'

'Sounds champion. Are you saying, you want to go back too?'

'Yes.'

'When?'

'This afternoon?'

'I thought we were going to see the lads at Norwich on Saturday?'

''Boro are playing Villa – should be a cracker. Lefty Wright says he can always get tickets for 'Boro home games.'

'Done.'

Rob always was a jammy bugger, thought Richie as the helicopter circled the hospital grounds.

Col made the *Erica B* fast in her usual berth alongside the rat-ridden wooden jetty and, soaking wet, stepped out on to dry land. He hadn't had time to change into his wet-weather clothes, had just slipped an old waterproof on over his Sunday-morning-at-home clothes and it had leaked everywhere. There was a police car waiting, a few routine questions, but he gave them his number and said he'd really quite like to get home and dry. They were good blokes and they understood. They offered him a lift but he said he'd prefer to drive himself. He was desperate for coffee, preferably with a big fat slug of brandy in it. He felt wide awake and curiously flattened, all at the same time.

Everything had happened so quickly. It was barely an hour since he'd dropped Carole off at her hotel on the edge of Dunwich. A lot had happened in that time but he just wanted to put it behind him now. The sun was warm and bright but it wasn't warm and bright enough for him. He almost wished it were winter, so he could curl up in front of a big roaring fire in his living-room.

He turned off down the rutted track that led to Crab Bay, still trying to make sense of his experiences and his feelings about them. In the end he didn't bother. He just accepted what life threw up. In his heart, though, he was glad. He'd got those lads out of trouble and he thought he'd stood up to the test all right. He'd been out on the *Erica B* in worse weather than that but never single-handed. There'd been a time when, trying to pull the second lad onboard, she'd suddenly reared up in the swell and he thought both of them were going to end up in the drink. He was glad it was all over. He wanted nothing more than to get back to his comfortable routines.

He parked the Volvo at the back of the house as usual. He had the place to himself. There wasn't any sign of life in any of the adjoining houses, and he didn't expect there to be.

A movement caught his eye. He half-turned and there, by the side of his house, was the most beautiful girl he had ever seen in his life, an absolute vision. Her blonde hair was wet and it clung to her forehead like she'd just stepped out of a tropical forest – he remembered an ad for creme bath he'd made ten years ago. Her t-shirt was soaking wet too and he could see how prominently her nipples stuck out. The only other clothes she had on were a pair of skimpy summer shorts and they were soaked too. He could see very clearly the outline of her bum, nice and peach-like. He'd not seen anything like it since Ursula Andress in *Dr No* – only this was better.

'Hi!' she said in a foreign accent – French, most probably.

She looked at him quizzically.

'You're the man on the boat, right?' she said at length.

'What do you mean?'

'Just now,' she said. She turned – that softly curved bum again – and made a gesture in the direction of the sea. 'You rescued those two boys. I saw it all.'

He looked at her again. She was absolutely stunning.

'You're soaking wet,' he said simply. 'You'd better come inside and get dry. Would you like some coffee?'

Of course, after she'd told him how she'd come into Crab Bay trying to find a call box so she could phone for a cab, because she couldn't walk back to Dunwich wringing wet like that, and after she'd found that it was out of order, and after she'd found that no one was home at any of the houses, and after she'd said she'd discovered that Col's front door was unlocked and was just about to try it when she heard his car approach, and after they'd both of them got warm and had coffee with a big fat slug of brandy in it, then of course they went to bed together. It seemed, in the circumstances, to be the natural thing to do.

The suddenness of his erection surprised even him. Without consciously thinking about it, he had crossed the room and taken her in his arms, crushing her to him. She was wearing an old sweater and a pair of jeans that just about fitted her – they'd shrunk far too much for him, or maybe he'd put on weight? – and yet she still looked ravishing. Her body was voluptuous, warm and dry now, and her tongue sought his, tracing its way over his neck, her hands all the while pushing up under his shirt.

Blood roared through his head as they paused for breath and

then they kissed again, with ferocious intensity. Time, at last, stood still. She dropped to her knees and pressed her head against his groin, with its burgeoning erection. She looked up at him, admiration in her eyes. She thinks of me as a hero, he thought. He'd never known that before because he'd never done anything particularly heroic, but it was a nice feeling, nevertheless. And the extraordinary skills she could display with her mouth and tongue! For one so young, she was amazing.

Then she was busy with his zip, roughly yanking his jeans down as he pulled his faded denim shirt off and over his head. His cock lolled there, stiff and ready for her. She took hold of it in one hand, gently stroking it as she licked around the top of his thighs, her cheeks brushing against his thick pubic hair. Then her lips closed over it and he felt himself transported into another realm.

He opened his eyes to see her looking up at him, a smile playing around her features. God, she was beautiful. Who was she? Where had she come from? It was like a dream. She nibbled around the tip of his glans, her tongue gently playing with the sensitive little hole at the end of his cock, then swooping down and taking as much of him as she could into her mouth. She did this over and over again, teasing him into gentle madness. After each deep suck, the pause became an aching void of anticipation. And then, just as swiftly, his longings were gratified.

He glanced down at her deep cleavage, her breasts swelling full and ripe, her nipples pressed hard against his thighs. God, he wanted to suck her, to press his cock against the warm fullness of bosom that seemed to invite him to nestle there. He could see her legs slightly parted, the fleshy lips of a pussy that he wanted to suck and fuck so very badly. First Carole and then this. It was unbelievable, it was every young man's dream.

He saw how her hand slipped down between her thighs,

seeking out her own private pleasures. Col sensed something quite different to the emotions of the early morning and those strange, surprising hours he had spent with Carole. There had been an inevitability about their coupling but there was also a faint nervousness, an unsureness that was completely lacking now. It was the difference between something he felt he ought to do and something he knew he wanted to do. Both had their place, both were feelings he could handle. Here in this sunlit room, with birdsong in the garden and a heavy sultriness already hanging in the air after the fury of the earlier storm, he abandoned himself to the realm of the senses.

As he felt his seed rising within him he took hold of her head with both hands. Her cheeks were engorged with his fullness, her eyes closed as though she were dreaming. There was a wildness in him now, a red mist that seemed to be descending on him, a delicious lewdness of thought. He caught sight of her buttocks, her breasts swinging as she leaned forward. Here he was, being sucked off in his own living room at nine-thirty in the morning by someone he had never met in his life – he didn't even know her name and he didn't care. He let out his pent-up breath, made a sound that was half-groan, half a cry of triumph, and then his seed boiled over into her mouth in thick, succulent pulses of pleasure.

'There,' she said at length, when she had time to compose herself. Her French accent was divine. 'That was nice, wasn't it?'

He felt like he could sleep for a thousand years but no, that wish at least would not be granted him.

'Do you think you could give me a lift back to Dunwich?' she said quite casually.

He looked at her. She was entirely without guile. She had enjoyed it just as much as he had.

'All in good time,' he said simply. Time was something that, for once, he had plenty of.

'That's fine,' she said. 'But could you let me have something to eat first – I'm starving. And then you can take me to bed.'

Also available from LIAISON, the intoxicating new erotic imprint for lovers everywhere

SLEEPLESS NIGHTS

Tom Crewe & Amber Wells

While trying to capture the evening light in a Cotswold field, photographer Emma Hadleigh is intrigued to discover she has an audience. And David Casserley is the kind of audience any smart young woman might be intrigued by – he's charming, he's attractive and he's sensational when it comes to making love in a cornfield. What's more, like her, he's single. But single doesn't necessarily mean unattached. And, as they are both about to discover, former lovers and present intrigues can cast a long shadow over future happiness . . .

0 7472 5055 3

THE JOURNAL

James Allen

Before she married Hugo, Gina used to let her hair down – especially in the bedroom. And though she loves her husband, sometimes Gina wishes he wasn't quite so straitlaced. Then she discovers that there is a way of breathing a little spice into their love life. Like telling him stories of what she used to get up to in her uninhibited past. The result is the Journal – the diary of sexual self-analysis that Hugo writes and which Gina reads. When she tells her best friend Samantha what it contains, the journey of sensual exploration really begins . . .

0 7472 5092 8

*Also available from LIAISON, the intoxicating
new erotic imprint for lovers everywhere*

HEARTS ON FIRE

Tom Crewe AND Amber Wells

*In the beginning it is a simple business arrangement.
Anna makes a living out of rich, powerful men and
Michael is just another name on her list. Then things
begin to change. He gives her status, she offers him
escape. And, as their intimacy deepens, they discover
what a dangerous road they are travelling together –
through murder, revolution and the white-hot flames of
uninhibited desire . . .*

0 7472 5115 0

VOLUPTUOUS VOYAGE

Lacey Carlyle

*Fleeing from an unhappy engagement to an unsuitable
American, naive but passionate Lucy Davenport embarks
for England accompanied by her schoolfriend, Faye. They
sail on the luxurious ocean liner, the SS Aphrodite,
whose passenger list includes some of the 1930's most
glamorous socialites – and dedicated pleasure-seekers.
With five days of the voyage ahead of them, it's an ideal
opportunity for two unchaperoned young beauties to
sample all the erotic delights their sensual natures crave!*

0 7472 5145 2

Adult Fiction for Lovers from Headline LIAISON

SLEEPLESS NIGHTS	Tom Crewe & Amber Wells	£4.99
THE JOURNAL	James Allen	£4.99
THE PARADISE GARDEN	Aurelia Clifford	£4.99
APHRODISIA	Rebecca Ambrose	£4.99
DANGEROUS DESIRES	J. J. Duke	£4.99
PRIVATE LESSONS	Cheryl Mildenhall	£4.99
LOVE LETTERS	James Allen	£4.99

All Headline Liaison books are available at your local bookshop or newsagent, or can be ordered direct from the publisher. Just tick the titles you want and fill in the form below. Prices and availability subject to change without notice.

Headline Book Publishing, Cash Sales Department, Bookpoint, 39 Milton Park, Abingdon, OXON, OX14 4TD, UK. If you have a credit card you may order by telephone – 01235 400400.

Please enclose a cheque or postal order made payable to Bookpoint Ltd to the value of the cover price and allow the following for postage and packing: UK & BFPO: £1.00 for the first book, 50p for the second book and 30p for each additional book ordered up to a maximum charge of £3.00.
OVERSEAS & EIRE: £2.00 for the first book, £1.00 for the second book and 50p for each additional book.

Name ....

Address ....

....

....

If you would prefer to pay by credit card, please complete:
Please debit my Visa/Access/Diner's Card/American Express (Delete as applicable) card no:

Signature .... Expiry Date..............